TO STEPHEN

ONE

He should not have done it.

He might have got away with murder once – twice even – but six times was pushing anybody's luck. And he had never really had what you would call good luck. Martin sighed and looked out of the window at the December night, his breath frosting the pane of glass that felt so cool against his forehead. He had not bothered to turn on the lights – he felt safer in the dark. The clock of the video recorder glowed ice-green. As he watched the liquid crystal display, the lower left-hand stroke of the figure eight vanished so that 10.58 became 10.59.

It was then that the patrol car turned into Clissold Avenue. The tyres made only the discreetest of squeals. Martin stepped back. There were plenty of reasons why the police should happen to be driving down here. Even so, his armpits began to prickle and the stabbing pain above his left eye returned. He clenched his fists, forcing the nails into the palms of his hands. Jesus Christ.

Martin Rudrum had never believed in God. The Rover pulled up outside. There was no point in making a scene. Or was there? He was not bored now.

TWO

It was a moment of rare perfection. The mahogany drop-leaf dining table gleamed in the soft light of the beeswax candles. Serried ranks of silver cutlery stood to attention. His guests took their places, flapping freshly laundered napkins onto their laps, clinking their glasses of champagne together in anticipation of what they knew would be an excellent, if unexciting, meal. Outside, Saturday was dying, the last of the September daylight lingering softly; dusk did not begin to describe it. Martin looked out of the window across the park to where the extravagant spire of St Mary's soared into the azure sky. The slats of the black venetian blind seemed as permanent as prison bars.

He had slaved all day for this moment: now the hard work was over and he could sit back and enjoy watching other people having a good time. He liked entertaining and tonight was a special occasion: this was the first dinner party he had given since finishing the renovation of his top-floor, one bedroom flat.

'It must be awful not to have a separate dining room,' said Nicola as she drained her glass, again. In the candlelight her hair was the colour of old gold. Her thin red lips tried to avoid smiling but failed. Martin looked at her, trying to decide if she was being mischievous or just her usual bloody-minded self. Alex sniggered.

'We can't all live in NW3,' Martin replied as he gave her a refill.

'Yes please!' said Michael.

'Yes please!' said Rory.

'Me too,' said Trudi and winked at Martin. He had no idea who she was except that she had arrived with Alex. Alex was one of his oldest friends, a gay who found it amusing to dine out with bimbos hanging off his arms. Blond and blue-eyed, Alex himself appeared to be a typical himbo. In fact he had a brain to match his beautiful body. It was just that he did not bother to use it much. Martin supposed he should be grateful that he had chosen to bring only one good-time girl. There was not a lot of room in his home.

'I'll just get another bottle,' said Martin. 'Tuck in. Don't let your smoked salmon get cold.' Isobel followed him into the kitchen. The wild rice was spluttering away. Its scummy spray had dried out on the hob, a rash of scabs. He immediately wiped them away with a damp dishcloth.

'You OK?' asked Isobel, who was standing behind him watching. She slipped her arms round his waist and pressed her right cheek into his shoulder. She kissed the nape of his neck.

'I am now.'

He turned to face her and kissed her on the lips. She drew away. 'Don't start,' she said, wagging her finger at him. 'You promised to behave.'

'Can't a man even kiss an old flame nowadays?'

'Not when there are people waiting.'

Cries of 'Where's the fizz? Where's the fizz?' were coming from next door. The loudest voice belonged to Michael, the berk for whom Isobel had left him. Martin swore and took another bottle from the fridge. He felt like braining the bastard – but that would be impossible. Mr Michael Ford, successful TV producer and stud extraordinaire, may have had a lot between the legs but he did not have much between the ears.

It was during the main course – chicken with grapes in a cream and brandy sauce – that Martin decided to kill them. They were all drunk, himself included, but his mind was obstinately lucid. It was one of those evenings when he knew that no matter how much he drank euphoria would elude him.

Arvo Part had given way to the Pet Shop Boys and, although the volume had remained constant, everyone had raised their voices. Alex was explaining how the duo were rumoured to have got their name. Toothless hamsters and clawless gerbils had something to do with it.

'Of course there's a much simpler way to produce exactly the same effect.'

'How, how, how?' begged Trudi, singing for her supper. Her tan was remarkable. It was as if she had been steeped in gravy browning. 'Go on then, tell us,' prompted Rory who was still holding Nicola's hand. Martin found public displays of affection irritating. 'Well,' continued Alex, looking round the table to check that he had everybody's full attention and smiling when his eyes met Martin's, 'the first thing you need is a lemon, the fresher the better. Then you place it in the microwave on high for one minute. I repeat, one minute – you don't want fried fruit all over the joint. When the bell pings, take the lemon out of the oven and after a few seconds it will be just the right temperature to stick up your arse. You see, the radiation makes it go all mushy inside and it's much safer than suffocating small animals.'

'That is truly gross,' said Isobel. 'I feel sick.'

'So do I,' said Martin. 'At least it gives new meaning to the phrase, I must go now the pips have gone.'

Everyone laughed, Trudi loudest of all. The curls of her peroxide perm bounced up and down. Martin always became flippant when he was bored and he was often bored. Under the table a bare foot was rubbing the calf of his left leg. The trollop winked at him again.

'Do I detect a hint of disapproval?' Rory sat back in his chair and linked his hands behind his head. His rugby-player's shoulders bulged massively in the Davies shirt. His one blond eyebrow was raised above both green eyes.

'Are you addressing me sir?' Martin asked his old schoolmate. 'Indeed sir. I was wondering what exactly had provoked that moue of distaste I saw upon your lips. After all, most things have passed between them.'

'Fuck off!'

'Now boys, let's not fall out,' said Michael in a tone which clearly announced that he would like nothing better than a full-scale table-top battle. 'Is there any more wine?'

'Red or white?'

'You mean there isn't any more champagne?'

'You know there isn't,' said Martin. 'It's not my fault if couples only bring one bottle. If you couldn't carry two, a magnum would have been perfectly acceptable.'

'It must be awful to be poor,' said Nicola, smiling as Rory pressed her paw once more. So it *was* bloody-mindedness.

'I wouldn't know,' said Alex.

'Neither would I,' commented Michael. 'Although it might be interesting to find out.' Isobel hit him.

'You wouldn't like it,' said Trudi.

In the few minutes it took for them to guzzle the chocolate mousse Martin studied the faces of his friends. Every so often the peace was broken by a murmured 'mmmm' or an exhaled 'aaah' but no one was going to go to the trouble of making conversation while greater pleasure was available for less effort. The host did not eat. He had every confidence in the cuisine but none at all in his physique. He had a hatred of flab. As a child it had taken several diets and iron willpower to dispose of his stubborn puppy fat and once his spare tyre had gone he had vowed never to be overweight again. One of his fiercest rows with Isobel had been caused by a playful allusion to his incipient 'love-handles'. He despised obese people. You could not blame anybody else for self-indulgence. He loved good food but constantly had to keep himself in check. It sometimes seemed that his whole life had been based on self-deprivation.

Alex was licking the sticky stuff off the back of his spoon. Trudi, a fitness fanatic, was stirring hers as if she were assessing how many calories it contained. Rory and Nicky were feeding each other – he might as well have given them baby food – whereas Michael, true to form, was wolfing his down and on the point of finishing. He watched Isobel slowly spoon the rich mixture into her mouth, her brow creased with the concentration of gaining maximum taste from each little bit. Because she was bending over the table, her jet-black hair had fallen forward. As she sat up to push it back from the sides of her face, using – as always – the thumb and little finger of her right hand, she glanced at Martin. Her eyes glinted. The skin covering her high cheekbones was flushed by the expensive toxins. His heart lurched. He still loved her. When Michael died she would come back to him.

THREE

A horse had kicked him in the stomach. Although Martin took every step to avoid hangovers he could not fully escape the consequences of drinking kir, champagne, chardonnay, medoc, port and Sambuca all in one evening. Before he had finally flung back his duvet and fallen into bed he had forced himself to down a litre of mineral water and four Nurofen to preempt dehydration and a headache. It was either that or blowing chunks into the toilet bowl. And he had been too tired for that.

It had been after 2am when Alex and Trudi eventually left, Trudi pressing a crumpled card into his hands as she stuck her furry tongue down his throat. Alex had already reached the front door and was using his remote-control key-ring to beep out a jingle on his BMW, the lights of which flashed on and off in time with the beat. Disco nights. It was a long time since he and Alex had been gripped by Saturday night fever.

'Call me,' whispered Trudi in his ear. 'I want to find out if what Isobel says is true.' With that she was off – her tight black moire dress rustling as she tottered downstairs in her white stilettos but not before she had pressed a hot little hand on his groin.

The memory of this caused a wave of nausea to sweep over Martin. He had not been celibate for two years just so that he could boldly go where most men had gone before. The sofa felt particularly comfortable today. He did not want to move. There was no need to, fortunately. He had cleared away the debris and polished the dining table before going to bed and he had washed up before breakfasting on orange juice and coffee. His hands still tingled from the hot water. You had to have it hot to kill the germs.

Now everything was in order. The only give-away was the sickening smell of stale cigarettes which seemed to cling to the new carpet and furniture. Martin did not smoke. The fresh air blowing through the flat would soon get rid of it. But how would he get rid of the red wine that Nicola had knocked over? Her initial horror had dissolved into giggles.

'Never mind Martin, it will soon be time to get another one. How long have you had this one? A month?'

He had refused to give her the satisfaction of losing his temper and, while Isobel was busy dousing the spot with Badoit, had gone into the kitchen to fetch the salt.

'You are a proper little housewife aren't you?' exclaimed Michael who, by this time, was down to his boxer shorts.

It was a constant source of wonder to Martin how such stupid people managed to hold down jobs in television.

The bitch could not have done it in a worse place. She had not spilled it on the black and white geometrically-patterned rug which could be washed but bang in the middle of the largest expanse of carpet in front of the window. The salt had worked to some extent but it still looked as if someone had been shot. A satanic mess had turned wine into blood. Nicola would pay for it with the claret coursing through her own veins.

It had gradually dawned on Martin over the past few months that he no longer liked any of his friends. He did not like himself either but that was a different matter – he could live with that. Each one of them proved Oscar Wilde's definition of a cynic as someone who knew the price of everything and the value of nothing. They themselves were worthless. Look at the way they had behaved last night.

★

'Enough of this tittle-tattle,' said Rory. 'Let's play a game.' The meal was over and the first bottle of port was dead.

'How about hump the hostess?' suggested Alex. He winked at Martin.

'He'd enjoy it too much,' replied Rory.

'I bet he would,' said Michael. Isobel refused to rise to the bait.

'Bags I go first,' pleaded Trudi. 'I'm having such a good time.'

'You're not supposed to be having fun,' said Nicola. 'Dinner parties are for those who don't like enjoying themselves.'

'There speaks the poor little rich girl,' sighed Martin. 'She's so glutted with pleasure only the opposite registers. I propose Truth Or Dare.'

'You would,' said Isobel. 'You're the only one who is not in a relationship. You're just like Nicola, you want to cause trouble as well.'

'I aim to please,' replied Martin beaming. 'Well?'

'Alex isn't in a relationship, are you darling?' said Trudi. '
Oh yes he is, *darling*.' Michael did not bother to hide his disgust. 'You're married to a trolley-dolley aren't you dearie?'

Alex lived with an air steward called Keith. They spent more time apart than together. Alex blew Michael a kiss.

'Why do you get so homophobic when you're squiffy, possum? Is it because gay sex is the one thing you've always wanted and never dared to try?'

'Shut your fucking face you fucking sausage jockey or I'll shut it for you.'

'Love it, love it, love it,' murmured Nicola.

'Michael please be quiet,' said Isobel.

In the end they decided on strip Trivial Pursuit. Although Martin felt extremely self-conscious in such aerobic and athletic company he had no qualms in playing because he knew that he could beat the lot of them.

'It's not fair,' whined Trudi, her breasts bobbing in the candlelight. 'Martin and Rory haven't taken anything off.'

'That's because we've had the benefit of a public school education,' said Rory, smirking.

'I thought that public school was where you were taught to bare your bum all the time,' said Michael. Alex and Nicola found this very amusing. Even Isobel, looking magnificent in her black silk lingerie, was smiling.

'Come on,' continued Michael, looking at Trudi. 'What gangster couple was riddled with 104 bullets?'

'I don't know,' wailed Trudi. 'Somebody help me.'

Alex leaned over and whispered in her ear, tweaking her left nipple as he did so. She giggled. 'Bonnie and Clyde.'

'Shit,' said Rory. 'Now we'll have to wait even longer to see if she really has got an all-over tan.'

'Well you know I have,' said Nicola, sliding out of her Janet Reger and standing stark-naked over the board. Michael stared in silent bliss. Martin knew what she was doing. She was bored and insisted on being the centre of attention. 'Courtesy of the Maldives,' said Nicola.

'Put it away dear,' said Alex. 'I can feel a draught.' Nicola gave a twirl and then went and curled up on the sofa. Michael's eyes followed.

'Pay attention,' said Martin. 'It's your turn. What – as usual that should be which – two countries share the Khyber Pass?'

'How the hell should I know? It's near Pakiland isn't it?'

'No clues,' said Martin.

'Get 'em off, get 'em off, get 'em off,' cried Alex, pointing at Michael's polka-dotted shorts.

'You'll have to show us your own Khyber now,' giggled Trudi, pleased with her wit.

Martin was not going to give the arrogant sod any more time. 'The answer is Afghanistan and Pakistan.' He looked at Isobel. She was revelling in her partner's discomfort.

Michael did not move. He was not usually so bashful. He seized every opportunity to show off his tall, gym-sculpted body. His long dark hair, liberated from its ponytail, framed his strong, open face and brushed his freckled shoulders. There was a glimmer of fear in his grey eyes. Martin was puzzled. People told him that he was tall, dark and handsome and yet he looked nothing like Michael. He would have given anything for a body like that. Why was Michael acting as if he were almost ashamed?

Finally Michael lumbered to his feet. 'Ask and ye shall receive.' He turned his back on the audience and stepped out of his underwear. His backside was his best feature. And then all was explained. He swung round to reveal a swaying erection. Now it was Alex's turn to look pleased.

'Michael, I'm impressed.' He licked his lips.

'Dream on, bum-boy. This all belongs to Izzy.'

'Thanks a lot,' said Isobel angrily. 'You do fancy Nicola don't you?'

'Time to go home,' said Rory.

✲

When he tidied up Martin found – besides the wine stain and the usual vile pot pourri of peanuts, cheese, crumbs, fag ash and bitten-off finger nails on the carpet – an empty cigarette packet behind the sofa and a pound coin down the side of one of the cushions. Someone had poured a glass of port into the pot of his umbrella plant and someone else had scratched the rag-rolled wall by the door – just to prove, no doubt, that it was not Osborne & Little wallpaper. The kitchen mirror was speckled with the foul fall-out of squeezed zits and, on the newly-laid Amtico tiles in the bathroom, there was a puddle of piss. They were all swine. Swine to be slaughtered.

FOUR

Lying on the black sofa-bed – which he had chosen because it did not look like one – Martin let the unseasonably warm breeze ruffle his hair. Sunday morning was his favourite time of the week. As a child it had meant wallowing in bed listening to the strains of Radio 3 which drifted up from the kitchen where his mother was frying bacon. During the week she tuned in to Radio 2 and chuckled as Terry Wogan burbled on about the DG. Now he continued the tradition by switching from Radio 4 to Radio 3 every weekend. He had not distanced himself from his parents as much as he thought.

On the other hand Sunday evening was the worst time of the week. It was a spiritual nadir, a hangover from the past. Sunday evening was the only time he had felt homesick at boarding school. If there had been an exeat, it was the time when sons and heirs had to be delivered back to the prison-house. Again, music played a part. After high tea each study would thud to the sound of the Top 40 on Radio 1 but few pupils ever heard Number One because the evening service in the school chapel began at 7pm. Martin, though, had been one of the few souls to rise at 7.30am so that they could take Holy Communion in the local church. This was a case of pragmatism not dogmatism. Prompted by thoughts of home, many boys telephoned their parents on Sunday evening. It was much easier to do this when the majority of them were droning their way through hymns ancient and modern. Following the morning service, the schoolboy communicants would hare back to swap their uniforms for jeans and T-shirts in time for breakfast. Sausages – it was always sausages on Sunday – were infinitely preferable to a wafer and diluted vino.

He was now 28 but the depression remained the same. The thought of another dead weekend and the start of another week just like the last sent his spirits plummeting. He and his parents still called each other on Sunday evening. They took it in turns. They rang even if there was nothing to say. His mother was the worst. Agonising silences, punctuated only by static, would intersperse the usual questions about work, weather and queries about any 'special lady' in his life. When he finally replaced the receiver – a farewell could last as long as ten minutes – he felt drained. Every hiatus underlined the lack of communication. The real conversation lay in the sub-text. He loved his parents but resented the emotional hold they exerted over him. It was the same with Isobel.

About last night. Why, as Michael had so amply demonstrated, had it been such a cock-up? He had chosen his guests with care. Seven people. Three girls and four boys of every sexual persuasion. Rory, Michael, Isobel, Nicola and Trudi were straight and Alex was bent. That left him, the walking moratorium. But it was useless to insist on such strict definitions. Michael seemed ripe for seduction and Rory occasionally had a pash on one of his sixth-form students. The latter did not need to work – his father had died when he was ten leaving him a fortune made from bottling gin – but he taught economics at an independent school in Hampstead that appeared to cater almost exclusively for the sons of wealthy North London Jews. And then there was his fiancée Nicola who attracted more than her fair share of Sapphic adoration.

Perhaps the age span had been too narrow. All of them, apart from Trudi, had been born within five years of each other. She had surprised everybody by announcing that she was only

25: prolonged exposure to ultra-violet light had prematurely wizened her skin. Michael, although in many ways the least mature, had been the eldest at 33. Trudi had also been useful in extending the social scale. Thanks to her presence, the whole gamut from the gutter to the gentry had been seated around the table. What had seemed suspiciously like C&A had been exchanging fibres with Cerruti. Cockney had been dropping aitches while the aristocracy had been dropping trousers. Michael's father was a duke; Nicola's papa, a lord. Martin's dad was a doctor; Isobel's daddy, a businessman who bought and sold anything and everything, legal or not. Alex's old man was an old man. His son put it about that he was a dustman but no one besides Martin believed him. But all of them, with the possible exception of Trudi, had a lot more money than him. And Martin liked money.

It had been unwise to invite people whom he loathed but the fact that he liked very few people had made it almost inevitable. His guests had detected his animosity; no wonder they had rounded on him. Disapproval is infectious. Martin had resented their spoilt brat routines while simultaneously wishing he could have joined in with them. His bourgeois sensibility made him censorious and jealous. There was no such thing as enough cash. It was better to be rich and miserable than poor and miserable.

His motives for giving the dinner party had been dubious in the first place. When it came down to it he had been showing off. It was no good trying to impress those better off than oneself. But he could not help it: he was proud of his flat.

★

14A Clissold Avenue had been a dump when he bought it. For once his timing had been right. As a freelance journalist it had required as much charm and false self-confidence as he could muster to persuade his bank manager to authorise his mortgage. He was an excellent bull-shitter. He had honed his gift of the gab studying English Language and Literature at university. Discussing novels that you had not read was ideal training

for writing on subjects that you knew little about. Martin had
sailed through his O', A' and S' Levels with the minimum of
effort and attempted to enter Oxford in the same way. He failed.
During his first term at Leeds he had stridden in fury through
the wet and windswept streets, torturing himself with images
of the cosy ancient college that was forever closed to him. An
idyll lost through idleness. For the first time in his life he knew
what it was like to be an also-ran.

The friendly banker said yes and Martin moved in. The
property market boomed for the last time in a decade as couples
rushed to take advantage of the joint tax relief that would soon
be abolished. House prices soared beyond the reach of most
first-time buyers. He was almost grateful that Isobel had
walked out when she had. Until then they had been sharing
rented accommodation in Hackney – Isobel preferred to let out
the Bayswater mews that her father had given her on her 21st
birthday. Now his own flat was exactly the way he wanted it –
give or take the odd stain.

Nothing was out of place. It was so neat that it looked more
like the set of a stage-play, or a page from a mail-order catalogue, than a home. The square living room had a fearful
symmetry. As in many other bolt-holes in the capital, the
alcoves on either side of the cast-iron fireplace contained dwarf
cupboards and bookshelves up to the ceiling which, as this was
the fourth floor, was not very high. The fireplace still retained
the original decorative black and white tiles. Above it hung a
framed poster advertising a Royal Shakespeare Company
production of The Comedy Of Errors. A large bowler-hatted
figure stared out of it. His blue face had bowler hats for eyes.
The sofa-bed was positioned directly opposite. It was flanked
by identical waist-high bookcases made out of black wood. On
the top shelf of each stood an identical art deco lamp, a crescent
of frosted glass. The drop-leaf dining table was positioned
beneath the large window where the black venetian blind trem-
bled in the draught. A tall white vase filled with black plastic
tulips was set in the middle. Across the room, facing away from
the window, a dual-pedestal desk squatted. Its battered oak

was inlaid with dark green leather and a million scratches. The drawers had brass handles that rattled every time they were closed. A computer took up most of the left side; the unruly umbrella plant, a souvenir of Columbia Road flower market, most of the right. A red lamp and a red pen-holder matched the red cushions on the sofa. A television and video recorder sat on the left-hand cupboard; a compact disc player on the right. Its two Bose speakers were sited on the bookshelves either side of the chimney breast. Alex dubbed the whole set-up 'anal'.

The four-storey house had been built in the 1840s and converted into three flats in the early 1970s. The basement and raised ground floor formed a maisonette that belonged to a batty old maid with artistic pretensions. The fumes from the acrylic polymer she used for sculpting permeated the entire house and caused collective headaches. Martin enjoyed seeing her two cats – Pyramus and Thisbe – snoozing in the back-garden sun. The third floor belonged to a young couple, both teachers, who seemed to spend most of their spare time bonking. Their bedroom was directly below his. When she came, Georgina screamed 'Yes! Yes! Yes!' whereas Paul just gave a protracted growl. In his frustration Martin suspected that the performance was entirely for his own benefit. To begin with he had tried to ignore them but now he wanked along with them, picturing the labouring lovers who were only feet away. His own orgasms were soundless.

The bedroom was the same size and shape as the living-room. The rest of the flat consisted of a small hall that led down three steps into a galley kitchen and a bathroom beyond. The latter was separated from the former by a tiny lobby which was little more than a cupboard formed by two doors. An overhead shelf fixed to their lintels held a wine-rack. The previous owners, in an attempt to make the bathroom and lobby seem larger, had covered the walls with full-length mirrors. Martin had removed all of them except the one behind the bathroom door. He did not like mirrors, especially when he was naked. But even when fully–clothed he would always avoid catching his eye in one. He did not like what he saw.

The lower part of the flat was tiled in grey and white Amtico that formed a zigzag pattern; the upper part was carpeted with the grey pepper-and-salt broadloom that Nicola had so kindly christened. Except for the kitchen, which was painted white, all the walls had been rag-rolled with a mixture of white and two greys. A frieze with a cross-hatched motif of black and grey ran underneath the cornices in the living-room and bedroom. Martin found the total effect soothing. The way in which the antique structure blended with the modern interior design was a source of deep satisfaction.

Such clinical neutrality was offset by the hundreds of books whose covers provided splashes of colour. Most of them were in the living-room but Martin's library had grown to such an extent that there were now packed book-shelves in the bedroom, kitchen and bathroom. All of the books were arranged according to format and alphabetical order: Absire to Zameenzad, Ackroyd to Wolfe, Achebe to Zinoviev, Adams to Woolf and Aristophanes to Zola. Azed was another reason for liking Sunday morning.

☆

The crossword in the *Observer* magazine was set by Azed. He had obtained his apt pseudonym by reversing Deza, the surname of a Spanish inquisitor. His fiendish puzzles, which used bars instead of black squares, were filled with many obscure and archaic words. Nothing gave Martin greater pleasure than completing a difficult crossword. The appeal was threefold. First of all a vast vocabulary and an ability to look at familiar words in a new light were required. For example, in the language of crosswords, 'distress' could mean to cut someone's hair off, ie to dis-tress. A sense of humour and an academic curiosity also helped. Secondly, a good crossword held out the possibility of success. It was proof that order could be achieved out of chaos. As in a detective novel, the clues led to a single correct solution even though both authors and writers did their best to mislead. The golden rule was not to say what one meant but to mean what one said. Like reading, crossword solving was a solitary pursuit that brought one into contact with some brilliant minds. It was also fun to delve into the massive word-hoard of the English language. Words were all there was. In the beginning was the word. The word of God. Martin did not think it was a coincidence that reversing the initials of the father of all dictionaries, the Oxford English Dictionary, spelled out DEO.

However, his favourite book, his desert island choice, was Chambers Dictionary, the bible of cruciverbalists. All human life was here from 'aa: a type of scoriaceous lava with a rough surface and many jagged fragments' to 'zythum: a kind of beer made by the ancient Egyptians – much commended by Diodorus Siculus, a writer of the first century BC'. Some of the definitions were opaque – 'Norite: a gabbro with a rhombic pyroxene' – but others betrayed a pawky wit: 'Eclair: a cake, long in shape but short in duration', 'pycnogonida: the sea-spiders, a class of marine arthropods with more leg than body'. Martin, a living definition of lankiness, knew exactly what the lexicographer meant.

Finally, crosswords were symmetrical. In Azed's puzzles all the various components were contained within a unique black and white grid. Nouns and verbs, adjectives and adverbs – the nuts and bolts of speech – were fixed in an unchangeable pattern. The familiar and the strange combined to produce a beautiful balance.

✮

Today it took him thirty minutes to complete the Azed. It never took him more than an hour. He usually polished off the daily one in *The Times* in ten minutes. His personal record stood at five. He sat at his desk doodling. Nutty Nietzsche may have been right when he said that the thought of suicide was a great comfort but he had neglected to mention that the thought of killing others was a great joy.

The problem was not who but how. He scribbled the names of all his guests on a piece of foolscap. Michael, Izzy, Rory, Nicky, Alex and Trudi. Suddenly he realised something that made him feel hot and cold at the same time. M, I, R, N, A, T:

their initials, when rearranged, spelled out his first name. The anagram could not be the result of some subconscious plan because he had not invited Trudi. He had not known who Alex would bring. It was an auspicious start.

What else did these people have in common? Nothing except that they had all been stuffing their faces in this room less than twelve hours ago. He was the only common factor. Apart from himself and their partners, the guests had never met each other before. Alex always insisted on seeing Martin by himself. Moreover, the chances were that none of them were likely to meet again. He could not recall any exchange of telephone numbers other than Trudi's lascivious farewell. No one had said with the sweetest insincerity, 'let's do lunch'. He practised cultural apartheid and kept his friends segregated. This allowed him to adapt his personality to suit the particular circumstances. As a teenager he had often toyed with the idea of becoming an actor but the insecurity and low pay of the profession had deterred him. Instead, as an accomplished liar, he had drifted into journalism. It was simply a question of believing what one said while one said it.

The safest start would be to begin with Trudi. She was a virtual stranger to him and as such he had no motive to kill her except, of course, a desire to do so. He had no doubt that he was more intelligent than most policemen. They were usually working class oiks or members of the lower middle class on the make. No wonder the statistics suggested that fewer crimes were being solved each year. For every murderer caught two others got away. Who would miss a whore masquerading as a masseuse? Alex had told him last night that he had no intention of contacting her again. There was a huge gulf between thought and deed but it only required a little determination to cross it.

★

Trudi would not be his first victim. There had been a couple of near misses during his childhood – he had a vicious temper – but the honour of being corpse number one had gone to eighteen year-old Darren Watson. Martin did not know his name but he was occasionally visited by the startlingly vivid image of his bare buttocks.

Since Alex earned £60,000 (plus bonuses) per annum as a PR executive, and since Keith, his 'significant other', was eligible for substantial discounts on air fares, they were able to go on holiday whenever they chose. Martin was invariably asked to housesit: 'We know *you're* not going to make a mess,' said Alex. They also left both their cars in his charge.

Martin had learned to drive at the age of seventeen but he did not have a licence. At the time driving lessons had provided him with the perfect excuse to leave his bedroom where his parents thought he was revising. It had not been easy to persuade his father to teach him but the tuition was immediately cancelled when he was accused of 'laying rubber' while practising setting off. His irate father had made him pay for a full set of new tyres for the Volvo. Volvo. Latin for I roll. That was as close as his father would ever come to a roller. A Corgi model of a blue Silver Shadow sat on top of Martin's television.

The keys to the Golf and the BMW were kept in a drawer in the kitchen. Two years ago, on a Tuesday evening in November, Martin decided to go for a spin. As it was some time since he had been behind the wheel of a car he opted for the Golf. He did not want to risk damaging the BMW even though it was a company car. Arsenal were playing at home that night so he waited until 11pm before venturing out on to the streets. By then the police and their horses, the clampers and hot-dog caravans, the supporters and their cars had all gone home. Soon he was speeding through the thoroughfares of N5, N7 and N1, relishing the power of the turbocharged German engine.

It happened as he was weaving his way back down the side-streets off the Holloway Road. A group of three or four football fans were staggering about on the pavement outside the darkened pub from which they must have been ejected. The lager louts were singing their heads off, their hot breath billowing out in the freezing air. Even in this horrid orange light he could tell from the colours of their scarves that they were not local supporters.

Both sides of the narrow avenue were lined with cars, bumper to bumper. Inside the two rows of terraced houses their owners were busy snoring, fucking and farting. When the young visitors saw the Golf coming towards them they changed their tune to 'Yuppy bastard! Yuppy bastard!' and one of them, surprisingly agile for a drunk, scrambled across the bonnet of the nearest motor, stood in the centre of the road and pulled down his jeans and Jockeys, bending over as he did so.

Martin floored the accelerator. The delightful thrust which pressed him back into the ergonomically-designed seat had scarcely passed when he reached the boy. His bare backside shone lily-white in the headlights. Martin just had time to notice an angry red pimple low on the right buttock when he hit him full on. He disappeared under the car, the front left tyre bumping slightly as it crushed his out-flung arm. The caterwauling ceased.

He did not stop. What was the point? It was just like smearing a pigeon.

FIVE

The little brass hammer ricocheted between the two bells with savage glee. Martin had chosen such an alarm clock because he wore ear-plugs. They did not stop sound banging his ear-drums – they muffled it. The wax pellets were a prerequisite of any prolonged slumber. He could not block out the ubiquitous background noise of people's lives: unanswered telephones that the starlings had learned to imitate, slamming doors, rumbling reggae, tinny radios, revving engines, wow-wowing car alarms, trilling burglar alarms, screaming jets, yelling drunks, wailing sirens, howling dogs, mewing cats and mewling brats.

Monday morning. His heart sank. His stomach knotted as he resisted the temptation to pull the quilt over his head and hide in bed all day. He could phone in sick. Now was the time to put the flat up for sale, to quit London, even go home to mummy and daddy, go anywhere as long as it was away from the physical and emotional anarchy that raged outside. He got up.

If he found it difficult to go to sleep, it was equally difficult for him to wake up. Every day greeted him with a pseudo-hangover. He seemed to overdose on the chemicals that were released into the bloodstream while the brain snoozed. Black coffee helped but the hike to the tube station was more effective.

It riled him that dwelling on the wrong side of a road could result in an inferior address. He was a postcode junkie. The socially desirable area of N5 lay just across Green Lanes but he lived alongside Clissold Park, one of the largest expanses of dog-shit in Western Europe, and a jewel in the crown of N16. The fact that he had an 0171 telephone number was little compensation. His walk to work crossed the boundary between Stoke Newington and Highbury. Today he would cross another boundary. He would go beyond the pale.

☆

Routine was important. It was a way of controlling the flux of daily existence that always seemed about to engulf him. If the slightest item on his mental checklist had to be altered he was unsettled for the rest of the day. Getting dressed – he lay out his clothes the night before – shaving, washing and making the bed all had to be accomplished before the radio news at 8.30am. He then had fifteen minutes to eat his breakfast and to check that he had not won the Portolio stocks and shares game in *The Times*. He hated being hooked by this bingo for snobs but was terrified of missing an easy opportunity to collect a couple of grand. Having glanced at the arts reviews – if the opinions of his fellow critics did not chime with his own they were the droolings of ignorant bastards – he had a further fifteen minutes to brush his teeth, have a dump, set the video and get out of the flat in time to get to the post first. More often than not the lazy devil shoved the letters for the whole house through the letterbox of the basement flat. This morning, however, a few envelopes were scattered on the doormat. There was never very much on a Monday. Today's glad tidings consisted of a circular for Romeo and Juliet, two letters for the fruitcake downstairs and a Barclaycard bill for himself. He owed Visa almost five thousand pounds.

He had other debts. His ever-extending overdraft was approaching three thousand pounds. He had borrowed five thousand pounds to pay for the installation of central heating and to modernise the kitchen and bathroom. The carpet had been bought on interest-free credit but he had used other bits of plastic to finance the finishing touches to the flat. The money that his father had 'lent' him had gone nowhere. All his monthly salary went on servicing debt – he had no disposable income at all. And champagne did not come out of a tap.

Love and money. Money and love. The basic ingredients of life and he had neither. Martin tightened his grip on the handle of his grey attache case, crossed Highbury New Park and entered the alley that led into Kelross Road. The right side of his forehead began to throb. He pulled out the strip of pink tablets that he carried at all times and popped two into his mouth. Nowadays a migraine was never far away.

When he reached Highbury Park he automatically glanced at his fake Gucci. It was 9.07. He was on schedule. A bit of rough in Reeboks, ripped denims and a white T-shirt was climbing down a ladder that was propped against the side of a corner shop. He had just finished pasting up a new poster on the billboard that covered the whole upper half of the house-wall. He had not made a very good job of it. Some of the sections overlapped, others had a gap between them. The ad featured a black and white photograph of a thirtysomething man in an overcoat and trilby dragging his girlfriend along a pebbly beach. In the foreground, a bottle was stuck in the stones. There was no mistaking the message which was couched in a handwritten script, presumably intended to suggest a cavalier attitude: *Lanson champagne – why not?* Why not indeed. Highbury was as good a place as any for hedonism. It demonstrated how affluent the neighbourhood must be if it was worthwhile advertising fizz. Either the hidden persuaders had been reading his mind or they had captured the zeitgeist. Why not?

Here was the paunchy man with the beard coming up the hill, hands, as usual, stuffed into the pockets of his green anorak. Here were the smart but flustered parents dropping off their darling Emmas and Olivers at the playgroup on their way to Docklands or the City. Here was the obese old woman without a bra, her flaccid breasts drooping down either side of her like empty panniers. He saw these people every weekday morning but they never acknowledged each other. Each one of them was running along their own private rut.

Even in the last compartment, all the seats were occupied. As he swayed in sync with the other strap-hangers, trying to inhale as little as possible of the fetid mixture of germs, dust, sweat and toothpaste fumes that swirled about him, he relived his favourite fantasy of working on a herb farm. Fresh air. No people. No noise. Lots of money.

At Caledonian Road a secretary-clone got on. Instead of brandishing a tabloid she tugged a paperback out of her handbag and stuck her nose in its pages. By craning his neck he could just make out the title. It was *A Guide To British Bats*.

✻

At the office three 'While You Were Out' messages awaited him. The first was from Isobel thanking him for dinner and confirming that she would see him for lunch on Wednesday as usual. The second was from Alex asking him to call and the third was from an angry left-wing playwright. In his review Martin had confessed that he had walked out of the ranter's latest effort and had advised others not to walk into it. He threw all three in the bin.

Martin was the features editor of a weekly arts magazine. *Streetwise* took up the fifth floor of the mirror-clad monstrosity in Covent Garden which housed all the British titles of an American publishing conglomerate. He was one of the very few hacks who did not grin at himself each time he entered the building. The latest circulation figures were on his desk. They had gone up yet again. He had no idea why. He peeped over the top of his cubicle – which was made out of chipboard covered in blue hessian – and met the twinkling eyes of his assistant, Araminta King. She was nibbling a chocolate croissant. Araminta had a fantastic figure and knew it.

'*Bonjour*, Marty. How are we this manic Monday morning?'

'We feel like shit. *We* have a fucking migraine.'

'So what else is new?' He frowned.

'Ah diddums. Let Araminta see.' She replaced her croissant in its paper bag and came round to him tut-tutting. She began to massage his temples. The scent of Chanel No 5 wafted up his nostrils. 'There, there,' she crooned. 'Minty's here. Everything is all right.'

'Everything is not all right… I think I must be suffering from the male menopause.'

'I know what you need.' She transferred her attention to his shoulders. 'My, how tense you are.'

'Money. I need money. Lots and lots of money,' he moaned, wriggling under her probing fingers.

'Poppycock. Just ask daddy like I always do.' She tossed her long dark hair over her shoulder. 'I had something rather more physical in mind.'

Araminta may have been eccentric but there was nothing irregular about her body which was at this moment in such pleasant proximity to his own. He knew he had as much chance of getting her into bed as he had with Isobel while Michael was around. In other words none at all. There was no harm in playing along though.

'You're supposed to be getting rid of my stiffness, not giving me more.' She laughed, kissed him on the top of his head and spun his chair round before answering the phone on her desk.

He sighed and picked up his own.

'Alex? It's Martin.'

'Hello queenie. Thanks for getting back to me.' He resisted the urge to slam down the receiver.

'What do you want?'

'Can't I just ring to find out how you are?'

'Of course – but I know you better than that. Come on, out with it.'

'Well. First I wanted to congratulate you on a splendid evening on Saturday. Sorry about Trudi. I thought she'd be good value. As I told you at the time, I will not be renewing her acquaintance. She has been airbrushed out of history.'

'I should damn well think so. Where did you meet her?'

'In the health-club that she works in. It's more of a knocking shop actually, a place for rubbing dicks.'

'Who does the rubbing? Trudi?'

'Possibly. I don't know. The only action I've ever seen has been between consenting male adults.'

'Oh. Right. Perhaps you should take Michael there.'

'I've already thought of that. Saturday was a real eye-opener. I'd kill for an arse like that.'

'So would I.' For a moment neither of them said anything.

'Ah well,' said Alex. 'I can't spend all morning gossiping with you. Is it today that you're interviewing Dan Salter?'

'It is.'

'Good. Be a darling and get his autograph for me. Ask him to sign a photo or something and make sure he puts lots of kisses.'

✯

The interview was to take place in a hotel off Piccadilly. The inevitable pack of paparazzi were loitering outside, whiling away the hours chatting up excited girls who should have been at school. He found the PR woman sitting in the lobby with a couple of crewcut acolytes. She apologised and informed him that they were running thirty minutes late. Martin had been on time.

After his third cup of coffee he was taken up to the top floor.

His guide pointed him in the right direction then returned to the express lift. A security guard stood outside the suite and, having frisked him and searched his case, he knocked on the door. Martin was surprised to feel butterflies flutter in his stomach.

The room was filled with the unmistakable aroma of french fries. Dan stood talking to what Martin assumed to be various members of his entourage. They were all men whose long hair lay on the shoulders of their Italian suits. They looked like archetypal hangers-on, losers who made a living out of ligging. There was no sign of the latest actress girlfriend. She was probably out shopping.

'Hi!' The boy wonder led the way into another reception room and closed the door behind them. 'We won't be disturbed in here.'

Dan Salter was the latest product of the Hollywood hunk machine. He was blond, he was tanned and he bulged in all the right places but, in essence, he was just a smile on a stick – even if the stick was beautifully carved. As the full force of this dental device was unleashed upon him, Martin felt his knees turn to mush. Once the knuckle-crushing handshake was over – having been held just that little bit too long – they sat down on facing sofas. Both of them leaned forward and adopted the legs apart/hands together position.

'OK. Fire away.'

He was accustomed to the sense of disappointment that follows the realisation that movie stars, literary whizzkids or childhood heroes are just ordinary people after all. There is no wonderland on the other side of the mirror. There is nothing behind the cinema screen. Dan had made his name doing stupid things in invisible helicopters and nuclear-powered Porsches. Fortunately for him, acting scarcely came into it. In the flesh he was not that good looking. There were no personal lighting designers or make-up artists on call today. Nevertheless, Martin was keenly aware of his physical inferiority and, to compensate, adopted an intellectual approach. This was not a good move. Salter did not understand the questions.

'Say what?'

'Do you think it would be fair to say that *Black Friday* is yet another allegory of the Vietnam War?'

'Um, yes. What's an allegory?'

'Would you rather I asked you what your favourite colour is?'

'Look. Don't get all mad-assed with me. I'm not dumb you know.'

'I wasn't for one moment suggesting that you were.'

'Sure, sure. It's green.'

'Sorry?'

'My favourite colour. It's green.'

After a further half-hour of verbal ping-pong Martin could not help liking the meathead. Dan was doing a job just like he was – except that he was being paid a few million dollars more. And he had really appreciated the answer to his last question.

'What do you like most about success?'

'The mega-bucks,' said Dan and treated him to another all-American grin.

★

Back in the office, Martin munched a pastrami on rye sandwich and pondered how he was going to spin such straw into the week's cover-story. The phone rang. He had forgotten to take it off the hook.

'Hello, handsome.'

'Who's that?'

'It's me, Trudi!' He choked on the last piece of bread. 'Hello? Hello? Is anybody there?'

'Excuse me. I was just dying.'

'Oh that's all right then.' She giggled. 'I had a triffic time Saturday night. I want to thank you in my own special way. Are you doing anything tonight?'

'Why?'

'Do you fancy a massage?'

He found the badly-printed card that she had given him in his wallet. 'Let My Fingers Do The Walking At Fighting Fit:

TRUDI JORDAN.' There followed a telephone number and an address in Camden.

'Don't worry about being seen,' continued Trudi. 'I know how shy you are. We close at 9.30 tonight. If you come at ten we'll have the place to ourselves.'

'Promise?'

'Promise,' said Trudi. 'It will be our little secret.'

'OK,' said Martin. 'Why not?'

SIX

Martin aged eleven. A new boy at Lancaster Royal Grammar School. It was not a public school but the governors liked to pretend otherwise. There were two boarding houses, Light Blue and Dark Blue. Martin was a member of the former. Martin was the odd boy out.

The school was financed by direct grant and therefore needed to supplement its income by taking in boarders. Three-quarters of the pupils were day-boys who had passed their eleven-plus. Boarders did not have to be as bright. Many resident students were the stupid sons of wealthy businessmen from Colne, Burnley, Blackburn and Manchester. Martin, who came from genteel Chester, had hoped to go to the local grammar school but the Labour government had earmarked it for conversion to a comprehensive the very year he had been due to enter it. His father insisted that this was a stroke of luck – even though it was going to cost him a fortune – because he was now justified in sending his only son and heir to his alma mater. His mother hated the idea. Martin was in two minds about it: he certainly did not want to rub shoulders with the dimwits that should have been shunted off into the secondary modern but being away from home for months at a time was a daunting prospect. However, when they went shopping for all the items on the inventory that had been sent to them – four shirts, white cotton; four shirts, grey cotton; eight pairs socks, grey wool; eight pairs underpants, white cotton etc – he felt a mounting excitement. It was just like preparing for Mallory Towers or St Clare's.

On a sticky Sunday evening in early September 1974, his proud father and tearful mother handed him into the care of Mrs Gittings, matron of Barton House. They had timed it so that they would neither be the first nor the last to arrive which was fine – except that every other boy was wearing his new school uniform whereas Martin was dressed in casual clothes. There had been some discussion on this point but it had been decided that jeans and the yellow jersey that he had got for his birthday were more suitable for the weekend and the long journey ahead. Mrs Gittings took him upstairs to change. When the red-faced Martin came down his parents had gone.

Barton House provided an ideal start for novice boarders. A large converted house at the end of a terrace, it stood further down the hill on which the main body of the school was sited. The boys slept in bedrooms not dormitories. Instead of one massive bathroom there were several small ones. On the ground floor there was an echoing table-tennis room lined with lockers, a library with an over-sprung sofa that often doubled as a trampoline and a TV room with more ancient armchairs. Viewing was strictly regulated. The cellars had been converted into a makeshift lab where Airfix kits could be assembled. It was down here that the boys had to clean their sensible shoes every evening after prep. If it was not exactly a home from home it was infinitely preferable to the impersonal, institutional School House where the older boys spent hours skidding along the lino-lined corridors in their socks. It was here that the First Years ate their meals with the rest of the boarders.

Grey-haired Mrs Gittings was known as The Git or The Stick Insect. Although she was only 35 she accentuated her age to enhance her authority. Martin, made all too aware of his puppy-fat by his footballing peers, complimented her on her slim figure. He was rebuked for making personal remarks and awarded his first 'notch'.

'Notches' were a system of black marks that were totalled up each week. The punishments meted out accordingly ranged from lines and daily duties to a beating with a slipper adminis-tered by Mr Douglas the swaggering House Master. Martin was shocked – he was only being friendly. Such an outrage would not have happened in Enid Blyton.

The first couple of weeks were nerve-racking. It was not easy to make friends. The fact that he did not wish to spend every available second kicking a ball about in the yard laid him open to accusations of being a cissy. So did his accent. Compared with the flat vowels and harsh consonants of Lancastrian, Cestrian – especially when one had been brought up to 'speak properly' sounded positively la-di-da. The other boys mimic-ked him. When he retaliated with sarcasm and snobbery his persecutors would turn their attention to his hair. His father believed in a short back and sides: the masculine style was a smart one that did not require a lot of titivation. But this was the seventies, the age of shaggy manes and sideburns. Although the boys were not allowed to let their hair grow over their collars, they still had much longer hair than Martin. He was polite and posh; they were rough and ready. He was homesick.

After the day's lessons, and as the day-boys dashed down the hill towards the town and their own homes, the boarders of Barton House would gather in the kitchen where the tuck boxes were kept on wide wooden shelves. It was in these small chests that the boys kept their sweets, biscuits and cakes and hid their teddybears. Martin liked the warm cosy atmosphere and lingered there, but was embarrassed to eat very much in case someone called him 'fatty'. It was in here, if anywhere, that he began to feel he belonged, that it would be all right, that he would be able to stick the next seven years. The schoolwork was no problem, it was outside the classroom that the trouble started.

On Tuesdays and Fridays at this time, Matron sorted out the laundry. Every item of a boy's property had to be labelled; his clothes identified by Cash's name tags. When Martin's mother had come to sew these into his new clothes, she had assumed, like her son, that this was to prevent them being stolen and had therefore, to confuse the thief, stitched the tags in the least obvious of places. This caused Mrs Gittings a lot of grief. One particular Friday, when Martin was valiantly trying to counteract the feeling that he would much rather be at home – weekends were particularly boring, there was so much time to kill – that she exploded with exasperation.

'For God's sake Rudrum, why do you have to be different? Why can't you be more like Patterson here?'

He flushed with humiliation as a flaxen-haired Rory stood and smiled.

SEVEN

Martin aged fourteen. On Monday afternoon the Third Years had their games period: rugby in the winter, cricket in the summer, athletics and/or cross-country running in between. Boarders were expected to play at the weekend as well. Martin hated rugby but loved running. He was not a team-player. Consequently he was not too distressed when, one Saturday morning in January, his stockinged-feet slipped on a set of shiny granite stairs in School House. Instinctively putting out his right arm to break his fall, he merely succeeded in breaking his right arm. It hurt and it made him throw up but, once his arm had been cocooned in plaster, the dull ache was a constant, not unpleasant, reminder that he was off games for the next six weeks.

Those excused games were not allowed to profit from their free time by, for example, reading a book in a warm classroom: they were required to stand and watch their fellows rolling about in the mud.

It was only natural that the boys who were forced to scrum down against their wishes took every opportunity to curse the reluctant spectators. However, a plaster cast acted like a magic shield – no one could be expected to take part with a whole limb out of commission. Even so, one games master suggested that he might like to go for a run. Martin courteously refused.

Lancaster Grammar had two sets of sports pitches, the Old Field and the much larger Memorial Fields. The former were the preserve of the First XV and other school teams who practised constantly. The latter were a five minute walk away from the school and although, being on the top of the hill, they overlooked the city and Morecambe Bay beyond, they were an unpopular venue for several reasons. The lower side of the fields bordered a council estate which surrounded the local secondary modern. Not surprisingly, the pupils of this dump for drop-outs looked upon those of LRGS as stuck-up representatives of unwarranted privilege and seized every opportunity to abuse them verbally and physically. Indeed, it had been known for them to ambush hapless first year boarders as they made their way back to Barton House after prep. Rumours would occasionally circulate of epic rumbles being conducted in Market Square: Stanley knives glinting, bike chains flailing, Doc Martens stomping faces to pulp.

But such shenanigans paled into insignificance compared with the toxic threat of Nightingale Farm. This establishment ran alongside the northwest corner of the fields. Its purpose was to extract the oils needed for the manufacture of soap from what was left of animal carcasses when the butcher had taken his cut. The leftovers of death were transported from abattoirs by the skip-load. As the lorries trundled up the hill past the school they left behind a foul trail of blood and shit on the road. The tarpaulins meant to hide the putrid remains – and prevent the overfilled dumpsters spilling their contents – were often badly tied and it was not unusual to find a cow's hoof or sheep's head in the gutter. The boys nicknamed the hell-hole Nightmare Fart.

The sobriquet was an accurate one. With its sheds of rusty corrugated iron, its gurgling boilers, labyrinthine pipework and smoking chimneys – all surrounded by high-fences and spotlights – the ramshackle factory resembled a baby Belsen. The men in rubber aprons who ran it were not the tidiest of operatives. Bits of bodies lay strewn all over the place. If water from a hosepipe failed to shift the offal it stayed there. The stink was overpowering and an ill wind often carried the ripe smell of corruption down into Lancaster. Those who lived nearest to this eye- and nose-sore organised a campaign called STENCH: the Society for the Termination of the Excessively Nauseating Community Horror. Nothing changed.

Normally only a thin wisp of grey smoke emanated from the main chimney but sometimes the refinery would go into overdrive, the machinery would shake, and the incessant rumble grow into a roar. As soon as this happened the master acting as referee would blow his whistle and both teams would run pell-mell for shelter in the vandalised changing-rooms where they would watch the wisp mushroom into a black cloud that would slowly drift over where they had just been gasping for breath. Anyone caught out in the cloud would find that it contained flakes of charred bone. The miasma would hang over the playing fields for at least fifteen minutes.

Pitch number five was separated from the farm by a bank. It was on here that the skivers would position themselves because it afforded them a good view of both the game and the local holocaust which exerted an unhealthy fascination. As dusk fell the reddening sun turned the snow on the Lake District peaks a salmon pink. The sea shimmered in the icy light. The invalids shivered. Bored, Martin turned his back on the yelling boys and watched as yet another skip tipped its cargo of corpses into the pit that fed the vats of cooking innards. There was a gap in the fence just here. Holding his nose, he decided to take a closer look. Blenkinsop, a boy with a permanent cold, followed.

On this side the tussocky grass grew right up to the rim of the cement well. The ground was crisscrossed with small narrow paths that were rat-runs. The hecatomb was a heaven on earth for vermin. Martin stood on the edge and gazed down at the carnage. Eyes frozen in terror met his. Viscera glistened moistly. Horns protruded from the noisome stew.

It was then that the fat rat scuttled over Blenkinsop's foot. He screamed and jumped forward, shoving Martin into the pit.

Although the mass of carrion looked solid it actually floated on a witches' brew of blood, ichor and diarrhoea. He went straight under. The freezing liquid shot up his nostrils, eeled down his back, trickled inside his cast and swamped his shoes. Kicking his legs as best he could, he tried to reach the surface but kept knocking against heads, hooves and horns. He began to panic.

An iron hook on a pole, and then another, clawed into his gabardine and yanked him out, intestines trailing off his limbs. Martin sneezed, coughed and retched. His hair was plastered to his head. A rheumy film covered him all over. Rinsed in red, he looked as though he had just endured a monstrous birth. As a filthy handkerchief wiped the scum from his face he blinked and saw his schoolmates gripping the fence with both hands and peering at him in silence. He puked again.

When they saw that he would survive the hooting began. In the ambulance Martin started to recover from the shock and held on to his master's hand. It was then that he discovered the constructive side to fury. He would show the bastards.

Three months later Blenkinsop was badly injured when the front wheel of his ten-speed racer spun off as he hurtled down-hill into Lancaster.

EIGHT

Martin aged 16. His puppy fat had wasted away. It was as though his body had used the surplus energy to fuel its sudden growth in height. Puberty had been kind to him and – apart from a few stubborn spots on his shoulders – left his skin unravaged. His features had begun to take on the form they would have for the rest of his life. His body clay, until now an amorphous mass, had begun to harden. His emotions still had some way to go.

June. Exam time. Martin lay in Duncan's arms. There were only three more weeks of term to go. The thought of a summer vacation would usually have filled him with relief and excitement but this year was different.

'God, I wish they were over,' murmured Duncan. He was eighteen and in the middle of sitting his A' Levels. 'It's all right for you. O' Levels are a doddle.'

'You'll be fine. Don't worry. You said that they'd gone quite well so far.'

'Yes I know. It's just that I can't wait to get out of this place. I can't believe that after seven years I'm finally going to walk out and never come back. There'll be no reunion dinners for me.'

Martin was silent. He had been determined not to bring the subject up but now Duncan had done so there was no point in holding back. It had been gnawing at him for weeks. Obsessed with yesterday and tomorrow, he had little time for today.

'Well?' Duncan tightened his grip on his shoulder and kissed him. 'Cat got your tongue?'

Martin was frightened. He knew what was coming. It was inevitable. In some ways it was remarkable that they had lasted this long.

Duncan felt his heartbeat quicken. 'You're not going to go all girly on me are you?'

Martin laughed. The two boys were lying naked on Duncan's quilt. They were on top of the sixty-foot tower which joined the headmaster's house to School House. It was a hot night. Above them the Evening Star was rising. A parapet, three feet high, ran round the top of the tower. In one corner there was a flagpole that was only used on special occasions such as the Queen's birthday or Founder's Day. Access to it was via a trap-door. Because there was not much space, the boys lay across the trapdoor, making it impossible for anybody to surprise them. The only problem was that someone might lock them in by slid-ing home the bolt on the underside of it. But this was unlikely – no one else ever came up here at night. It was an eyrie, an ideal place for trysts.

As the prefect of Dorm 4, Duncan's study/bedroom was the one that lay off the staircase inside the tower. This made it very easy for him to drag his bedding onto the roof. And because Martin was in Dorm 4, anybody who saw him leaving would think that he was on the way to the bathroom. If anyone knew about their relationship they had not mentioned it. After all, Martin and Duncan were not the only ones. Perhaps the fact that Duncan was in the First Fifteen gave them some degree of immunity.

It was in the bathroom that he had first noticed Duncan. Although he had taken part in the wanking competitions that were a feature of Lights Out in the second and third years – the last to come on the digestive biscuit had to eat it – Martin had only entertained an academic interest in the bodies of other boys. However, his speed in climaxing had provoked ribald comment. With Duncan, though, it had been different. For a start, Duncan was not a boy but a man. As he stepped out of the shower, water streaming off his muscles, Duncan caught Martin's glance of admiration and grinned. The white teeth, slick black hair, brown skin and unselfconscious ease made his heart flip. Confused and embarrassed, he hid his face by bending over the sink.

The following Saturday he went to watch the home game against Sedbergh. Duncan was in the second row of the scrum. The annual fixture was a traditional needle match and the brutal way in which the players cannoned into each other made Martin wince. Clouds of steam came off them, their ragged breath leaving contrails in the frigid air. As the sun sank and the two teams tired, the spectators ran up and down the sidelines to keep warm. Lancaster were winning and Sedbergh did not like it. Fists began to fly. The younger boys loved it. Then Duncan's shorts ripped. The whistle went and the game stopped. Duncan trotted over to the coach who was waving a spare pair. Such incidents were not uncommon.

Without a moment's hesitation, Duncan took off what was left of his own pair and stood in front of the sizable crowd in his jock-strap. Martin's mouth went dry. As he put on the new shorts, Duncan noticed Martin and winked. That night, after Lights Out, Martin knocked on Duncan's door. The perfect prefect was waiting for him in the bottom half of a purple tracksuit.

Martin's father had a thing about homosexuals. Whenever footballers, ecstatic at scoring a goal, threw their arms around each other, he would hide his discomfort by blowing kisses at the TV screen. 'Bloody nancy-boys. I'm going to leave the country before they make it compulsory.' Martin did not see what all the fuss was about. Having had sex with Duncan, he was surprised to find that he did not feel guilty. The forbidden nature of their friendship, instead of detracting from the pleasure, increased it.

They spent the night together two or three times a week. When it was warm enough they went to the top of the tower, otherwise they stayed in Duncan's room. He would hanker after the sense of security he felt in Duncan's arms for the rest of his life. Duncan was like the brother he had never had. His mother had recently told Martin that he was actually her second child. Her first son had died aged six months. Although he concealed the fact from his parents he was haunted by his brother's death. He had always wanted an older brother, someone to look up to, someone to look out for him. He had not realised that he was a surrogate.

By 'girly' Duncan meant 'emotional'. The two lovers may have been of the same sex but their relationship was still based on the attraction of opposites. Martin thought that it had a sexual symmetry. Duncan was short and stocky; he was tall and slim. Duncan was brilliant on the field but comparatively dull in the classroom; Martin was bright on paper but stupid on the pitch. Endomorphic and ectomorphic; brawny and brainy. Only their feelings were out of sync.

'What's going to happen to us?' said Martin.

'I'm going Inter-railing round Europe with Steve and then – all being well – I'm going to Durham University. You're going to get grade As in all your O' Levels and then come back and do the same in your A' Levels and then you're going to go to Oxford.'

'That isn't what I meant and you know it. What's going to happen to us?'

'Nothing.'

'Nothing?'

'Martin, you know I'm very fond of you…'

'Careful! You almost said love then.'

'You know I'm very fond of you but we can't go on seeing each other like this. It's been good while it's lasted but the time has come to move on to other things.'

'You mean career, car, wife, house, kids and pension plan.'

'Sarky, sarky!' He tried to kiss Martin but he pushed him away and stood up.

'Sit down you fool. Someone might see you.'

'I don't care. You know I love you. You can't just suddenly stop seeing me.'

'I won't stop seeing you. We'll keep in touch. We'll still be friends. We can visit each other. Sit down.'

'Why is it that I don't believe a word you're saying? We've been together for ten months. Are you saying that it's simply been a question of my mouth being better than your hand?'

'Shut up. Shut up.' Now they were both angry. 'For God's sake sit down.'

'Why should I, you bastard? I knew that you didn't feel about me the same way I did about you, but I did think that you felt something for me.'

'I do. Why do you think it's lasted this long? If it was only a question of sex I could have found someone else easily enough.'

'And I suppose I couldn't?'

'I wasn't suggesting that. Look…' Duncan sat up and held out his hand. 'Come on, come here. I was really hoping it wasn't going to be this way.'

'So was I.' Martin wanted nothing more than to lie down beside Duncan again and nuzzle him but he stepped back instead. 'I love you Duncan. I can't bear to give you up.' He stepped onto the parapet.

Duncan shot to his feet.

'Stay there,' warned Martin. 'Don't come any closer.'

He had no intention of jumping. Perhaps Duncan should be made to jump instead.

'Please Martin. Don't do this to me. We'll get caught. I don't want to be expelled after all this time. I'll do anything you say but you're behaving like an idiot.'

'Perhaps. Perhaps. Stand over there, against the other side.' Suddenly they heard voices. Before Duncan had time to react, Martin leapt across the top of the tower towards him. When he saw the baleful light in Martin's eyes, Duncan quailed but his strength saved him. He caught him in his arms and pulled him down onto the quilt. Martin burst into tears.

The incident ensured that Martin and Duncan did not even remain friends. Martin continued to write to Duncan for a couple of months. He received no reply. Duncan could never decide whether Martin was going to jump, to push him over the edge of the tower, or kill both of them in a ludicrous sort of lovers' leap. Whatever the intention he was well rid of him. He really had been fond of him. He was a funny, affectionate boy.

Martin's mother had often accused him of having an old

head on young shoulders. He had read enough books to know that first loves were not last loves – even if they were often the most intense. Perhaps the end of the affair proved that men were not supposed to love each other, that what he and Duncan had been up to was evil. Girls believed in fidelity, in pairing for life. Perhaps his instincts were female rather than male.

It would be thirteen years before he had sex with another man.

NINE

He had seen enough television to know how to make things difficult for the police. The cardinal rule was to leave as few clues as possible. The keyword was ordinariness. It was important to stick to routine as closely as possible.

'How's the Salter piece coming along?' said Araminta.

'Slowly. I've transcribed the tape but his laugh is the most interesting sound on it – that and my own voice of course.'

'Can I borrow the tape when you've finished? I'll get Sebastian to jiggery-poke a copy of it so that we can use Dishy Dan's vocals on our answering machine. It will be quite a coup!'

'Your wish is my command.'

'You are sweet. I don't know why some girl doesn't come along and snatch you up. You'd make someone a lovely hubby.'

''Thank you.'

'What are you doing tonight? Are you off to the theatre?'

'Nope. All I've got in store is an evening with my carpet slippers and pipe.'

'You lucky thing. I wish I could stay in now and then. It's such a bore being a social butterfly. One of Seb's friends is having a birthday bash. You could come along if you like.'

'No thanks. I think I'll stick to being a couch potato.'

'Oh well. I'll see you tomorrow. If you change your mind give me a ring.'

'I will.'

That would do for an alibi. If he needed one.

★

As with any other social occasion he had to decide what to wear. It was not an easy choice to make – he did not have many cheap clothes and the cheaper they were, the more difficult it would be to trace any fibres back to him. Similarly, black would be the safest colour. In the end he opted for a pair of white Marks & Spencer boxer shorts, black Levis 501s, a white T-shirt and a navy blue woollen sweater which was also from M&S. With his black leather jacket – the older, less expensive one; not the one he normally wore for work – and black training shoes, he looked as if he was going to the ICA, not out to murder a whore.

Accessories. A tenner and his front door key were anonymous enough.

It would be necessary to truss Trudi up at some stage but he had not got any string and he did not want anybody to remember him buying some. Superglue would have to do. He would take a pair of black shoelaces as well. They might come in useful. Finally there were the rubber gloves.

The gloves were not of a household variety such as Marigolds but genuine surgeon's gloves. His father used them at his practice and often brought a box home for the daily who wore a new pair every week. Last time he had been at home Mrs Muckalt had given him six packets: 'You never know when you might need them.' How right she was. They not only hugged the skin but they were also virtually transparent. In a dim light it was impossible to tell if someone were wearing them. He ran through his mental checklist and tut-tutted: he had nearly forgotten a clean handkerchief.

He ate dinner watching *Brookside*. Fifteen minutes to go. He did not want to arrive early, just as the last bum-bandits were leaving. He did *The Times* crossword and had a pee. Now he was ready.

He had decided that the underground was the safest method of travel. Bus routes offered more clues. Taxis were out of the question. He changed from the Piccadilly line to the Northern line at Kings Cross. As the filthy, hot carriages rattled their way along the giant drains, he hid behind a copy of the *Evening Standard*. His horoscope for the next day promised well-earned relief from tension.

He had always disliked Camden. It was nothing more than a glorified rail-junction: the domain of dossers and drunks; the place where pine furniture was pushed at the poor. The tube station formed a promontory round which the one-way system of traffic swirled in a vortex of exhaust gases and grit. Snatches of music belted out, Vivaldi competing with reggae, Mozart trouncing rap. He, too, was stuck in his own one-way system. There was no going back now.

An old codger in a moth-eaten ulster, the face above his daglocked beard marbled with dirt, staggered up to him.

'Twenty pee for a cup of tea?' Martin neither stopped nor looked at him.

'Fuck off grandad.'

He turned into Camden Road.

☆

The door was open. He dropped the latch and listened. He could not hear any voices. Somewhere Kylie Minogue was being strangled. How apt. He put on the gloves.

The lino in the middle of each step had lost its pattern where countless, heavy-breathing men had climbed the hill to climax.

There was a small reception area on the landing with a desk and two imitation-leather couches. A livid green cheese-plant stood on one corner of the desk. It was so alive it seemed artificial. Robert Mapplethorpe prints hung on the white walls. The stairs continued up to the next floor, but straight ahead another door led into a cramped gym. It was from here that Trudi emerged. She was wearing a short white overall and had her peroxided hair tied up in a ponytail. Her arms were full of soiled towels. Instead of curling up his lip in distaste Martin beamed.

'Hello sexbomb.'

'Hello handsome. How about a sunbed?'

'Why not?'

She dropped the towels and started up the stairs, hitching up her overall as she went. She had nothing on underneath. He followed, licking his lips in a mixture of nervousness and lust. Araminta was right – he could do with a quickie – but it would be tantamount to leaving a calling card. Besides, every second here was a second of danger. He shifted his erection into a more comfortable position.

The second floor consisted of a narrow corridor lined with three numbered doors on each side. Was it his imagination or was the lino actually sticky? Trudi went into Room 6. A large sunbed ran along one wall. A shower cubicle took up most of the remaining space but there was just room for a plastic chair. It was very hot.

Trudi slipped off her unbuttoned coat and came towards him.

'Come on slowcoach.'

Before her puckered lips had time to reach Martin's, he gripped her round the throat with both of his hands and squeezed as hard as he could. She tried to knee him in the groin but he was holding her at arm's length. She tried to scratch him with her chipped fingernails but he fended her off with his outstretched arms, squeezing and squeezing, the fingers of each hand gradually interlocking with their counterparts round the back of her neck. She was certainly putting up a fight. He watched in fascination as her eyeballs bulged in their sockets. The whites of them were decorated with a delicate tracery of tiny pink lines like the ones found in the glaze of old china. Her mascara began to run, streaking her bronzed cheeks. He kept on squeezing.

When he could bear the ache in his hands no longer he let go. She dropped to the floor. She had not made a sound. Kylie Minogue was still wailing. He put his hand on her heart and was annoyed to detect a faint beat. There was no time to lose.

He turned on the sunbed. The fluorescent tubes flickered into life, flooding the cubby-hole with ultra-violet light. He set the control switch as high as it would go. He picked up Trudi with a grunt and spread-eagled her on the scratched perspex surface. He took the Superglue from his pocket and daubed some on all four corners of the bed then pressed the back of her hands and the outsides of her feet onto it. It really did hold fast in seconds. He sealed her lips. He did not want her screaming for help. Some of the adhesive trickled out of her mouth like saliva. The little tart was brown all over: Rory would have been pleased. Now he was going to tan the hide off her.

As he gazed down at the girl's defenceless form, he could not resist stroking her V-shaped bush. V for velvet. Vulva. Vagina. Venus. Venereal. Vice. Victim. He felt no remorse. She deserved her death. Casual ties always led to casualties.

He stood up and lowered the top of the human toasted sandwich maker as far as it would go. Even if the glue melted, Trudi would have no room for manoeuvre, assuming, that is, she ever regained consciousness. He tied the handles on the middle of each side together with the shoe laces. He turned off the light, closed the door and left her to fry.

He had been in the health joint less than ten minutes and yet he could already feel the difference. It had been better than sex. And it was so easy! There were so many ways to kill a human being. As he made his way home – slightly flushed and gently shaking – he entertained himself by listing all the alternatives. He had never been so clear-headed. It was almost impossible to recall the agony of a migraine… There was shooting, stabbing, drowning, smothering, poisoning, burning, freezing, baking and hanging. You could bludgeon someone's brains out, scare them to death and even crucify them. None of these methods appealed to him though. Next time he would try something really different.

TEN

He watched as a policeman and a policewoman got out of the Rover. When the doors were closed they made the kind of satisfying thud that only expensive models provide. The white roof of the car was blazoned with 5X9 in black letters. A fluorescent strip on the side of the vehicle glowed lemon-green in the light from the porch. It was very quiet. The male officer, who had been driving, joined the female on the pavement. They both looked up at the house. Martin darted away from the window.

The gate creaked.

ELEVEN

That night Martin slept soundly. He woke early and without the faintest throb of a headache. He was alive and ready for anything. As his father would have said, today was the first day of the rest of his life.

It took him a while to find his tracksuit. When he had lived with Isobel he had gone running every morning. Sometimes, to his delight, Isobel had joined him. Loping round Victoria Park they must have seemed like an ad-man's dream: healthy and wealthy, getting and spending, racing towards a joint success that lay straight ahead. It was different nowadays: he did not know where he was going but he knew he had not got there.

He was halfway round Clissold Park and he still had not got a stitch. He was sweating rather heavily though. Geriatric mongrels sniffed about in the dewy grass. Their owners, afraid of conversation, skirted each other warily. Martin kicked and increased his pace. This was the only time when he was glad that he had long legs.

Green Lanes was choked with rush-hour traffic, each car, like a mechanical dog, nose to tail with the one in front. A purple-grey pall hung over the jam, poisoning the air that he was gulping. It was a no-win situation.

He returned in time to buy a carton of orange juice from the milk-float that was whirring and rattling up the street. Not many people had milk delivered – bottles did not stay on doorsteps very long. As he wallowed in the hot bath and sipped the juice he suddenly realised that he was happy.

✷

By lunch-time the treadmill had made him as tense as ever.

'Hello. It's me.'

'Hello.'

'Thanks for the photo. Dan The Man gave me five kisses. It's fabulous. You should have seen the biker who brought it. He was a vision in leather. Young too.'

'I'm glad you like it. I told him that Alex was my sister.'

'Well I suppose we are sisters in a way.'

'I think the term you're looking for is blood brothers.'

'If you say so. Not feeling bitter and twisted are we?'

'No more so than usual.'

'Good. Guess what I did last night.'

'Oh I don't know. Shared a few lines with the entire Arsenal team in a jacuzzi of champagne?'

'No. I've done that. Not far off though. You remember I told you about that art dealer called Theo I met at the gym? You know, the one with the immaculately shaved arse.'

'Vaguely.'

'Come off it. You were as moist as hell when I described him.'

'Alex. Please. Just get on with it.'

'Yes, well, as I was saying, Theo took me to meet a friend of his who lives in this mansion in Highgate. He's a millionaire, owns a lot of trees apparently. Anyway, I expected him to be old but he's only 23! And he's got the biggest cock I've ever seen.'

'How do you know?'

'I'm coming to that. After dinner, Theo and John suggested we have a threesome. I said no but once I'd sniffed poppers a few times I thought what the hell, you're only young once, so we all went into the sauna. When I saw this *thing* between John's legs my heart nearly stopped. It was one of those moments when you've just got to have it even if it kills you. And he had no trouble getting it up. He wanted to fuck me but there was no way I was going to let him put it up me so I made him fuck Theo instead. He was in absolute agony. I loved it.'

'Martin are you all right?' Araminta had noticed his horrified expression.

'Yes. It's Alex.'

'That explains it.'

'Who are you talking to?'

'Sorry. It was Minty.'

'Stuck up cow. What does she want?'

'Nothing. Go on.'

'Oh. All of a sudden we're interested are we? Nothing like a mention of size to make your ears prick up is there?'

'My interest is purely academic.'

'I bet. Well, after John had come, Theo said he felt sick and left us to it. It was bliss. On the way back Theo told me he could actually feel the willie poking his stomach. Can you imagine?'

'I'd rather not.'

'John's invited me to his family's chateau for the weekend. His parents are in Japan. It's not that far from Paris. He said I could bring a friend. Do you want to come?'

'No thanks. It wouldn't really be my scene.'

'What do you mean? Fabulous wealth, fabulous surroundings, fabulous boys and fabulous drink and drugs. It's as close to heaven as we're ever likely to get. Think about it.'

'OK. I will.'

Alex was right but he knew that he would not go to France. He would only feel nervous and insecure. Orgies were what other people took part in. He was cursed with self-consciousness, the bane of the middle classes. He would be unable to blinker the all-seeing eye that monitored his eternal progress. The only way he could obviate this disassociation of sensibility was to achieve such a level of abandon that he did not care what the mental spy-in-the-sky was recording. But this solution involved the consumption of so much alcohol and/or illegal substances that in the event he was scarcely capable of performing. The catch-22 meant that he never caught anything.

The double bind did not stop there. Whether at work or play, Martin tried to accomplish what he had to do as quickly as possible. In the office such efficiency led to accusations of cutting corners but he always ensured that the quality of his work did not suffer. Slowness was no guarantee of value. At home, if he were solving a crossword, he tried to complete it as fast as he could. In his thesaurus taking one's time and wasting one's time were synonymous. He would often dash home, unpack his case, shower, put on his comfort clothes – faded jeans and a sweater that his mother had knitted – make a coffee and slump onto the sofa only to think, now what? Beating the clock had been a means of beating boredom but now he was bored even when he was busy. Tired of the old, he was afraid of the new. The more he packed into each hour, the more time there was to kill.

He was a control freak. If there was nothing to do it meant that order was being maintained. If crosswords were useful in occupying the mind there was nothing more useless than a filled-in crossword grid. He saw them as symbols of victory in the battle between setter and solver but such contests were necessarily unequal. An unsolvable crossword was pointless. Each diagram was a means of patterning the random, of structuring flux. He strove to give his own life a regular shape. He did the same things at the same time every week. He went shopping on Friday evenings, did the cleaning on Saturday mornings and wrote the cheques to pay the bills on Monday evenings. Externally strong, he was internally weak.

Tuesday evening entailed *The Bill*, cauliflower cheese and the *Listener* crossword which had re-emerged in *The Times* on Saturday. Tonight though, he had an excuse for his haste: he had something to read.

He had found the address book in Trudi's handbag which he had searched before leaving Fighting Fit. It was a tiny black notebook with red corners. Gold letters on the cover spelled out LITTLE BLACK BOOK. He had slipped it into his pocket along with the thirty pounds from her purse. On the way home, having dumped the rubber gloves in a litterbin, he had bought a bottle of Lanson from the local off-licence. He opened it now and gazed at the memento mori.

He felt a slight reluctance to touch it. The book was the only piece of evidence that connected him to the corpse. If need be he could say that Trudi had left it here on Saturday. Even so, he would have to get rid of it. He took another swig of champagne and picked it up.

Many of the grimy pages were dog-eared. They contained dozens and dozens of names, most of them male. The potential for mischief was immense. When the chance of making serious money finally came into his hands, he could do nothing about it because any action would immediately place him in jeopardy. He smiled at the irony.

In addition to the alphabetical lists of names, there were headings such as 'Leather', 'Scat' and 'Kids' with more names beneath them. He shuddered and turned to R. There, at the bottom of the fourth page, was his own name. He turned to F for Fenton and, sure enough, there was Alex's number. Something else caught his eye. The last name in the section was Ford. Michael Ford. He riffled back to R. The same biro had been used to record the name and numbers of both Michael and himself. He had not given Trudi the *Streetwise* number but, if she had not asked Alex for it, she could have found it in any copy or simply called directory enquiries. His home number was ex-directory and so was Michael's. He must have slipped it to her on Saturday. He could just hear him tell her, 'you'd be ideal for my next series.' How could he do this to Isobel? Michael was famous for his wanderlust but Isobel had always insisted that he was faithful to her. Now his suspicions had been confirmed.

He stared at Mr Blueface in his bowler hat. He stared back. Did Michael know that Trudi was going to see him? The bastard might have dropped in on her last night before he turned up. He did not let the grass grow under his ass. It was essential to find out. Mr Ford was now a double liability. Both Isobel and himself would be better off without him. Michael would be stiff number two.

TWELVE

Isobel came breezing into the restaurant just as she always did, pushing back her hair, laughing, slightly out of breath. Black curls, white teeth, red lips. Martin kissed them and, holding her padded shoulders so that she could not move away, kissed them again. He enjoyed letting the watching businessmen know that Isobel was his. It did not matter so much that she was not if they thought she was. They sat down at their usual table, an air of complicity between them. He liked to think it was because they only really felt at ease when they were together.

'Hi.'

'Hello, mon petit choux. Ça va?'

'Ça va. Ça va. Et tu?'

'Ça va bien. Très bien.'

Ever since they had started seeing each other as friends – about six months after they had broken up – Isobel and Martin had met for lunch on Wednesday. The rendezvous was always the same, a French restaurant just off Leicester Square. It reminded him of their favourite holiday together. The summer of 1987. Sunrise at Alyscamps, the ghost of Van Gogh lurking among the rough, bone-chilling sarcophagi… Midday in Nîmes, basking on the top row of the amphitheatre, a cool breeze evaporating the sheen on their upper lips, making their nipples erect… Dusk on the Pont du Gard, the mistral running its fingers through their hair, Germans whooping in the icy water below… Midnight in Avignon, getting sloshed on Côtes du Rhône. For a whole month they did not fight.

Chez Albert was a bastion of good bourgeois cooking. The onion soup and coq au vin were legendary – nouvelle cuisine had made no inroads here. A plush banquette ran round the walls which were covered in red and gold flock. Pictures that could be bought in any branch of Boots hung above the tables and their starched white cloths. The house wine was served in carafes. The cost was calculated on how much you drank – what was left got poured back into the vat.

They clinked their glasses together and said 'salut'. Martin reflected that there was little to show for their years together. All he had, apart from a few photographs and memories, was bitterness, a bitterness that he was forced to hide. In the first place he had had to feign forgiveness so that Isobel would agree to see him. It had not been easy. It never occurred to him that he might be the cause of the break-up.

'I've got something to show you,' said Isobel. She handed him a sheaf of photocopies that were stapled together. 'I found this in Michael's study.'

Martin looked at the shabby booklet. It claimed to be The *Steroid User's Underground Handbook*. In fact it was a sort of amateur PiMS, a pharmaceutical catalogue.

'Samizdat for iron-pumpers. Whatever next?'

Leaning over the table, Isobel fingered through the pages until she found the right one. 'Look at this.'

Among the entries for Exoboline, Durabolin, Methandriol, Nolvadex and Prednisone, the one for Growth Hormone was ringed:

Injectable, 10 unit vials, 4 to box. Wow, is this great stuff! It is the best drug for permanent muscle gains. It is the basic pituitary hormone that makes your whole body grow. People who use it can expect to gain 30 to 40lbs, of muscle in 10 weeks. If they can eat 10,000 calories per day. It is about $600–$800 per 4 vials. We think this to be another best buy. It has been very hard to get in the past as it was made from the pituitary glands of rhesus monkeys and is illegal for general sale in the USA. It is now being made from 'smart' E Coli bacteria at Baylor Medical School in Texas. Usual dosage has been 2 units every three days.

This is the only drug that can remedy bad genetics as it will make anybody grow.

A few side effects can occur, however. It may elongate your chin, feet and hands but this is arrested with cessation of the drug. Diabetes in teenagers is possible with it. It can also thicken your ribcage and wrists. Massive increases in weight over such a short time can, of course, give you heart problems. We have heard of a power-lifter getting a heart attack while on GH GH use is the biggest gamble that an athlete can take, as the side effects are irreversible. Even with all that, we LOVE the stuff.

'Terrific prose style. Is he taking this shit?'

'I don't know. I doubt whether he can get hold of it.'

'Why has he got this thing then?'

'He says he wants to make a documentary on the subject. There are rumours that some people are so desperate for the hormone that they have bribed undertakers and pathologists to remove pituitary glands from corpses. Can you believe it?'

'Yes I can. If this stuff is as good as they say it is then I wouldn't mind trying it as well.'

'Martin, for God's sake. You'd eat bits of dead people just for the sake of a better body?'

'Why not? The stiffs aren't going to miss their glands. Besides, it says here that the Yanks are producing it artificially now. A beautiful body is a desirable thing. I've often wished that I could swap a few of my grey cells for a muscle or two. Clever people and hunky people are ten a penny. It's the combination of the two that is difficult to come by. Physique and intellect perpetually warring within a single frame – that's my idea of perfection.'

Isobel sighed.

'Sometimes I think that you and Michael are more alike than you know.'

'Well you left me for him. It stands to reason that there must be at least one quality in both of us that you respond to. Obviously you prefer a little more meat and less IQ than I could offer.'

'Cut it out. Are you ready to order?'

During the meal Isobel admitted to him that Michael was taking a drug to enhance his musculature.

'It's called Pregnyl, an extract from the urine of pregnant women.'

'You might as well just go to placenta parties and have done with it. It would probably be cheaper too.'

'Don't be gross. Seriously Martin, I'm worried about him. He swears that the only side effect is water retention but I'm not so sure. Will you talk to him for me? I'm going to Milan for a couple of days tomorrow. Why don't you call him and suggest a drink?'

'Me talk to him? Why me?'

'Stop being ingenuous. You know he likes you, and I know, deep down, that you like him too. All that banter is just his way of flirting with you. He knows you get off on it. I can't ask anybody else. I trust you.'

'I'm glad you feel this way but if your joyboy wants to become the Michelin Man why should I interfere? You forget that he is still my rival.'

'You shouldn't think of him like that. There's no going back, Martin. Just be glad that you met me first. Michael got me second-hand.'

'I want you back.' Isobel flushed.

'I know you do. I know you do.' She swilled the wine round the bottom of her glass.

'I still love you. There hasn't been anyone else.'

'Please don't let's get into all this again. I want you to do me a favour. If you won't do it just say so.'

'I will do it. Of course I will. You know I'll do anything for you.'

'Thank you.' She kissed the middle finger of her right hand and pressed it to his lips.

'Just answer me this one question. Don't worry, it's not that difficult. I realise that Michael, with or without drugs, has got an infinitely better body than me. I realise that he earns a lot more than me as well. Was it either of these things that made you leave me?'

'Of course not. You do have a low opinion of me don't you? I'm not saying that such things didn't play a part in my decision but there was a much more important reason.'

'What? I wasn't unfaithful. I didn't beat you up. I tried to give you what you wanted.'

'I know you did but you wouldn't give me what I really wanted. I was frustrated and, to be absolutely honest, bored. We were so married. We had got as far as we were ever going get. It was stalemate. You hid yourself from me. Deep down inside you there is a locked strongbox with the real you inside and try as I might, I couldn't get in. You wouldn't let me in. Yes you were affectionate, yes you loved me but I always sensed that when it came down to it you were holding yourself back. It was as if you were saving yourself for someone else. In the end I couldn't stand it. Michael is so open, so genuine. What you see is what you get. And, just as importantly, he lets me be what I want to be, not what he wants me to be.'

'I'm sorry I asked,' said Martin.

✶

On the way home he was almost relieved to see MURDER OF A MASSEUSE on the front page of the *Evening Standard*. So Trudi was dead then. He had begun to think that she might have survived. If she had it would have been his turn for a grilling then. The headline was at the top of a single paragraph which merely stated that Trudi Jordan, 25, had been found strangled on Tuesday morning in the Camden health-club where she worked. Clearly the police had omitted all the juicy details. Perhaps they were afraid of triggering copycat crimes. Beware of imitations. No doubt the tabloids had, or would, go to town on it for a day or so. Exposés of the steamy world of saunas. The dangers of rubbing strangers up the wrong way.

Would an inspector come to call? He rather thought not.

THIRTEEN

Michael and Isobel lived on the top two floors of a large Victorian house that had been built on the brow of Highbury Hill. Not only was the property, in the words of the estate agent, in an extremely sought after location, but it was also an architect-designed residence. The walls of the upper storey had been replaced by tinted glass that sloped inwards at an angle of 75 degrees. Its owners could see out but *hoi polloi* could not see in. Martin called it the lean-to.

Isobel's trip to Milan was a golden opportunity. He had been racking his brains to come up with a suitable method of despatching Michael. Yesterday's lunch had provided the necessary inspiration.

For a woman whose job depended on dissembling and deceit Isobel was full of trust. As the publicity director of a publishing house she was responsible for pushing books to those who could not read and promoting unreadable books to those that could. She was helped in this by a selective memory.

While co-habiting with Martin she had managed to lock herself out of their flat on three separate occasions. The first time she telephoned Martin who came home from work to let her in. The second time, afraid of what he would say, she called the fire brigade. The third time she just smashed a window and clambered in. It was a couple of days before Martin noticed the new window. It was much cleaner than the rest. In the end she persuaded him to let her hide a spare key in one of the window-boxes. The procedure worked after a fashion. When they were eventually burgled the intruders used a sledgehammer.

Martin was more subtle. He knew that Michael and Isobel no longer set their alarm system because it was a sophisticated one – Isobel could not cope with a different code each month. The love-nest was reached by way of its own front door and two flights of stairs. The maisonette below belonged to a retired and retiring rock star. During his rare visits to the capital he appreciated his privacy. Therefore it was probable that, somewhere in the vicinity of the big, black, shiny front door with its lion's head knocker of tarnished brass, grinning letter box, proud 1A, spyhole and TV intercom – a key was hidden. All he had to do was find it.

On Thursday morning he left the office telling the receptionist that he was going to do an interview. She did not ask who. He took the tube to Kings Cross and changed on to the Victoria line. It was a blustery day, the sky a bruised mass of grey, black and white scudding clouds which made the sun appear in fits and starts as though someone were playing with a light switch. The rain, when it came, fell at an angle that suggested that the same person had now decided to empty a giant watering can over Highbury Fields. Any sensible person would have stayed indoors.

He turned up his collar and kept his head down. Not many housebreakers wore a Burberry. The trick would be to appear as natural as possible, to pretend that retrieving the key from its hidey-hole was an everyday occurrence. Michael would be at work now – he was certain of this because, complying with Isobel's wishes, he had called him yesterday. Michael had said that he would love to meet for a bevvy but it would have to be on Friday evening because tomorrow he was going to be busy brown-nosing a bigshot American producer whom he hoped would be his passport to the US. Martin doubted it.

He swept past the clock tower that never seemed to work and, using his arm, pushed open one of the tall black wrought iron gates. He crunched across the gravel and went round the side of the house to the door. He could only be seen from the flats across the road.

Where was the key?

The doorstep was flanked by a pair of reproduction mud-scrapers that showed no sign of having ever been used. A door-mat, blazoned with OH NO NOT YOU AGAIN, lay in front of it. Too obvious. A terracotta tub, complete with moribund gera-niums, stood to the right. The tamped earth was undisturbed. Then he saw the nesting box. He put on his rubber gloves.

It was nailed to the high wooden fence that separated the garden from the neighbouring one. As a des-res it did not amount to much. It was old and streaked with a livid green lichen which at least served as camouflage. There was no fancy design or thatched roof – it was a mass-manufactured living space, a council house for bluetits. The front of it had the usual small round hole for an entrance and a piece of dowelling for the doorstep. A hinged lid formed the sloping roof. He lifted it up and, standing on tiptoe, peeped through the hole. There was no one at home. He groped around. At first he found nothing but a few bits of dry grass and leaves but then his fingertips touched it.

He put the key into the Banham lock and turned it. The door opened. He braced himself for the tell-tale whine of the alarm which provided ten seconds to tap in the code on the keypad before all hell broke loose. It did not come. He wiped his feet and crossed the threshold. He closed the door and re-locked it. He took the steps two at a time. He liked this pad. It was a shame he could not linger.

The maisonette was topsy-turvy. The lower floor contained the hall, bathroom and three bedrooms; the upper one, without external walls, comprised one vast space which combined a living room and an open-plan kitchen. He climbed the spiral staircase that formed the axis of the apartment.

Yards and yards of parquet flooring glowed in the dim light. The windows were tinted gold, throwing into relief the minute squares of yellow in the Persian rug which lay in front of the freestanding fireplace. The carpet was the one concession to fussiness and colour. Elsewhere black and chrome ruled. Two Eileen Gray sofas faced each other. A large Alastair Thain composition in a cast-iron frame – a photographic crucifix of Joseph Beuys – was bolted to the single white internal wall. He strode through the kitchen area admiring the gleaming marble work-surfaces and opened a drawer just to delight in the silent smoothness of its runners. Nothing was out of place. It was hard to believe that dozens of dinner parties had been prepared in here but he had been a guest at several of them. Michael was an excellent cook.

He went downstairs. The bathroom was unoccupied. The drip-drip of the shower put him in mind of the Chinese water torture. As if to prove the power of suggestion he felt the first jab of a migraine. He swallowed a couple of pills.

The bed in the master bedroom was unmade, the goose-feather quilt flung back. He stood beside it and sniffed the pillow on the right. Isobel always slept on the side furthest from the door. The faint aroma of her favourite scent brought tears to his eyes. It sent him hurtling back to the nights when he would deliberately lie awake just to appreciate the warm and fragrant fug of her company. Four long black hairs, letters of an unknown alphabet, squiggled across the dented pillowcase.

The second bedroom, which doubled as a study, was tidier – probably because Michael seldom worked at home. The transparent telephone on his desk made him sigh – Michael's spontaneity was so predictable. Time and again the careful cultivation of taste was sabotaged by a sudden lapse into naffness. It showed that he was not sure of himself.

The third and smallest bedroom had been converted into an impromptu studio. Most of the space was taken up by the Nautilus multigym, a Heath Robinson contraption that allowed the body-builder to develop a whole variety of muscles depending on which direction they chose to face: north, south, east or west. A padded bench, along with an exercise bike and a rowing machine, lined the walls. It was exhausting merely to look at them. He was still stiff from his Tuesday morning run. A pair of dumbbells and an assortment of weights had been left on the floor. It was these that interested him.

The doors on this level were of a solid, four-panel design.

The sheen of their brilliant white gloss was pleasing. They had originally been self-closing but Michael had unscrewed the plates that attached the chains and counterweights to them because the constant slamming had got on his nerves. Martin planned to balance sufficient steel between the top of the door and its lintel so that when Michael entered the room his head would cave in.

It was not a fool-proof gambit but the element of chance appealed to him. As long as he used the correct weight and left the door ajar at the precise angle it would work.

He picked up a disc of cold blue metal that claimed to be 10kg. It was too light but would do to experiment with. He positioned the door then placed the weight on top of it at the end furthest away from the hinges. The lintel, of course, was slightly higher but, with the door open wide enough, the weight hardly tilted at all and, because it was heavy, there was little danger of it slipping off. Holding up his hands to protect his head, he slid out of the gap into the corridor. Right.

He pushed open the door. The weight fell straight into his waiting hands. He had judged it wise not to let it drop to the floor in case Geronimo was at home below. Excellent. If ten kilograms might bounce off Michael's bonce, twenty kilograms should crush the numbskull. The pair of leaden Frisbees fitted together perfectly. By the time he had finished setting them up his arms were aching almost as much as his head. Michael would see the weights if he looked up as he entered but such an action was unnatural. His penchant for soft lighting worked against him.

✫

He pulled the front door to and locked it. He smiled at the 1A. One across would lead to two down. He replaced the key in the bird box and, having closed the gates, took off his gloves as he headed for Highbury Fields. He could just see Michael, full of beans as usual, barging into the gym, his grin turning to a grimace as his skull split open.

His migraine began to dissolve.

FOURTEEN

He tried to put the dead-fall out of his mind. He lunched with a couple of colleagues and for once did not object when they ordered a third bottle of wine. He felt like celebrating. His cover-feature on Dan Salter had met with approval. Now all he had to do was proof it and oversee its lay-out. The chromalin, the colour plate off which all the covers would be printed, had already come in. It made Dan look extremely toothsome.

That evening he felt at a loose end. He watched *The Bill*, ate his cook-chilled tagliatelle and did the crossword but, all the while, he was aware that he was waiting for something to happen. The sword of Damocles was hanging still. The telephone remained stubbornly silent. He had to be realistic. Michael would probably not get back till late – there was plenty of time left for some serious sycophancy. And even if he was at this very moment pushing open the door to his death, the blood already gushing from his head, who would discover him? Isobel was not due to return until Saturday and he had no idea when their little treasure proved her worth. The most likely turn of events would be for Michael to pour out of a cab at midnight then roll straight into bed. Hangover permitting, it would be tomorrow morning before he entered the gym.

By 10.30 he had decided that he had made a mistake. He should have known better. Such a plan meant that he was not in control. Its success depended on other people and not on himself. He was not normally a passive person. Ambushes were both cowardly and erratic. Henceforth he would be in at the kill. He sat fuming at the TV. The telephone made him jump.

'Martin. Martin is that you?'

'Yes it is.' He did not recognise the voice.

'Martin, it's Michael. Something dreadful has happened. She's dead. Isobel's dead. I've just found her. I don't know what to do.' The shock was sobering him up. 'I don't know what to do. She's dead.' He began to cry.

Martin felt something die deep inside him. A lone candle in the blackness had been snuffed out. He felt very tired.

'Stay there, Michael. Stay where you are. Don't touch anything. I'm on my way. Don't worry, I'll be with you as soon as I can. Call the police… Michael, are you listening?'

'Yes.'

'Call the police.'

FIFTEEN

When Isobel had lunched with Martin she had forgotten that her departure for Milan had been postponed for 24 hours. It was only when she turned up at the publishers in Soho Square, hurriedly-packed Louis Vuitton in hand, that her secretary reminded her that her flight was not until midday Friday. She spent the morning fielding phonecalls and attending to general administration but, expecting to be away, she had not made a lunch appointment or arranged any meetings for the afternoon. In the end she decided to go home and skim-read one of the manuscripts that formed a jagged stalagmite on the floor of her office.

✭

When in London, Geronimo went to ground. He never rose before 2pm.

There was nothing to get up for in this God-forsaken country. It was so cold, so wet, so fucking boring. His accountant had made him buy the duplex. Bernie had a lot to answer for. He rolled over in his waterbed and tried to let it sway him towards sleep. The joys of jet-lag: you were perky as hell when you wanted shut-eye, dead to the world when you wanted to waken. He scratched his balls and sighed. It was no good, he would have to take two more Temazepam. He was fed up with drowsing – what he needed was coma.

Three hours later Geronimo was dead to the world when Isobel left the land of the living. The almighty thud – which threatened to crack the enormous Louis XIV mirror screwed to his bedroom ceiling – barely punctuated his black-and-white dreams. And, as Isobel's life-blood slowly began to seep through the plaster – forming a heart-shaped stain – Zachariah Taylor snored on.

✭

It was only after she had paid the cabbie and he had driven off, leaving behind a bouquet of diesel, that Isobel remembered that she had not got her keys. She had not forgotten them: she had been so worried about losing them in Italy that she had deliberately left them behind. Michael had promised to meet her at Heathrow when she flew back. No matter – she would use the secret spare. Dumping her bags on the doorstep, she fetched an empty dustbin and, having overturned it, clambered up to retrieve the key from the nesting box. She would hold on to it for now: she would probably need to pop out for some milk later. She replaced the dustbin and went inside.

By four o'clock she was tired of reading. The copious cups of coffee she had drunk in a vain attempt to remain alert had simply made her jittery. She would work off her nervous energy in the gym.

A suggestion that the hinges needed oiling had scarcely formed in her brain when the first ten kilos dropped onto her cranium, smashing her to the floor with a silent scream. A second later – clunk – the second weight fell end-on onto the first and widened the split in her skull. Red and green burst into her eyes but she did not see them. Pain – pure, clean, naked pain – ballooned in her head but she did not feel it. She was dead.

Black blood poured out of her nostrils. Saliva trailed out of her mouth. The twenty kilograms continued to press down. The medulla oblongata, cerebellum and cerebrum crushed together; the dura mater, arachnoid and pia mater became one. A ghastly porridge-red, grey and no colour at all – was squeezed out as circuits blew, cells shut down and canals were drained of their vital fluids. Her glossy hair became a sodden mass. The twitching stopped.

When, hours later, the body-baggers finally peeled her – with a sickening tug – off the white carpet, her right cheek was embossed with the abstract pattern of its tiny woollen tufts.

SIXTEEN

So the booby had escaped the booby-trap. He slammed the front door and stepped into Clissold Avenue, banging the gate behind him. The cherry-picker swooped away and soared higher and higher towards the orange clouds of night. The irising lens watched him beetle through the quiet streets.

He was breathing heavily when he turned into Highbury Hill. The circus had come to town. Blue and white crime tape stretched from one gatepost to the clock tower and then back to the other gatepost. It formed an oblique triangle as if to symbolise the relationship of Michael and Isobel and Martin. The papery plastic fluttered in the breeze like bunting, enhancing the carnival atmosphere. *Carnem levare*, to put away flesh. That was what they were here to do.

An ambulance, two patrol cars and a police van were parked every which way in the wide road giving passing motorists the perfect excuse to slow down and rubberneck. The flashing lights – blue, red, white and amber – created an open-air disco which threw into lurid relief the faces of the spectators who clustered, like marabou storks on the edge of a grassland fire, ready to feast on the misfortune of others. The light streaming from the uncurtained windows of the surrounding houses silhouetted yet more sightseers. The buildings resembled giant advent calendars. It was an eerie scene: in spite of all the activity nothing broke the silence except the odd burst of static from a walkie-talkie. The effect was simultaneously strange yet familiar – like coming across tinsel in May or daffodils in October.

The cinema and television screens had been pulled back – the film set had become the reality. The camera moved in for a close-up.

Martin approached one of the constables on sentry duty and explained who he was. The bluebottle said nothing but raised the tape so that he could duck beneath it. He walked through the open gates and round to the front door of 1A where another crusher stood on the step. He could feel the adrenalin coursing through his veins.

'Straight up, sir.'

'Thank you. I know the way.'

At the top of the stairs yet another plod asked his name and told him to wait before clumping up the spiral staircase. Flashlights flared in the gym. Finger-print experts dusted for dabs. A WPC, wiping her mouth, emerged from the bathroom.

'Feel better now do we?' enquired a young uniformed officer in an Essex whine.

'Fuck off.' She was about to continue but when she saw Martin she disappeared into the master bedroom instead. Her sidekick followed and closed the door.

'You can go up now sir,' said the doorman, returning to his post. 'God knows how they got all that poncey furniture up there.'

'They used a hoist,' said Martin.

When Michael saw him he leapt off the sofa, threw his arms around him and burst into tears. Surprised by this explosion of spontaneous emotion, Martin felt his own eyes begin to prickle. Without removing his arms, he led Michael back to the sofa and sat down beside him.

'Very touching.'

'Shut up, Monkton. Mr Rudrum? I'm Detective Chief Inspector Herbert and this is Detective Sergeant Monkton. I'm sorry about that last remark. He pretends to be a hard bastard but he's a big softy really. He didn't mean any harm.'

Martin looked at the younger CID man. He was in his early twenties. His black, collar-length hair was slicked back with Brylcreem. He was attractive in a cheap kind of way. His regular features were covered in a pallid, spotless skin – too much white bread and lard as a kid.

'I'd forgotten that they'd lowered the height requirement for policemen,' said Martin, meeting Monkton's gaze. 'Still, they must pay you enough if you can afford to get blood on Paul Smith threads.'

'Blood? Where?' said Monkton anxiously. He twisted round to check the back of his trousers. When he saw Martin smiling Herbert told him to shut up again. He sighed. Mauve bags sagged beneath his bloodshot eyes. His crumpled skin fit him like a second-hand suit.

'What time was it when Mr Ford here called you?'

'About 10.45, I think.'

'What did you say to him?'

'I told him not to panic. To stay where he was. Not to touch anything and to phone the police. I told him that I'd be round as soon as I could.'

'Why?'

'Why what?'

'Why did you say that you would come straight round here?'

Martin glanced at Monkton. He was smirking. 'Sorry. I missed that. What's so funny?'

'Take no notice of him,' said Herbert. 'Answer the question.' It was time to up the ante.

'Isobel was dead. I wanted to know what had happened. I still want to know what has happened. Michael was in a right old state. He needed my help.'

'Did it never occur to you that you could have been in danger? For all you knew Mr Ford could have killed Miss Walker.'

'Nonsense. Michael wouldn't hurt a fly.'

'I'll hurt who ever did this,' said Michael, sniffing. 'What did you think had happened?'

'I didn't know what to think. I was under the impression that Isobel was in Italy.'

'So was I,' said Michael. His voice began to crack.

'How many other people knew that she was going to Milan?' Milan, not Italy. They had clearly got some answers already.

'Loads I should think. Certainly most people at her place of work.'

'When was the last time you saw Miss Walker?'

'On Wednesday. We had lunch together.'

'Is it true that you asked her to live with you?'

Martin blushed and removed his arm from Michael's shoulder. 'No it is not. I told her that I still loved her.'

'I'm sorry, Martin,' said Michael. 'You should have known that Isobel always told me everything. We had no secrets from each other.'

'I did know,' said Martin, lying. 'I'm not ashamed that I still feel the same way about her.'

'Miss Walker was an old flame then?'

'Yes. Yes she was and I'd appreciate it if you would stop calling her Miss Walker. Her name is Isobel.'

'Was,' said Monkton.

'My, aren't we the sensitive one? Why don't you go and do something useful like beating up a baby? What is this? A Youth Opportunity Programme? You do know that I'm a journalist? I should have thought that you'd welcome the chance of some good PR. God knows you need it.'

'Mr Rudrum, this is not getting us very far. I've told you, ignore Sergeant Monkton. He's seen too many episodes of The Sweeney.' Monkton wandered off and pretended to study the Alastair Thain. 'Will you please tell me what has happened.'

'You might as well see for yourself. We need someone to identify the body. Mr Ford doesn't wish to return to the room. He's had a very nasty shock.'

It was typical. When it came to the crunch the macho ones always lost their balls.

✯

It must have gone like clockwork. She had not even had time to close her eyes. The weights had been removed and placed in polythene bags. She lay as she had fallen, her limbs askew. A doll no longer loved by a child. Men in overalls buzzed about her. He could tell they were waiting to cocoon her in the black human hold-all. It had to be now.

With a low moan Martin sank to his knees and clasped Isobel's left hand. It was cold and hard. The floodgates opened. Once he had started it was difficult to stop, his grief came welling up in convulsions. He kept his head down and remained on his knees sobbing. He was sorry. He was so sorry. Presently he felt the inspector's gentle hand on his shoulder.

'Come on.'

For a second he thought that he was being arrested. They went into the largest bedroom. He sat on the bed and hugged Isobel's pillow.

'Mr Rudrum, you must understand that I have to ask you these questions. It's simply a matter of routine.' Christ, they really did come out with such lines. 'Can you give me some indication of your whereabouts today?'

'You mean do I have an alibi?'

'If you like. Until we get the pathologist's report we won't know the time of death but it's clear that the victim has been dead for some hours.'

'I was at work on *Streetwise* magazine from ten till six. I spent the evening at home alone.' It was by no means a watertight alibi but an apparently unbreakable one would be more likely to cause suspicion.

'Were you in the office all day?'

'No. During the morning I went in search of a CD that has both Janacek's 'Glagolitic Mass' and 'Sinfonietta' on one disc – I was bored – and then I had lunch with a couple of colleagues.'

'Didn't they miss you while you were shopping?'

'No. I told the receptionist that I was going to do an interview. *Streetwise* is a laid-back kind of place. Within reason you can come and go as you please.

'And did you find what you were looking for?'

'Unfortunately not.'

'OK.' He did not seem suspicious. 'Can you think of any

reason why someone would want to murder either of your two friends? At this stage it seems likely that Mr Ford was the intended victim. Who would want to kill him?'

'Anybody who had seen his programmes.' Martin giggled. 'I'm sorry, I'm becoming hysterical.'

'It's all right. Shock can affect you in many ways. Isn't Mr Ford good at his job?'

'Oh he's very good. That's the trouble. There's an insatiable appetite for junk TV and Michael does his best to help feed it. I should know – I have to review the stuff. I have to say though that balancing weights on top of a door seems rather a dodgy way of killing someone, don't you think?'

'Yes I do. And yet it appears to be a professional job. There's no sign of a forced entry. Indeed we've yet to ascertain how Miss Walker, Isobel, got in. She had left her keys with Mr Ford. For the moment we have to assume that she obtained a spare from somewhere, possibly from a colleague or neighbour.'

There was a knock on the door. Monkton entered.

'That long-haired plonker from downstairs is going on about who's going to replace his priceless silk rug. He wants to know when you're going to interview him.'

'Give me two minutes.'

Good. He was feeling exhausted. Monkton closed the door behind him. 'It's just occurred to me.'

'Yes?'

'On Wednesday Isobel told me that Michael was investigating the sale of illegal drugs in Britain – steroids, monkey glands, stuff like that. He had expressed an interest in making a documentary on the subject. It must have been a last-ditch attempt at respectability. He had these wild ideas about exposing a black market in human pituitary glands. Of course all this could just be bluster. Believe it or not, in spite of everything, Michael and I have become good friends. Anybody will tell you that. I don't want to get him into trouble but, then again, I don't want him to get killed.'

'I understand,' said Herbert, rubbing the stubble on his chin. 'This is interesting. It might be relevant. We'd better have another word with Mr Ford. You're not suggesting he takes such drugs himself are you?'

'Not at all. Anyway, they're supposed to be extremely difficult to get hold of – that's why so much money is involved.'

'Thank you. You've been very helpful.' He stifled a yawn. 'When you've given your address and phone numbers to the constable on the door you can go. You'll have to come in and make a formal statement in a couple of days and, as a regular visitor to the flat, your finger-prints will have to be taken for the process of elimination. Would you like someone to take you home?'

'No, thank you. It's not far. I need some air. Besides, I don't think I'll get much sleep tonight.'

'You'll be surprised,' said Herbert. 'You'll sleep like a log.'

Martin got off the bed.

'What about Michael? Shouldn't I stay with him?'

'There's no point. We'll be here for some time yet and I do need to talk to him again.'

He took his leave of Michael and said that he would call round to see him tomorrow afternoon. It would be Friday – it was technically Friday now – but after tonight neither of them would be going to work. After he had told Monkton that it had been a pleasure to meet him he went downstairs and out into the cold. The ghouls had vanished.

When he was safely out of sight round the corner he gave a little skip. It had been an Oscar-winning performance.

SEVENTEEN

Torschlusspanik. Fear caused by the sound of closing doors. The Germans meant it metaphorically – an awareness of opportunities slipping away, knowing that you were stuck in a one-way system, that you had reached the point of no return – but Martin felt it physically on Saturday morning when he made his statement at the police station in Holloway.

The brick walls of the interview room were painted cream. The WPC who had vomited in Isobel's bathroom was standing by the door. He was sitting at a table facing an empty chair. If the pigs were trying to unnerve him they were failing. They might suspect him – he seemed to be the only person with an obvious motive for topping Michael – but they had no concrete evidence. Michael had told him that the house-to-house enquiries had not produced a single person who had witnessed anyone leaving the scene of the crime. Geronimo had heard nothing. Apart from Isobel and Michael, the only other known key-holder was the charlady and on Thursday she had been visiting her grandson in Catford. No one else's fingerprints had been found in the flat. The Coroner's inquest had been postponed pending further investigation.

✷

'They told me that they can't even rule out the possibility of suicide,' said Michael, ignoring the blaring horn of the driver whom he had just cut off.

'Well the way you're driving could certainly be described as autodestructive,' replied Martin, 'but there's no way that Isobel would have done such a thing is there?'

'Absolutely not. Anyway, I think that whoever it was must have been after me. I don't mind telling you I've been glad of the security system. If we'd used it before, this might never have happened.'

'True – but if the killer did get in without a key then they would have probably been able to deal with the alarm as well.'

'The whole business has been a fucking nightmare.' A motorcyclist overtook them on the inside and, in response to Michael's flashing headlights, gave him the finger. 'Dickhead… I really miss her you know.'

'Of course you do. So do I. The best thing to do is to try and put it all behind you. I know it's easy to say and hard to do but look upon today as the end of the horror. That's what funerals are for – they're of no use to the dead. They provide a service for those who are still alive.'

They were on their way to bury Isobel. Her family lived in Sussex. She was to be interred in the graveyard of the Saxon church next-door to the village school that she had attended as a little girl. He was dreading the ceremony but enjoying the journey.

Michael, like most overgrown kids, loved sports cars. So did Martin. His current model was a scarlet Toyota MR2.

'With those initials, this should be my car,' said Martin. 'What does the ad say – 'passion and control in perfect harmony?'

'Action speaks louder than words,' replied Michael. 'Watch this.'

He pulled up at a set of traffic lights. The drivers either side of them gave them the once-over. With all the sizing up that was going on it was like being in a communal shower. When Michael revved the engine, his fellow competitors on the starting line – an Escort XR3 and a Saab Turbo – followed suit. Two seconds before the red light was joined by the amber Michael stamped on the accelerator. By the time the others had reacted the lights were on green and Michael had left them behind with a screech of his tyres. 'We have lift off!'

'Yippee!'

It was exhilarating. Ten seconds later the same procedure began all over again.

They crossed the Thames – he had already crossed the Rubicon – and entered the mazy mess of the South Bank. Inner-city decay gradually gave way to suburban sprawl which, in its turn, ceded to the relative splendour of exurbia. As the buildings became lower, and the spaces between them got wider, he began to breathe more easily. The congestion cleared. They zoomed along with Aretha Franklin. It had been one hell of a week.

★

Although Martin claimed to be an atheist he appreciated the solace of faith. On the rare occasions that he revisited Lancaster he would slip into the priory by the castle and spend half an hour simply sitting in one of the pews. As a member of the school choir he had sung there on Founder's Day and at Christmas. But fond memories did not bring him back – he was drawn by the peaceful atmosphere. It was only at such times that he experienced anything remotely like tranquillity. It was as though he left himself behind or found a mental escape-hatch. If benighted fools liked to call this state of mind a manifestation of the Holy Ghost or some other mystical mumbo-jumbo then that was up to them. He preferred to think of it as a taste of things to come – not so much an afterlife as oblivion, the nihilist's nirvana.

The vicar stumbled his way through his address, mixing up the number of Isobel's brothers and sisters and getting people's names wrong. Martin stared at the oak beams in the ceiling. Sky-pilots did not have much to do and most of them could not even do that. In the God Squad the living was easy. In return for murmuring comforting noises at the appropriate times, members received tea with parishioners, free accommodation in desirable residences and a reasonable salary. Their days, mapped out according to the ecclesiastical calendar, were an unceasing round of commemoration and commiseration. The uniform, if not exactly drag, was a drawback but the choirboys must be a great compensation.

He had wanted to throw a red rose on to the coffin but Michael had disapproved of the gesture saying that it was a melodramatic cliché which smacked of emotional oneupman-ship: 'Besides, her parents wouldn't like it.' Isobel's family were of good yeoman stock and dyed-in-the-wool Tories. Catholicism in choice or creed was anathema to them. Martin and Michael were united in their dislike of the clan. Their feel-ings were reciprocated. Mr Walker considered journalists and TV producers to be on a par with debt-collectors. When it was the turn of the former suitors to throw a handful of dust into the grave both men wept.

After the ceremony Herbert and Monkton mingled with the mourners.

Martin ignored them but Michael had a few words with them. They had agreed not to stay for the wake so, having doled out their condolences, shaken the necessary hands and kissed the requisite cheeks, they sneaked away.

'Thank God that's over,' said Michael.

'Your turn next,' murmured Martin.

By the end of the evening he had changed his mind. When they had arrived back in Highbury Michael suggested that they have their own wake and celebrate the girl who had brought them together. After the third bottle of champagne they sprawled on the floor laughing and crying and even hugging each other in a half-ashamed way. As he watched Michael chop the coke – a token of good will from the American producer – into lines with his gold Amex card Martin realised that he would be in fear of losing his charmed life for at least another month. It would be safer to wait. He had eluded him once but he would not get away again. He was going to derive maximum satisfaction from his demise. He would save the handsome fucker till last.

EIGHTEEN

Martin aged seven. A precocious child. A boy who looked and listened, who observed grown-ups with a mixture of admiration and fear. They were unpredictable – it was difficult to gauge their reaction to anything you might say. They could do whatever they wanted whenever they wished. No one told them what to do, what to eat, what to wear and when to go to bed. If school was so important why did they answer his queries with fatuous phrases like 'ask no questions, get no lies', 'them that ask don't get', 'curiosity killed the cat', 'that's for me to know and you to find out'? His father was always going to see a man about a dog. This one in particular puzzled him. He was allergic to cats and dogs.

Walnut Close derived its name from the magnificent specimen that grew in the middle of the cul-de-sac. It was a spindle tree: all the houses looked directly on to it, all life in the close revolved around it. The children in the neighbourhood would gather beneath its branches after tea to play Grandmother's Footsteps, tig or simply to mooch about on the grass. If anybody attempted to climb the tree at least one window would open and a young parent call out to tell the culprit to get down. Sometimes the kids would try and sneak away to venture further afield but it was not easy. Dusk was the best time for escape – just before the streetlights flickered on, glowing pink, then red, then orange as the moths and daddy-long-legs began to dance attendance.

Martin's parents lived in one of the two new detached

houses which stood on either side of the entrance to the close. The other houses were post-war semis, pebble-dashed and privet-hedged. Because Martin did not actually live in the close, every time there was an argument some future politician pointed out that he should not really be in the gang at all, let alone be its leader. But he was six months older than his nearest rival and taller than all of them. He was also, so he told them, the cleverest. Why else would he be going to prep school when they all had to go to the local primary school? He received more kudos from the fact that his parents never called him in to bed. They did not realise that he always promised to be home by a prearranged time. An old head on young shoulders did have its advantages when it came to infant realpolitik. But it also had its disadvantages. For instance, knowing what to say in a certain situation without really knowing what it meant.

Andrew was Martin's best friend. He had brown eyes, brown hair and brown skin. It did not matter that his parents had no money. Perhaps you had to be poor to be Catholic. They went to each other's house for tea; Andy came with him when his father took him swimming; and their mothers went shopping together. Andy's father, a large man in a dusty navy-blue overall that smelled of sweat and potatoes, was a driver for an agricultural supplier. His swarthy skin prompted Mrs Warrington – an endless source of gossip who lived next-door – to say that he had gypsy blood in him. Sometimes he beat Andy with his wide, age-worn belt. This made Martin cry. He was afraid of Mr Kelly.

One evening, when there was just the two of them beneath the walnut tree, Andrew and Martin had a fight. Andrew had brought his Action Man out with him. Martin did not like dolls of any sort, although teddy bears were OK. He thought dolls were for girls and said so.

'So is skipping.'

'No it isn't.'

'Yes it is. My mummy said.'

'Well tell your mummy that boxers skip as well. I've seen them doing it on telly.'

'That's not the same as skipping in the street with Jane and Claire. My mummy says that you're a cissy.'

There was that word again. It was usually women who called him that. Just because he preferred reading to kicking a ball about. He was not a softie though. That Andy should think he were upset him.

'I am not a cissy.'

'Yes you are.'

'No I'm not.' Martin snatched the plastic toy from him. 'This is a cissy toy. I don't play with dolls.'

'Give it back to me.'

'No.'

Andrew punched him on the nose and tried to grab his Action Man back. Martin hit him in the face with it. His eyes were watering from the blow but he had not got a nose-bleed.

'Cry-baby!'

'I am not crying, you pig.' He kicked Andrew in the shins. He fell over. Before he could get up Martin held on to his shoulders and straddled him, ignoring his flailing fists. 'Surrender.'

'Never.' He bumped his head on the grass. He started to wail. His mother opened the window. She wore a black and white striped trouser suit which looked more like a pair of pyjamas.

'Leave my Andrew alone, you big bully. Pick on someone your own size. Stop fighting this minute.'

'He started it. He called me a cissy. He said that you called me a cissy.'

'And so you are. Now leave Andrew alone.' Martin got off him. He scrambled to his feet and ran home without his toy. Martin threw it after him.

'I am not a cissy.'

'We all know what you are, you little devil. If I catch you hitting Andrew again, there'll be trouble.'

'Yes, and we all know what you are.' Martin had not got a clue what the expression meant but it produced the desired effect. Mrs Kelly glared at him and, muttering something under her breath, closed the window with a bang. He stood there trembling with anger and excitement. Well that had shut her up. Seconds later Mr Kelly emerged from the side of the house. His boiler suit was unbuttoned to the waist. A forest of black hairs sprouted out of his chest. He was carrying his belt.

Martin turned on his heels and legged it down the close. He went through the side gate – the other gates of the property were on Meadowsway around the corner – ran up the path and locked the back door behind him. He hoisted himself onto the worktop so that he could peep out of the kitchen window. Mr Kelly stopped by the gate, looked up at the house then went away scowling. Martin slid off the worktop and tiptoed into the hall.

'Hello, you're back early.'

'Andy wasn't feeling well. Should I go and have my bath Mummy?'

'That's a good idea. Then you can come down and watch television for half an hour.'

'OK.'

The bottom of the bath had scarcely got wet when the front doorbell rang. Martin crept onto the landing. It was Mrs Kelly.

'I'm sorry to bother you, Margaret, but I just had to come and tell you. I've never been so insulted in my life. And by a child as well.'

'What's the matter, Bridget?' He expected his mother to invite her friend in but for some reason she did not.

'Martin and Andrew were fighting. When I told them to stop Martin called me a bitch.'

'That's not true! She's lying,' shouted Martin.

'Martin, come down here at once.' He did as he was told, slowly. 'Did you call Mrs Kelly a bitch?'

'No.'

'Now don't you go telling fairy stories to your mother Martin, it will only make things worse.' She smiled at him. When he saw the glint in her eye he knew he had lost.

'Well say something,' continued his mother. He could tell she did not know who to believe.

'I did not call her a bitch. Mrs Kelly is fibbing.'

'Apologise to her this minute. Go on!'

'I will not apologise for something that I have not done.' Before he had finished she had clipped him round the left ear, hard. She raised her hand to do it again.

'I'm sorry.'

'And so you should be young man. Still, there's no harm done. Good bye, Margaret.'

'Bye Bridget. I am sorry.'

'Don't worry about it. These things happen.' She closed the front gate and waved, a grinning two-legged zebra.

His mother closed the front door. As usual his father had remained out of sight in the drawing room. He never answered the door. Fighting back the tears, Martin hissed: 'How could you believe her and not me?'

'She must have had a good reason for coming to see me. I've told you before about answering back, you rub people up the wrong way. It's not what you say, it's the tone in which you say it. Now go and have your bath.'

As he tried to float in the hot water, blowing bubbles off the tip of his nose, he seethed with indignation. Yes he had been cheeky – but not without provocation. It seemed that words could have more effect than fists. It was inevitable that adults should side with each other but surely a mother should believe her own son? He could not even rely on his own parents. It was his first taste of betrayal.

NINETEEN

Martin aged nine. The summer holidays. He put down his Agatha Christie and lay back on the rug. He gazed up at the sun through the branches of the apple tree and let himself be dazzled.

'Haven't you got anything better to do?' His father came round the side of the house. He was carrying a pair of shears. 'There are plenty of weeds to pull up.'

4 Meadowsway was set square in the middle of its corner plot. Fences either side of the house divided the front garden from the back garden. The front garden was cut in half by the winding path that led from the front door to the gate. The back garden was bisected by a corrugated iron shed where sessions of you-show-me-yours-I'll-show-you-mine were conducted. A dense wall of shrubs prevented passers-by peering in. His father liked his privacy.

Although the total area of the grounds amounted to about half an acre, much of the space was taken up by a double garage, the shed, a swing, a compost heap, a vegetable garden and a pond. Martin loved the garden but hated gardening. His father was not keen on it either. The only way he could get his son to assist him was by bribing him with pocket money. But Martin had just received this week's allowance. It was too hot to work. He continued to lie there listening to the neighbourhood symphony of droning mowers, toddlers splashing in a paddling-pool, transistor radios and the clack-clack of a portable typewriter.

'I said, haven't you got anything better to do?'

'Not really, it's the holidays.'

'I could do with some help.'

He sat up and looked at his father. When he opened his eyes the world was black and white. Slowly the colour seeped back. His father was wearing a pair of khaki cotton trousers and a white open-necked shirt. He was sweating profusely. He had just finished cutting the front lawns and was exhausted because he insisted on using a manual machine. Motor-driven mowers apparently failed to roll the grass properly.

'OK. I'll just go to the loo.' He took his book with him.

Ten minutes later his father's voice floated through the open windows and into his bedroom.

'Martin. Haven't you finished yet?'

'Nearly.' He was in fact lying on his bed determined to complete a particularly exciting chapter.

'Martin?'

'God, if it's that important why don't you hire a gardener?'

As soon as the words were out of his mouth, Martin knew that he was for it. He leaped off the bed. His father was already charging up the stairs. He had ignored his wife's request to take off his shoes and was tramping grass cuttings into the carpet. Martin seriously considered jumping out of the window. It would do no good. Even if he broke both his legs he would still be punished. On the one occasion that he had tried to commit suicide by looping a tie round his neck, fixing it to one of the curtain rails in his bedroom and jumping off the windowsill – only to succeed in bringing the whole thing, curtains and all, crashing down around him – his father had beaten him until he could not continue for laughing.

It was only later that he realised that it was not so much his laziness and lip that had enraged his father as his blasphemy. 'God' was such a simple, three-letter word – dog backwards – but its utterance had nearly killed him. He had misread the situation. When his father burst into his bedroom, the door banging into the side of the wardrobe, the only clue to his fury was that the tip of his nose was white. His father did not go to church, he did not pray and he did not devote five per cent of his income to charity but even so he would not have the Lord's name taken in vain. Instead of using his open hands as usual, his father went at him with clenched fists and knocked him to the floor. He grasped his son by the hair and dragged him out onto the landing. The carpet burned his bare knees.

'When I ask you to do something, I expect you to do it immediately, without hesitation, without quibbling and without any backchat. Understand? Get up.'

He stood up, shaking. 'Yes.'

But he was not quick enough. His father's right fist struck him a glancing blow on the side of his head and sent him tumbling down four stairs. The staircase turned through two right angles. Martin cowered in the corner of the first halfpace, terrified. Stars – black stars with white edges – hovered in front of his eyes.

'I am sick and tired of the way you speak to me and your mother. It's time you bucked your ideas up. Get downstairs.' He gripped his left arm and pulled him to his feet. He shook him till his teeth rattled. He slapped him on the right cheek, on the left cheek and then let go. Martin fell down another four stairs.

'Get into the garden.'

He narrowly avoided a foot intended to speed him on his way, slid down the remaining stairs and skidded across the parquet flooring. His ears were ringing, his face was stinging, his whole body was aching. He could only think of one thing – to get away from this madman. He scrambled across the lawn, knelt down by the bushes and pretended to start weeding. Suddenly he was sick in the flower bed. He wiped his forehead and mouth with the bottom of his T-shirt and sobbed as he listened to his parents shouting in the study. He would be better off without them.

TWENTY

He sat on the edge of the couch and waited. He ran his hands through his hair. He twiddled his thumbs. He tried to whistle – but it was no good. He had never liked playing Hide and Seek. It was much better to seek than be sought. He stared at the face of the man with bowler hats for eyes. He had no mouth. He was unable to speak, laugh or scream.

He had been expecting the doorbell to ring but when it did his heart leapt into his mouth. He gagged and thought that he would have to spit it out. The sensation subsided and left behind a panicky pounding in his chest. He did not move.

The bell rang again.

TWENTY-ONE

Two weeks after Isobel's funeral Martin decided that he was in need of a break. He could not afford a holiday so the only option was to go home and see the old folks. The trouble was they were not that old. His father was 55 and his mother was 51.

As a child it had pleased him when his mother had been mistaken for his sister or his grandmother had been taken for his mother. As an adult it annoyed him that he would be as old – if not older – than his parents were now when he finally came into his inheritance. That was assuming he were not cut off without a penny in the meantime. Both his grandmothers were still alive: one serving time in a nursing home; the other fitter than himself and having the time of her life spending his grandfather's legacy. If youth were wasted on the young, money was wasted on the old. He needed cash, lots and lots of it, *now* – not when he was a middle-aged has-been.

★

The train pulled out of Euston with a jolt. He tilted back his first class seat. It was covered in a lurid orange material which highlighted the multifarious stains that blotched the clicked synthetic. In the boxy back-gardens of Camden, Primrose Hill, Kensal Green and Willesden nothing was stirring. The Flying Scot picked up speed. The two white humps of Wembley Stadium loomed out of the mist. He hated London but could not imagine living anywhere else.

'Coffee or tea, sir?'

'Coffee, please.'

The waitress placed a cup and a brown plastic disposable filter in front of him on the formica table and moved along the carriage. It was scarcely a quarter full. He had four seats to himself. He leaned into the aisle and watched her plump bottom shift beneath the tight black skirt. As she walked the nylon seemed to whisper 'yesyesyesyes'. Five minutes later a short, stocky man in his twenties arrived pushing a trolley. The sleeves of his white shirt were rolled up to display the tattoos on his forearms. Martin paid and was rewarded with hot water poured expertly into the filter. The waiter was also Scottish. His black trousers stretched across his pert buttocks too. Martin surreptitiously adjusted his erection. The trouble with boxer shorts was that they gave one's cock too much room to crow.

The scenery was more attractive inside than out. When the minions had returned to their galley he gazed out of the window and watched the scrap-yards, industrial estates and sewage farms roll past. Satellite dishes sprouted from the sides of council flats like alien fungi. There was nothing else to do in the North except watch TV.

When the express eventually trundled into Lancaster – on time for once – he felt ill. Every time the train decelerated the compartment filled with a faecal odour. The ticket inspector had insisted that it was the brakes and opened a window. Martin was consequently overjoyed to see the familiar skyline of castle and priory come into view. He was home.

✶

One week later he was bored out of his mind. He had stopped mistaking seagulls for jumbo jets; he had become accustomed to the softness of the water which meant that it took ten minutes to rinse the soap off one's face; he had even got used to his coffee tasting different. But the solitude that had at first been so soothing was now starting to unnerve him.

His parent's house was on the top of a hill that afforded

distant views of the Lune estuary. The surrounding pasture-land was gradually disappearing under the stealthy encroach-ment of a new housing estate. White plastic pillars disgraced the porches of every tiny residence. Their mock Georgian and Tudorbethan designs were enough to convert the most broad-minded egalitarian into a raging snob.

One morning, on his way back from the newsagents – his father read the *Daily Telegraph* – he decided to venture into Legoland. The developers had crammed as many properties as possible into the available space. It was as if someone had used houses instead of broken flagstones to crazy-pave the mead-ows. There was only one through road: all the rest were stubby cul-de-sacs that led off it at awkward angles. These were linked by a network of paths – the natives called them ' ginnels' – that occasionally opened out into redundant grassy plots where a lone seesaw or swing awaited vandals. He wandered through the maze peering over fences into virgin back-lots that waited to be turned into gardens. A couple of newspaper boys had finished their rounds and were walking back with their empty dayglo orange bags slung over their shoulders.

'My dad's got a BMW,' said the taller of the two. He had floppy blond hair.

'Mine's got a Jag.'

'Mine says he's going to get a Merc next.'

'When I buy a car it will be a Rolls Royce.' The other boy already had the makings of an executive paunch.

'Oh yeah?' The pretty one flicked the hair off his forehead. 'I'd rather have Porsche.'

Neither of them could have been older than ten.

✳

He sprawled on the sofa and listened to the gas fire expanding in its own heat. He could not hear another sound. Out of the window nothing moved. His parents were at work: his father at his surgery, his mother in an estate agency. His father had not permitted his mother to have a job while he was a child. The idea of his wife going out to work had been an insult to his manhood. He saw in it the scandalous suggestion that he was incapable of providing for his family. Having never picked up a duster in his life, he failed to understand that housework soon loses its novelty. His mother had given up a successful career with BP to marry his father. Cooking and cleaning, baking one week and dieting the next, were poor substitutes for life in a hectic office.

During his first term at Leeds his mother had rung him to say that she had got herself a job. He was touched by her excitement. It was as if she had been granted a second youth. Freed from the vacuous circle of church coffee mornings and flower-arranging, she made new friends and spent her evenings dining out with them instead of waiting to make his father's supper when he returned from the golf club at 11pm. Martin was glad of the extra income. Although the money did not come into his own hands he thought it might help to offset his father's disastrous attempts at playing the stock market. He had never forgiven him for selling the M&S shares that his godfather had bought for him on his first birthday.

His parents had moved back to Lancaster, their place of birth, one year after he had left the grammar school. He would have preferred to have been a day-boy but at least he had had the satisfaction of costing his father a great deal of money. They had returned to look after their parents, none of whom had ever lived anywhere else. First his paternal grandfather had died of a heart attack, then his maternal one had succumbed to a stroke brought on by sixty Capstan Full Strength a day and a fondness for bread and dripping.

He sighed and threw the paperback on to the floor. He had revisited his alma mater, meditated in the priory, read three novels and taken his mobile grandmother to Morecambe for the day. He could not put it off any longer – he would have to go and see grandmother number two.

Martin, like most physically healthy people, hated hospitals. He could still remember being taken to visit his great-grandparents as one by one they had dwindled away in their nineties: long afternoons of boredom, boiled sweets, hairy lips, whiskery chins and the smell of wee-wee.

☆

In spite of the many strenuous efforts made by its owners, the rest home still had the sullen atmosphere of an institution. On the surface it seemed a pleasant enough place for granny-dumping – a converted mansion in which the gentlefolk each had their own bedroom and bathroom – but there was no disguising the statutory fire-doors, smoke alarms and white tubular handrails. The heating was permanently on full blast. The suffocating warmth made the pungent aroma of air-freshener all the more noticeable. It cost £500 a week to stay in Craiglands but, thank God, the Rudrums were not paying a penny. Five years ago his grandmother had signed her house over to her son so that, when the inevitable day of reckoning arrived and she was deemed no longer capable of looking after herself, the authorities would discover that she had no assets to realise and were therefore required to finance her last years themselves. And why not? His grandmother never tired of pointing out that as a working woman she had paid her stamps all her life. It was only right that she should now get something back.

He arrived in the Twilight Zone soon after 3pm and was taken up to his grandmother's room by a smartly dressed nurse who asked a lot of questions. When she did not receive a response she stopped smiling and snapped, 'It isn't one of her good days.' He thanked her for her trouble and watched her flounce down the corridor which was lined with prints of hunting scenes. He knocked on the door softly and, when there was no reply, tiptoed in.

She was snoozing in a wingback armchair, her chin resting on a floral-patterned dress. He sat on the bed beside her.

'Nana?'

Her hair looked as if it had been permed that morning. The carmine varnish on her fingernails was unchipped. Her liver-spotted hands were clasped together in her lap. The rings on her fingers sparkled in the late sunshine. At least the swollen, arthritic knuckles would prevent an unscrupulous orderly trying to slip them off while she was asleep.

'Nana? It's Martin. I've come to see you.' He put a hand on top of hers and squeezed them. 'Hello-o. Is there anybody there?' With a grunt and a sniff she lifted her head and opened her glabrous eyes. It took a moment for them to focus.

'Hello, Martin. This is a surprise.' She rolled her tongue round her mouth then licked her lips. 'No one told me you were up here. Why aren't you down in London quaffing champagne?'

'Those days are few and far between at the moment. Anyway, it's good to see you.' He leaned over and kissed her powdery cheek. 'I must say you're looking very chic.'

'One tries, one tries. Appearances count for a lot. There isn't much to do in here except titivate yourself.'

She dozed off again. He got off the orthopaedic bed and went over to the double-glazed window. He pushed the net curtain aside and looked out over the well-groomed gardens. A middle-aged couple were pushing a swaddled skeleton round in a wheelchair. He did not want to be old. He turned his back on the dutiful children and let his eyes wander round the magnolia-painted room. There was a photograph of himself among those of her other grandchildren on the dressing table. He was in school uniform and grinning at the camera. That must have been just before he met Duncan.

'Has Robert still got that gun his father gave him?' He swung round almost guiltily, afraid that she had read his mind.

'A gun? Are you sure?' She might have been sleep-talking.

'Yes. Didn't he tell you about it? Your grandfather brought it back from France after the war. He said an American gave it him.'

'He kept that quiet.'

'Well ask him. It was quite a big thing. Goodness knows why your grandfather held on to it. He never used it. At least I don't think he did. There was some ammunition to go with it as well.' She rubbed her aching fingers. 'I sometimes wish I had it with me here. It's not nice being decrepit. Make the most of your life while you can. It's no good regretting things when it's too late to do anything about them.'

'Nana, don't talk like that.' His eyes began to prickle. 'You like being here don't you? They don't mistreat you do they? You only have to say.'

'Of course not. Besides, where else would I go? It's just that I get so bored some days. It doesn't matter that I can't have many left. These pills they give me make me so sleepy.'

'I understand.' He resumed his position on the bed and held her knobbly hands. 'I'll come and see you again before I go back to London. I promise.'

'Good.' Her eyelids began to droop.

He normally felt depressed after visiting his grandmother but not this time. A gun! Did his father still have it? If he had not sold it, where had he hidden it? Why had he not mentioned it? Guns did not leave much to chance. This was one heirloom he had to inherit.

TWENTY-TWO

The front door shut. He leaped out of bed naked and scuttled along the landing into his parents' room. The last vestiges of the nocturnal fug lingered in the warm air. The mirrors in their bathroom were still partially shrouded in mist. The unmade bed signalled the imminent arrival of the cleaner. If the gun was not in his father's wardrobe he would have to wait until the afternoon before extending the search. He could hardly ask Mrs Muckalt if she had seen a revolver lying about.

The key, as always, was in the lock. He turned it and shivered. The walnut door swung open, releasing an aromatic mixture of camphor, tweed and aftershave. He studied the layout of the contents, photographing it mentally. He prided himself on being able to leave things exactly as he found them.

The shelf above the hanging rail was stacked with a decade's unwanted Christmas presents: gloves of suede and leather, tubes of golf balls and sets of handkerchiefs, boxes of golf balls and handkerchiefs, argyle socks and garish silk ties – all still in their original packaging. They were gifts from grateful patients but his father was only interested in cigars and bottles of spirits. Even so he refused to send these superfluous items to a jumble sale or recycle them by giving them to distant relatives the following year. His moral code was quaint.

There was nothing else on the shelf except a clothes brush and a stack of techno-thrillers that reeked of suntan lotion. He knelt down. The bottom of the wardrobe was covered with shoes. He had not known there were so many shades of black and brown. Nothing. It was all suspiciously neat. Perhaps his mother had recently had one of her periodical clear-outs. There was only one place left to look: the attic.

✫

He spent the morning rooting around in the cobwebby garage while Mrs Muck chattered away to Jimmy Young. He had scoured it yesterday evening but he wanted to check that he had not missed anything. It was like an intransigent crossword clue: no matter how much you bludgeoned your brains it would not give up its secret but, if you let go and returned to it the next day, you had every chance of solving the damn thing straightaway. There were plenty of implements – spade, fork, hoe, dibber, scythe, mower, strimmer, rake, shears – but not the tool he wanted.

✫

Although he was not hungry he had to sit at the kitchen table and eat the beans on toast that Mrs Muck had 'cooked' for him. He lunched in silence as she chuntered on and dashed away with the steaming iron. Finally, after yet another cup of tea and a cigarette, she left at 2.30pm. She waddled down the road, trundling her shopping basket behind her. He fetched the step-ladders from the garage and carried them upstairs.

The entrance to the loft was a square panel set into the landing ceiling. It could not have been sited in a more dangerous position because the ladders had to be set up at the head of the stairs: if you fell out of the loft you would end up broken-backed in the hall. He did not suffer from vertigo. He climbed the creaky aluminium steps, pushing the panel up and to one side as he did so. A rush of cold air washed over him. He hoisted himself through the hatch and perched on the edge of the hole, his legs dangling in space. He swung them up into the attic and got to his feet.

Even in the middle of the garret it was impossible to stand up straight. Adopting a stoop worthy of Quasimodo, he sidled his way through the higgledy-piggledy piles of boxes on the chipboard that his father had laid across the central joists. The insulation was the dirty pale yellow of spiders' nests. In the far right-hand corner water slowly trickled into a cistern. Sparrows scrabbled on the roof.

He recognised two of the boxes as the ones holding Christmas decorations. They were exhumed with due cere-mony each December. Most of the others were in black bin-liners to protect their contents from condensation. He would have to undo each and every one of them.

After half an hour his fingers were numb and his back was aching. He had found his school exercise books; the love letters his parents had written to each other when they were younger than he was now; a suitcase containing a china tea service that had belonged to one of his great-great-grandmothers; his father's chest of medical instruments which he had used as a student in the fifties; several lamp shades; an old vacuum cleaner; and four antique chamber-pots which must have been worth a fortune – but not as much as his father's coin collection.

He had been a numismatist for as long as Martin could remember.

Each month a small Jiffy-bag would arrive from the Royal

Mint in Llantrisant. Inside would be a new coin – untouched by human hand – sealed in plastic and cushioned in a blue leatherette presentation case. He had also filled old coffee tins with pre-1947 shillings because they contained a higher percentage of silver. It was a magnificent hoard but he was too wary of burglars to display it. There was something miserly about the pursuit. It was an obsession worthy of Shylock, Scrooge or Harpagon. As soon as the collection of a lifetime passed on to him he would sell it.

He took up the last remaining canister. It was an ancient Peek Freans luxury selection biscuit tin. With the aid of a 1922 florin he twisted off the lid. Bingo.

It was wrapped in a mustard duster and lay in the tin diagonally, northwest to southeast. The rest of the space was crammed with loose ammunition. Real bullets. He picked up the gun gingerly. It was surprisingly heavy. And so cold it felt as though it were carved out of black ice. The barrel was much longer than he had expected. The six-shooter was nearly twelve inches in length. The handle was embossed with the logo of a young horse snapping an arrow in its teeth. It was a Colt.45. After checking that it was unloaded he replaced it in the tin and tidied everything else away. He hid the treasure trove under his bed.

★

All that remained of Freeman's Wood was a straight path between two rows of trees. He jumped over the stream at the bottom of the hill on which his parents lived and crossed the football pitch where teams of local factory workers clashed on Saturday mornings. This area of Lancaster was known as The Marsh. Clumps of willow trees shielded the playing fields from the unmetalled road that led to the new housing estate.

The muddy track was flanked by ditches and meadows dotted with sheep. Their black faces made their grey fleeces loom white in the fading light. Halfway down, the dirt turned to gravel as a disused railway line cut across the footpath. Once upon a time it had connected the city to Glasson Dock. Now it was a nature trail. The only wildlife to be seen was a pair of BMX riders.

After a quarter of a mile the path emerged onto the south bank of the river Lune. On the other side of the choppy water stood an inn known as Snatchems. In the eighteenth century, when Lancaster was a thriving port, any undermanned ship setting out to sea would make up its crew by grabbing drunks from the pub. Even today the watering-hole was cut off at high tide. To the left seagulls wheeled and screamed above the municipal dump. To the right the nuclear power station formed a black square on the horizon. The countryside was a wonderful place.

In summer there were often a few dogs walking their owners or fishermen escaping the wife. On a Wednesday after-noon in the middle of autumn there was no one about. He used to come jogging down here. It was a good spot for beach-comb-ing as long as you did not mind the occasional bloated corpse. Suicides were forever throwing themselves off Carlisle Bridge upstream. The desolate expanse of windswept marram grass was riddled with hidden channels which rapidly filled with the incoming tide. The path, however, continued on a ridge that veered towards Glasson Dock. He tramped on, the gun in the pocket of his Burberry banging painfully against his thigh. He realised now why these raincoats were favoured by shoplifters.

Ever since he had found the firearm he had been itching to try it out. He was slightly disappointed that it was not a .44 Magnum. Smarty Marty did not have quite the same ring as Dirty Harry. Nevertheless, just the knowledge that he now owned a gun made him glow inside. He was still uncertain what he was exactly going to do. He had been hoping to encounter a stray pooch but for once they had stayed away. Then he saw the car.

It was parked on the old railway line. A lane ran down to the river from the hamlet of Aldcliffe. It was possible to park in what was once a siding but many drivers simply used the track itself. It was a popular haunt of teenage lovers, courting couples and adulterers.

As the Lune meandered towards its estuary the distance between the path and the nature trail gradually narrowed to about 25 yards. Thereafter they ran parallel to each other, separated by the width of a single field. Martin clambered down the ridge and crept along until he was level with the Ford Orion. Although the windows were steamed up, the sinking sun silhouetted the two figures inside. A boss and his secretary no doubt. He lay on the bank and peeped over the crest. He was sure he could hear the suspension rocking. He would give them a bang to remember.

He slid down the bank and put one bullet into the chamber. He resumed his position and looked around. Nothing stirred. He rested both elbows on the ground and aimed the gun at the offside rear tyre. Biting his tongue, aware of his accelerating heartbeat, he gently squeezed the trigger. Nothing happened. He had copied the example of a thousand movies. No he had not. He giggled. It would help if he released the safety catch. He tried again.

The trigger had a double mechanism. The second click was immediately followed by a god-almighty roar that flung his arms into the air and left him face down in the grass. The momentary numbness in his hands was replaced by the myriad stabs of pins and needles. He raised his head. He had missed the tyre completely and hit the petrol tank instead. The family saloon exploded into a cauldron of flame. Tongues of blue, white and copper spurted out of the black smoke which billowed into the milky sky. It was a breath-taking sight, more beautiful than any sunset.

If the occupants screamed it was impossible to hear them. The initial detonation was succeeded by several smaller ones – crump, crump – that fuelled the inferno. Martin stared in appalled fascination. He had to keep blinking to prevent his eyeballs drying in the pulsating heat. His eyebrows seemed to have disappeared. He would have loved to stay but it was time for tea.

TWENTY-THREE

It was the end of British Summer Time but there was no turning back the clock for Martin.

He lay on the sofa listening to Janacek's Sinfonietta. He played it all the time now. Its Slavic steeliness haunted him. He especially enjoyed the third, moderato, section. There was something almost fascistic about the relentless cascading brass.

As the music swirled about him he considered his options for the coming evening. It had been good to return to London, to rejoin civilisation after three weeks in the sticks, but his initial excitement at the hustle and bustle of metropolitan life had, as usual, turned to irritation at the extra effort required to simply go about one's business. The capital was a crumbling hive. The elbowing crowds, crawling traffic, clinging dirt and incessant noise were debilitating. He seemed to spend his whole life wishing he were somewhere else.

Araminta had invited him to a party. The occasion was a fund-raising benefit for Albanian orphans. He could not afford to go. He could earn some money by getting on with his review of a 2,000-page biography of Ann Radcliffe but for some reason he was unable to summon up sufficient enthusiasm. He would watch *Blind Date* instead. The would-be impressionists made him cringe, the Waynes and Traceys in their glad rags made him sneer but, when a couple hit it off, tears would spring to his eyes. And then there was the additional pleasure of sussing out which of the men were really gay. There was always one.

'Leave it alone. It'll drop off.'

'Hello, Alex. Not everyone feels the need to beat their meat at every opportunity.'

'Speak for yourself. Anyway Sweet Pea, how are you? I haven't seen you for *ages*. We must do something very soon. Spend some quality time together. How were the old folks?'

'Ma and Pa Rudrum? The same as ever. Perhaps slightly battier. Then who can blame them? I'm slowly going out of my mind as well.'

'I know you are. Well do something about it. I couldn't live without my therapist. There's nothing more relaxing than lying back and listening to the sound of your own voice for an hour. It's bliss.'

'Yes, but some people haven't got fifty quid to throw away. You can come and talk here on my couch if you like. I'll only charge you half the going rate.'

'Thanks but no thanks. You only want to know what I say about you.'

'So you do talk about me then?'

'Of course I do darling. You're one of my bestest friends. I'm the one person who really cares about you. You may well laugh. Other people may say they care but when you're in trouble, who do you turn to? Well possum?'

'You.' Why was this conversation plunging him into depression?

'Ten out of ten. And just you remember it. Now what are you doing tonight?'

'I'm not quite sure. Araminta's asked me to this charity shindig but I think she just wants to show off her new boyfriend. He's a Swedish tennis player, apparently.'

'Lucky cow. I wouldn't mind being his ball-boy. Can I come?'

'I'm afraid not. It's by invitation only.' He did not want to be forced into going. If he went he would only wish that he had not. 'Pardon me for asking. I've probably had Sven or whatever his name is anyway. Bye!'

Martin did not like to be reminded that he needed other people. Self-sufficiency was his watchword. If you only relied upon yourself you would not be let down. It would be pleasant to have someone to talk to when you came home from work, to hold hands with in the cinema, to have something to hug in bed other than a pillow. But he had killed the one person he really loved. He was clearly meant to be alone. So be it. He would have his fun uncoupling twosomes. Trudi would probably have got married soon. He had spared her the ordeal of dragging up brats. He had saved a pair of fornicators the inevitable descent into mutual recrimination. He did like tidying up and so far there were no loose ends. His mother had told him in hushed tones about the incident near Aldcliffe. It had been some time before the victims had been identified. The general consensus seemed to be that it had been some sort of bizarre suicide pact. It just went to show how sex outside marriage was dangerous. He was not sure if his mother were joking.

When he woke up it was getting dark. He slowly got off the sofa and – stretching himself in front of the window – watched the leaves dropping off the horse chestnut trees. With their five lobes they looked like hands clutching at nothing.

After *Blind Date* he felt restless. He had known all along that he would stay in. The fact that he would be alone indoors while everybody else would be out on the town gave him a curious satisfaction. He would go for a run down to Kings Cross, collect an early edition of the *Observer* and get a cab home. He could do the Azed crossword then – before anybody else. Living in London did have its compensations.

When he returned he was greeted by a red number one flashing on his answerphone. It was Nicola, inviting him to dinner on Bonfire Night.

'It will be a quiet evening, just the three of us. You know how anti-social Rory can be.'

Perfect.

TWENTY-FOUR

It was an inspirational view. As the train lurched towards Oxford station he saw the dreaming spires pricking the blue sky. His spirits soared.

He was here to attend the annual dinner of The Crossword Club. Each member received a monthly pamphlet which contained two very difficult thematic crosswords, solutions to previous puzzles, reviews, letters and various competitions. Cruciverbalists, or advanced crossword solvers, were a rare breed; solving was a solitary pursuit. Consequently it was good to gather once a year and let off steam.

His bank manager had run out of patience and refused to extend his overdraft. A trip to Oxford was out of the question. When he had finished cursing Martin came up with a solution. He went to Elaine with a proposal for a feature 'on the increasingly popular but esoteric world of crossword addiction.' Using *The Times* Crossword Championships to back up his argument, he not only persuaded the sceptical but accommodating editor to finance his 'research' in Oxford but also to pay for a year's subscription to the club. He did not tell anyone that he had been a member since the age of sixteen.

After he had checked into the Randolph Hotel – his double room at the rear looked out onto a slate roof, he could have been anywhere in England – he set out to explore. He had to force himself to slow down – he had the rest of the day. It was against his nature to stroll.

He had been apprehensive about the visit. Being an Oxbridge reject, he was still uncertain as to what his reaction would be. His moods were becoming more and more unpredictable. However, the fact that these denim-clad dickheads cycling past him were enjoying a privileged education denied to him – even though he was their intellectual equal or superior – somehow no longer seemed to matter. Many of them were no doubt hoping to end up in a job like his – but other people's envy was no compensation for boredom. It was a sad state of affairs if the only thing that could stimulate him was a small grid of intersecting words. Apart from killing, of course.

He wandered round the colleges playing spot-the-TV-location. He still appeared young enough to be mistaken for a student. Oxford was the ideal setting for the dinner. From above, the various quadrangles and squares that surrounded Carfax would resemble a giant grid: crossroads and crosswords. He emerged from Blackwell's with a thesaurus of the Scottish language. It had cost twenty pounds but he felt better off knowing that a frizzel was the hammer of a flintlock pistol or gun.

★

As evening dress was not de rigueur he decided against a penguin suit. It would be more fun to play the London trendy. At 7.45 he went downstairs to the function sporting one of Alex's cast-off Katharine Hamnett ensembles. His mother always told him he looked better in blue.

The room was surprisingly full. Perhaps there was no such thing as being fashionably late in Oxford. At least he had been right about the sauce though: sweet and dry sherry was all that was on offer. You could not expect retired librarians and schoolmistresses to shell out for champagne.

Once he had downed a couple of Croft Originals he felt more favourably disposed towards his fellow puzzlers. He had chatted to a banker, a crime novelist and even shaken hands with Azed himself – he did have some work to do – but he had yet to encounter a bookseller, an accountant or a computer systems analyst. Floral frocks rubbed shoulders with suits from Dunn & Co. At 8.30 the bonhomous philologists were led into the adjoining chamber for dinner. Guests were invited to find their own places by unravelling the anagrams on the name-cards. To begin with, Martin was unable to locate himself. He was on the point of complaining that he had been overlooked when two words leaped out at him:

ANTRIM MURDUR. Somewhat unnerved, he sat down and met the cornflower-blue eyes of the woman seated opposite.

'This is a pleasant surprise. I was beginning to think that I was the only person here under thirty.'

'In that case I'm sorry to say that you still are. Never judge a book by its cover.' She flicked her long blonde hair over her shoulders and smiled.

'I'm amazed. I trust you don't mind my saying so.'

'Not at all. What's a couple of years among friends? How do you do?' She held out her slender right hand. Against her white skin her blood-red nails seemed almost shocking. 'I'm A SIREN'S ROMANCE.'

'Pleased to meet you, Nerissa.' It felt as though her eyes could see right inside him.

'And you, Martin. What brings you to this little gathering?'

'I'm writing a feature on crossword addiction for *Streetwise* magazine. I've been a member of the club for years though.'

'How interesting. I don't remember seeing you here before, although I do recognise your name. I buy *Streetwise* whenever I go up to London.'

'This is my first time.' He filled their glasses with the white wine that had just arrived. 'Do you live in Oxford?'

'Not far away. I've just moved into a cottage in a village outside Banbury.'

'Lucky you. I've decided that Oxford would suit me a lot better than North London.'

'I've lots of friends in London. Whereabouts are you?'

'Highbury.'

'Really? You must know Highbury Hill then.'

'Yes I do.'

'One of my oldest girlfriends and her lover have a house there. Number 40. They had to do an awful lot of work on it. The builders were in for yonks.'

'They must be loaded.' She laughed.

'They were.' Her two front teeth slightly overlapped each other. The single flaw enhanced the surrounding perfection. He wanted to explore it with his tongue.

During the meal he did his best to continue the conversation but the neighbouring old men were determined to have their share. In one or two cases Nerissa seemed to be the main reason for their presence. He was forced to make polite chitchat with other diners but he eavesdropped whenever he could. He thought he detected a slight Scottish accent. She looked stunning in that slinky satin dress. It was exactly the same colour as her eyes.

'I can see that our sexy lexicographer has made another conquest,' observed the crime novelist with a sigh. 'Don't get your hopes up. She was born to be that obscure object of desire.'

'You mean she's an ice-maiden?'

'I wouldn't go so far as that,' he continued, helping himself to more venison. 'It's just that she always comes by herself. She never mentions spouse nor swain.'

'Perhaps she has yet to meet Mr Right.' The chrome-domed writer smiled indulgently.

'I wish you luck. If I were forty years younger I'd give you a run for your money.' Martin was about to reply when he changed his mind. He asked a question instead.

'Does she work for the OED?'

'Yes she does – on the Concise to be precise. She is reputed to be a brilliant linguist. Professor Cameron is her father.'

'The author of *Magic and Mirth In Shakespeare*?'

'The very same.'

'Well that accounts for her unusual Christian name. It was an interesting work. I used it when I was at university.' He should not have said that.

'Here or the other place?'

'Leeds, actually.'

'Ah.'

As the port was passed round it was traditional to play a

simple elimination game that enabled solvers to show off their most obscure vocabulary. The subject this year was 'Fantastic Creatures'. Those who wished to take part sat together at one of the long trestle tables. The rest were free to watch or retire to the other reception room. When Martin saw that Nerissa was going to participate he joined in too.

The players took it in turn to come up with the name of a monster. If you could not conjure up a beast in Chambers you were supposed to make one up. Anybody could challenge an opponent to define their word. If it did not appear in the dictionary, or if the definition was wrong, then that player was out. Alternatively, if the monster did exist and was correctly defined, the challenger was out of the game.

Ten members lined up to begin. At first the pace was quite fast as, one by one, all the obvious animals were trotted out: leviathan, behemoth, kraken, cockatrice, basilisk, chimera, lycanthrope, hippocampus, hippocentaur, hippogriff. Mythology proved to be a plentiful source but once harpy, minotaur and gorgon had gone the game slowed down. Martin remembered that there had, in fact, been three gorgons and said 'Medusa'. Nerissa, who was sitting beside him, said 'Euryale' and her neighbour, a computer systems analyst, followed up with 'Stheno'. A blowzy, not to say boozy, middle-aged woman in a marigold twin-set immediately said 'poppycock' and was out.

'Who's that?' Martin asked the crime writer.

'God knows. I think she runs a secondhand bookshop.'

'She should try reading more of her stock.'

Fabulous birds rekindled the fight with phoenix being chased by roc, simurg and fung. This last, Chinese, contender was unsuccessfully challenged which left just five players. The novelist went out on a technicality because, although Lewis Carroll's snark was in Chambers, his boojum was not. The hiatuses were filled with drinking and thinking. Almost every contribution was being challenged now. The final quartet offered definitions without being asked.

Wasserman, a sea monster shaped like a man, was followed

by wivern, a cross between a dragon and a griffin. Martin proudly trumped this with wendigo, a man-eating North American Indian monster, but, with hardly any hesitation, Nerissa offered manticore, a lion/scorpion hybrid with a human head. Her accompanying smirk tempted a small, nattily dressed man with red-framed glasses, a professional crossword compiler, to challenge her. Nerissa was right.

'He should have known better,' murmured the crestfallen author.

The third man then suggested Arimasp, a gold-loving cyclops. Martin bit his lip. Even though he was racking his brains, he only had one teratism left. He was also getting a frightful headache.

'Monopode. A one-footed creature whose foot is so large that it can be used as a sunshade.' Everybody laughed except Nerissa. When no challenge was forthcoming she treated them to an explanation.

'It's genuine. Pliny mentions it in his *Naturalis Historia.*'

How the hell did she know? He had only come across it when he had been looking up monopsony. Detecting Martin's peevishness, Nerissa raised her eyebrows and blew him a kiss. He blushed.

For her own turn the beautiful bookworm posited tragelaph, part goat, part stag. A hush descended on the room. The gooseberry, as Martin had dubbed the computer man, submitted opicinus, half dragon, half fish. Martin was on the point of admitting defeat when Nerissa commented, 'I think you'll find that opicinus is an heraldic term meaning half dragon, half lion.' The adjudicator pronounced her correct. Now there was just the two of them. Nerissa flicked back her hair and said, with as much innocence as she could muster: 'Well, Martin, it's time to show us what you've got.'

It was a tactical mistake to arouse him because his quickening heart must have carried extra blood to his brain as well as his groin. Suddenly, he saw the light. As airily as possible he said: 'Tarand. A reindeer that changes colour like a chameleon.' The blue in her eyes darkened to a cobalt hue. He grinned. 'True or false?' The judge silenced the excited whispers with a 'sh'.

'Given that you are a journalist,' said Nerissa deliberately, 'and, given that I feel sure that I would have heard of Rudolph's colourful cousin, I challenge you.'

'I win! I win!' exclaimed Martin, punching his fists in the air. The referee announced that he was indeed the winner and, to an enthusiastic round of applause, the editor of the Crossword Club presented him with a bottle of champagne. Martin beamed.

'I don't know if they're pleased to see you win or just glad to see me lose,' said Nerissa, disconsolately. 'I won last year, and the year before.' She kissed Martin on the mouth. 'Well done. I'm impressed.'

'It was worth winning just for that,' he whispered in her ear, aware that they were being watched. 'To the victor the spoils. D'you fancy a nightcap?'

TWENTY-FIVE

The symmetry of her face was uncanny. Carefully cupping her chin in both hands as if it were bone china, he turned her head to the right and then to the left. Each profile was a mirror image of the other. Two almond-shaped eyes gazed at him from beneath the two blonde menisci of her eyebrows. A perfect pair of high cheekbones was separated by a straight nose whose small black nostrils resembled a pair of full stops. Her mouth, although most of the lipstick had now been kissed away, was still red; the upper lip, neither thick nor thin, was exactly the same size as the lower. As Nerissa watched his rapt expression, a smile played upon them. She twitched her nose.

'You look just like a Siamese cat,' whispered Martin. 'Here kitty, kitty.'

They kissed again.

It had been sometime before they had been able to get away.

Following his victory, more people were interested in talking to him. As he fielded the usual questions about where he worked and where he lived and what he thought of such and such a compiler, Nerissa stayed by his side. He was flattered. The jealousy of the dirty old men only increased his pleasure. He would have liked to leave the occasion trailing Nerissa on his arm but he agreed to wait for her in his room. There was no point pushing his luck.

He could not tune into anything suitable on the radio so he turned it off. A single bedside lamp provided the requisite half-light. When he went to stand the bottle of champagne in the sink – which he had filled with cold water – he realised that he was trembling. His head was throbbing too. He swallowed a couple of pink Migraleve and then a yellow one to make absolutely sure. The naffness of the situation did not stop him feeling nervous. Would she come? He hung up his jacket, took off his shoes and lay on the bed with his ankles crossed and his hands behind his head then immediately sprang up and ran to the bathroom to drain his bladder. So much for nonchalance.

As he scrupulously dried himself off he heard a knock. 'Room service!' The door had hardly closed before Nerissa had glued her lips to his and entwined herself about him. She was astonishingly strong. His tongue traced her overlapping teeth. They staggered across the cigarette-burned carpet and collapsed on the bed panting.

'Hi.'

'Hello.'

'Are you married?' he asked.

'No.' She ran a middle finger down the inside of his left thigh. Her nail made a slight scratching sound on the cotton.

'Where's that champagne?'

He opened the bottle in the bathroom to forestall any embarrassing accidents. When he returned Nerissa was stark naked. Her skin – which had clearly never seen the sun, let alone a sunbed – seemed almost to be lit from within. She lay on the bed, resting on her elbows. She made no attempt to cover herself.

'These will have to do,' he said, placing two tumblers on one of the bedside tables. His mouth felt very dry.

'No matter. It's what's inside that counts. Speaking of which – isn't it about time you took your clothes off?'

Even in this baggy suit, she could see that he was hard. Without bothering to undo all the buttons, he pulled the white shirt over his head and, remembering to take his socks off first, dropped his trousers to reveal a pair of paisley boxer shorts. His cock protruded from the flies. Slipping down the underwear caused his erection to bounce against his stomach. Martin stood there watching it nod and glanced quizzically at Nerissa. She giggled.

'That's just what we need – a swizzle-stick.' He filled their glasses and handed one to her. She moved over to sit on the side of the bed.

'Cheers.'

'Cheers.' She had a sip but, instead of swallowing, took Martin in her mouth. He could sense every icy bubble bursting against the tip of his hot cock. Some of the fizz dribbled out from her lips and trickled down to his balls. He groaned.

She behaved like a cat as well. When, at last, she let him enter – safely sheathed in rubber – her back arched and a deep-throated purr filled his ears. The hairs on the back of his neck stood up. She writhed beneath him, gnawing at his shoulders. To his surprise – and relief – it took him a few minutes to come. Whether this was due to the alcohol, or simply nerves, he could not tell. He was also unable to block from his mind an overhead shot of them fucking. In the event she ruined his orgasm by clawing his buttocks at the vital moment. He yowled in agony not ecstasy. Men were not supposed to leave blood on the sheets.

★

They were sitting on the bed, cross-legged and face to face. 'Wysiwyg,' said Nerissa.

'Sorry?'

'What You See Is What You Get.'

'And what do you think I see?'

'A beautiful, innocent girl who likes having her tits sucked.'

'If you want to be a mother I'm not the man.'

'Who mentioned babies?' She held her breasts out to him. The nipples were disproportionately large. As he nibbled her teats, he was suddenly reminded of blowing up a pair of water-wings. He could even taste the warm plastic of the valves. Was he afraid of getting out of his depth?

'Haboob,' she murmured, stroking the back of his labouring neck. 'Haboob is the Arabic name for a sandstorm.'

'Don't you ever stop working?' The ends of her hair, brushing and tickling his groin, had given him another hard-on.

'No I don't.' She pushed him back onto the bed and straddled him, holding down his shoulders as she rode her way to brutal satisfaction. The intensity of her desire was almost frightening. It was better the second time.

★

The bedside clock glowed in the dark. It was 3.27am. Nerissa was asleep. They lay in the same position, a double zig-zag, his arm around her waist. He had forgotten that sharing a bed was a technique to be practised like any other. The rhythm of her breathing interfered with his own. The effort of synchronising them made him even less sleepy. It did not seem right to wear ear-plugs. He wanted to turn over but was terrified of waking her up. He had pins and needles in his other arm. He was hot, he was exhausted but he could not go to sleep. Footsteps on the ceiling told him that he was not the only one. The central heating made a ticking noise.

At 4am he could bear it no longer and got up for a drink of water. He stared at himself in the mirror. Her teeth had left Xs on his skin. Crossbites. Now she stretched diagonally across the whole bed. He yawned again and looked down on her. A wave of tenderness washed over him. It was no good getting to like her – he would probably never even see her again. She had come too late. He had other things to do instead of getting embroiled with another person. He had to look out for number one. The feeling of compassion was superseded by one of claustrophobia. He wanted to get out.

He was about to ease himself reluctantly back into bed when he remembered that he had not done his daily press-ups. He might as well do today's as well as yesterday's.

Ten minutes later he was asleep.

TWENTY-SIX

'It's on! It's on!' cried a bronzed young man in a Yamamoto suit. He strode through the bar and into the brasserie at the back. He was carrying a portable phone even though their use was forbidden in The Club.

'What a plonker,' said Michael, waving to the waitress with a shaved head. 'I bet he's in PR. God knows why they let such people become members.'

'Because they have exceptionally large expense accounts,' said Martin, sinking further into the arms of a leather sofa. 'Size isn't everything.'

'You should know.'

They were both well on the way to being drunk. Three hours ago they had met for lunch in Soho. Thus far their main achievement of the afternoon had been to make it downstairs from the dining room.

Michael ordered another couple of Mexican beers, belched and, checking himself in one of the many mirrors, turned to Martin.

'So tell me more about Nerissa. She sounds exactly like my kind of girl.'

'Apart from being stunningly attractive, well-off and amazing in bed, she's far too intelligent for you.'

'Balls. If I got her between the sheets she wouldn't have time to think. I wouldn't mind sloppy seconds.'

He felt like hitting him but refrained – it was Michael's turn to pay. There was no point in getting worked up about a one-night stand. His objection to Michael's lust was not that it was directed at Nerissa – even though he had not set eyes on her – it was that he had apparently forgotten Isobel so easily. On the way back from Oxford he had been worried that he had been unfaithful to her memory. The last time they had met he had told her that he had not slept with anybody else. Perhaps it was guilt that had made him so itchy. But if he had betrayed her, Isobel had betrayed him first.

The next morning, after a slow, sleepy fuck and a shower, Nerissa had not dashed off but stayed for breakfast in his room. He was gratified to note that their conversation had no trace of sheepishness. They had both known what they were doing and had enjoyed it. The first thing that he had done on returning to the office was to order her a dozen red roses. Araminta had complained 'you never send me flowers' so he had ordered some for her too. His credit card might melt but it was all good PR.

Michael was talking to a pair of grey-hairs in grey suits. He invited them to sit down and have a drink with him but they declined, explaining that they were in a 'time-clench'. Martin watched them in a mirror. He thought he detected a patronising air about them but, after the glass doors had swung to behind them, Michael gave him a grin of satisfaction.

'Who were those two?'

'Bigwigs. TV top dogs. Head honchos with their hands on

the lolly. I've been trying to see that fat one for weeks to raise the necessary for my piece on pumping iron. He's agreed to see me next week. This calls for a celebration. Simon, a bottle of shampoo please!'

Martin sighed luxuriously. There would be no going back to work today. It did not matter – Tuesdays were always slack. The Club was the one public, or semi-public, place in London where he felt at ease. Lounging in this bar was his favourite form of relaxation, and yet, underneath the cool atmosphere, there lurked a subtle tension. Members cultivated carefree attitudes but they were all intent on observing and being observed. It was impossible not to look up and catch someone's eye. Oeillades cannoned round the crystal walls. The more famous the guest or member, the more they would apparently be ignored. The air-conditioned watering-hole was a hot-house of gossip, jealousy, networking and ambition.

The waiter brought the champagne and the perspex vacuum to keep it chilled. Once upon a time Martin had been embarrassed when his coevals had called him 'sir'. Nowadays he did not give a damn. Like the rest of the bar staff, Simon was dressed in black and white and had an expensive haircut. After a few drinks it was difficult to tell these chiselled clones apart. They were all equally attractive but this did not deter punters from awarding them marks out of ten for sex appeal.

'Seven,' said Michael, raising his glass. 'Salut!'

'Eight,' said Martin. 'Skol!'

The Yamamoto suit and mobile phone went by with a side-kick. They could hear the eager beaver telling her: 'It's on. It's on.'

'And what are you two sybarites toasting?'

'Hello,' cried Martin, lumbering to his feet to shake hands. 'Fancy seeing you here. How are you? Have a drink.'

'Well just one. I've got to run. We still haven't finished editing *Mindless Pleasures*.'

'Great title,' commented Michael. 'As Martin is clearly too pissed to effect an introduction, I'll do it myself. I'm Michael Ford.'

'Pleased to meet you. David Burnstone.'

'Ah, yes. I saw *Blue Murder*. I loved the bit where that hooker gets raped with a cactus.'

'Shut up, Michael. You're thinking of a different movie. Take no notice of him – he'll say anything at the moment. He's trying to get the dosh for his next project. He calls himself a documentarist.'

'I'm as susceptible to flattery as the next *auteur*,' said Burnstone with a smile. He was sloshed as well. Martin had interviewed the director two years ago, just before his third film – a sassy teen romance – was released to mixed reviews. Although he was in his mid-thirties he looked at least ten years older. Dark circles round his eyes gave him the appearance of a giant panda. This impression was enhanced by his short stature and wide girth. Wannabes were known to find him 'cuddly' or 'cute'. As a sex object Martin thought him a non-starter but as a friend he was both generous and useful. Following the publication of the – on the whole – favourable interview Burnstone had invited him to lunch. After that they had met every three months or so. In addition to their mutual interest in film, Martin was attracted to Burnstone's success and Burnstone was attracted to Martin's naive fascination with Hollywood. 'You're the nicest journalist I've ever met,' confessed Burnstone during their second encounter.

'And you're the nicest film person I've ever met,' replied Martin. They were smashed then too.

Michael and Burnstone were talking shop and ignoring Martin's theatrical yawns. When he had swilled down his second glass Burnstone got up to say goodbye.

'Must be on my way. Time is money. Thanks for the fizz. We must meet again soon, Michael. Martin, come to dinner next week. I'll give you a bell.'

He almost fell down the two steps that led into reception. Martin licked his right forefinger and chalked up a notch in the air.

'Now don't say I don't do anything for you.' Michael snorted.

'It took you all your time to get off your fat arse.'

'I have not got a fat arse.'

'I'll take your word for it.' He sniffed. 'Fancy a toot?'

'You bet!' He leapt to his feet. Michael sighed.

'Come on then.'

He followed Michael through the swing doors and down the narrow stairs to the cloakrooms, flashing a smile at the bimbo on reception as he passed. They entered the gents. More mirrors. Both cubicles were occupied.

'Christ, everyone's at it!'

'They could actually be laying a log,' said Martin.

'Laying something else more likely. I can't wait. We'll have to go next door.'

They beetled into the ladies. Fortunately, at this time in the late afternoon, apart from one of the three cubicles, it was empty. 'Why don't we get fresh flowers?' complained Martin. Michael bundled him into the furthest stall.

'Be quiet!' He put down the lid and took out his gear, a chrome kit that had clearly seen considerable use.

'Where did you get that from?'

'Isobel bought it me last Christmas. I thought I'd lost it after the funeral but I found it again.'

They fell silent for a moment. Someone washed their hands and left. Michael continued. His hands were shaking.

'There we are. Girls before boys.'

He did not need to be asked twice. He crouched down, took the proffered metallic straw and inhaled two of the wobbly lines – one per nostril – off the tiny mirror, making sure that none of the white powder remained. He sniffed again and tilted his head back against the wall waiting for the rush. Michael reclaimed the toot-tube.

'Nose-candy, yeah, yeah, yeah.'

As the drug took effect, Michael ran both his hands through his long black hair, then chucked Martin under the chin. They gazed into each other's dilated pupils. For a moment he thought Michael was going to kiss him. It was extremely hot in here.

'Yes!' breathed Martin. 'Who needs sex when you can have

this?'

'I do. Better still, have them both at the same time.'

'That's what's known as having your coke and eating it.' They laughed hysterically.

'I'm always giving you angel dust,' said Michael, wagging a finger.

'I'll pay you back. I promise,' said Martin. 'Even if it's the last thing I do.'

They did not linger for fear of losing their strategic position in the bar. Michael ordered another bottle of champagne. 'Why not?' said Martin. They had drunk half of it when the PR-man came back. There was no sign of the phone.

'It's off. It's off.'

He appeared to be on the point of crying. Martin looked at Michael and Michael looked at Martin. Tears streamed down their faces. Nobody else was laughing.

TWENTY-SEVEN

The inflatable green dinosaur glared back at him. It was a ridiculous creature; the designer's intention appeared to have been to create a tyrannosaurus for tots. It was perched on the top of a set of shelves in the subs' section. Over the months Martin had watched its rainbow colours gradually fade as layer upon layer of dust settled on its plastic skin. Now it had begun to deflate; its stubby neck was drooping. He almost felt sorry for it.

The office was virtually deserted. It was Friday lunchtime so most of the staff were in a pub around the corner. They would not be back till after four. One by one the computer screens blacked out into power-save mode. He had stayed behind to work on his crossword feature but all he could think of was Nerissa's hair grazing his glans. His cursor winked at him. He was bored. Glans, glandis – Latin for acorn. He was going nuts. Nothing made sense.

He had finally received a call from Nerissa thanking him for the roses.

'You shouldn't have done it.'

'I know.'

'They're lovely. It was very sweet of you.'

They had not had much to say to each other. The conversation ended with her promising to get in touch the next time she came to London. He did not hold out much hope. If she had been interested she would have phoned him sooner.

'What are you doing at your desk at this time? Have we been eating in class?'

'Hello, Alex.'

'Well don't sound too pleased to hear from me. How are you, Alex? How is Keith? How's your new job going? Thank's for calling me.'

'Is everything all right?'

'As a matter of fact it is. Thank you for asking. What's up with you?'

'I'm bored.'

'So what else is new?'

'Nothing.'

'Then this is your lucky day. I'm taking the afternoon off. Do you want to come shopping with me?'

'What for?'

'I don't know. What's it matter? I'll know it when I see it.'

'I haven't got any money.'

'Since when has that stopped you? I'll pick you up in twenty minutes.'

Alex had to sound his horn to attract Martin's attention.

'I thought you had a white BMW.'

'I did. I changed it for a black one. This is a later model with lots of extras. More chic, don't you think? Get in.'

They tore down Kingsway, crawled round the Aldwych and bunny-hopped down the Strand. It was only when they had negotiated Trafalgar Square and Admiralty Arch that Alex could put his foot down. Hightailing it down the Mall always gave Martin a buzz. Even though there were still plenty of leaves on the trees, bonfires smouldered in St James's Park. Carlton Terrace gleamed white against the overcast sky. Trendies traipsed in and out of the ICA.

'Wouldn't it be fabulous to live up there,' said Alex. 'You could drop in on Queenie for tea.' He slipped a tape into the removable cassette deck. The Pet Shop Boys belted out. Martin lowered the volume.

'Aren't you afraid of speed-traps?'

'Lighten up, Martin for God's sake. When you're as loaded as I am you'll understand that on-the-spot fines are a drop in the ocean.' He turned the music up.

The weekend exodus had already begun. Hyde Park Corner was gridlocked. Alex regaled him with his latest brief encounter, a plasterer from the Isle of Dogs.

'And before you say it, Jason was devastatingly handsome. He looked terrific in his denims and Doc Martens. I don't normally go for skinheads but in his case I made an exception. I was glad I did. His balls were as large as hen's eggs. Of course, he fell head over heels in love with me. It just goes to show the harder they look, the softer they are. It's so tiresome. Whatever happened to the Four Fs?'

'What do you mean?'

'Find 'em, fool 'em, fuck 'em and forget 'em.'

'Charming.'

'He was actually. It's amazing who you meet in Waterstone's these days.'

They had moved ten feet in as many minutes. Hemmed in on all sides by idling traffic, he began to feel trapped. He opened the tinted electric window.

'What are you trying to do? Kill us?' cried Alex. He shut it.

Martin tried in vain to open it again. The driver's controls over-rode the passenger's button.

'If you care so much about your health why don't you quit smoking and stop screwing around?' said Martin furiously.

'Temper, temper. I'm always very careful, you know that. And I'm going back to the hypnotherapist's next week.'

'How many times is that now?'

'It will be the fourth, not that it's any of your business. It only seems to work for about a month. The effect wears off.'

'You've got no willpower.'

'And you've got too much.'

They had got as far as the Sheraton Tower. 'Do you really enjoy being promiscuous?' asked Martin.

'Not as much as I pretend to.'

'I knew that. Why do you keep on doing it?'

'I'm bored, just like you.'

'What about Keith?'

'He doesn't know what I get up to. Besides, I'm sure he's no angel, either.'

'Doesn't it worry you? Aren't you afraid of catching something?'

'Not especially. Anyway, I have the test every six months. I know that doesn't mean I'm clear but it's still reassuring. The only safe sex is no sex and that is not the answer. I mean, look at you.' Martin had not told him about Nerissa. For some reason Alex did not like it when he slept with women. He lit another cigarette. 'It's a question of priorities.'

'But surely being in a relationship means that you are supposed to be able to trust your partner. Remember the concept of fidelity? Surely faithfulness is the bedrock of love?'

'Bullshit. How many relationships have you been in? One. And look what happened to that. You're too starry-eyed Martin. Keith and I live together because we don't like being alone and because it's cheaper to live as two than it is to live as one. All relationships are based on mutual exploitation whether it be emotional or economic. Now for the love of God give me a break.'

When they eventually reached the King's Road it took them another fifteen minutes to find a parking space. They ended up down a side-street behind Peter Jones. Alex, who made it a policy never to walk if he could ride, complained bitterly. He suggested getting a cab.

'Don't be ridiculous,' said Martin. 'How on earth are you going to cruise from the back seat of a taxi?'

'It can be done,' said Alex, rolling his eyes.

Martin had mixed feelings about Chelsea. He admired the endless terraces of white stuccoed facades and shiny black railings but he hated the residents for being able to live in them. That was why he enjoyed watching sixties films like The Servant – even he could have afforded to buy in Wellington Square then.

It was fun to be seen in public with Alex. Somehow it did not matter if people thought that they were gay. It was a relief to be able to camp it up a bit and if the numerous queens judged them to be a couple so much the better. Alex was his alter ego, a more attractive *doppelganger*, the man he should have been.

Christmas had already come to consumer-land. Martin's heart sank – he had yet to finish paying for last year's gifts. They trailed in and out of the boutiques, each with their own shop-fitted concept and thumping soundtrack, each with their own simpering assistants. He always felt self-conscious in such surroundings. He could wear the merchandise without any problem but, as he was purchasing them, he sensed that the minions were laughing at him for doing so. As he browsed around, trying to avoid glancing in the ubiquitous mirrors, Alex darted here and there, fingering sweaters, picking up shirts then immediately dropping them in disgust. He showed more interest in the customers than the clothes.

'Have you any intention of buying something?' said Martin, quietly.

'What? This rubbish? Certainly not. Come on, there'll be more action in Habitat.'

Single men floated around aimlessly. In the basement Alex decided to buy a dozen bunches of dried flowers.

'I'm exhausted. Let's have a drink.'

They found a table by a window in the first-floor cafe. From here they could look down on everyone. 'I shop therefore I am,' said Alex. 'You are what you buy.'

'Does that mean you're an armful of dead weeds?'

'Better than being a wallflower, darling.'

When he returned from buying two more coffees he found Alex talking to the man in the mustard duffel coat that he had been eyeing up downstairs. He seemed much younger close up. His fair hair flopped either side of his centre parting in the archetypal public schoolboy fashion. His cheeks were flushed with nervousness. Martin wanted to stroke them.

'Martin, meet Adam.'

'Hello.'

'Hi.'

He gave Alex his cappuccino and sat down. He did not ask Adam if he would like one. He made no effort to join in the conversation. He sipped his espresso and stared out of the window. He was used to being de trop and relished Alex's embarrassment. When it came down to it his libido always overruled his loyalty.

'Martin.'

'Yes?'

'Adam and I are just going to take a walk.'

'I see.'

'Should I meet you back here?'

'I can get a cab if you want.'

'That won't be necessary. I won't be very long.'

'I'll be in Marks and Sparks then. The food department.'

'OK.'

'Nice to have met you,' said Adam.

'Really?' said Martin.

As he toured the chilled food cabinets, basket in hand, he gradually regained his composure. He was reassured by the instantly recognisable packaging, the clean environment, the insistence on quality. What this store offered was no effort, no mess and no surprises.

TWENTY-EIGHT

He removed the cellophane and took off the lid. You did not get much for 25 quid. The bomblets nestled in their green tissue paper. They seemed harmless enough now – only the nitre pricking his nostrils hinted at what they could do. It was at least ten years since he had bought fireworks. Standing in the enormous queue at Hamleys, he had been amazed at the range of pyrotechnics on offer. Frantic assistants weaved in and out of the gaily-painted dustbins from which they extracted single fireworks the size of landmines. The top-of-the-range rockets seemed more like bazookas, their sticks the thickness of broom handles. There was enough gunpowder to fight a battle.

He picked up the fireworks one by one and put them into a Marks & Spencer carrier-bag. Traffic Lights, Snowstorm, Jack-In-The-Box, Vesuvius – their names had not changed since his childhood. As a child he had looked forward to the fifth of November for weeks.

The last quarter of the year had always been the most exciting time for him. After Halloween, Mischief Night and Bonfire Night, there was his birthday and then the build up to Christmas. Nowadays he was just relieved to have made it through another twelve months.

★

Before he had been sent away to school Martin and his parents had spent every Guy Fawkes Night at the Bradburys'. His father had met Mr Bradbury at the golf club and Martin had soon become friends with his daughter and two sons. Nick and Jenny were older than him but Stephen was younger. Martin liked going round to their house because it was larger than his own and there was a swimming pool in the garden. Mr Bradbury owned a chain of garages. Although he liked money he was by no means a miser. Mrs Bradbury – a small, slim crea-ture dwarfed by the beefy bulk of her husband – was forever complaining that he spent it faster than he could earn it. His habit of skinny-dipping at any time of the day or night caused scandalous delight among the neighbourhood wives, while his succession of flash cars prompted much envy among their Ford-driving husbands. In the end it was this latter passion that did for him.

In 1985 he was hot-rodding it down the inside lane of the M6 when the left front wheel of his Jaguar, from one of his own garages, came off. When the vehicle finally fetched up against the bulwark of a bridge, all that remained of the XJS was a badly dented can of mincemeat. Martin had been surprised by his mother's grief.

Every night a week before the big event – if he had been a good boy – his father would let him carefully go through their deluxe selection of fireworks and read the descriptions of what they were supposed to do. He would occasionally persuade him to light one in the back garden while he watched – lights out, curtains open – from the warm safety of the dining room. Martin thought that this was the height of naughtiness.

When the big day finally arrived he would wait in the garden for his father to come home from work so that he could watch the rockets streak across the night sky. At seven o'clock the three of them would walk round to the Bradburys', hand in gloved hand, singing 'Remember, remember, the fifth of November.' Mrs Bradbury always prepared a massive spread of treacle toffee and toffee apples, sausages and sausage rolls, baked pota-toes and baked beans, tomato soup and beefburgers, crisps and cashews. After the display they would all go inside to sip cocoa and listen to Mr Bradbury's quadraphonic sound system.

The combined Rudrum/Bradbury collection of fireworks was so large that after an hour or so the excitement would begin to wane. The mothers grizzled in the cold and the children – fed up of being cooped up in the open-doored double garage – would run around the garden zapping each other with the beams of their torches or writing their names in the frosty air with sparklers. The white-hot signatures lingered in the black. Mr Bradbury, who refused to have a bonfire because he said it would ruin his perfect lawn, nevertheless had a cavalier attitude to the firework code. Instead of, for example, igniting a roman candle with the taper that had been provided, he would light the blue touchpaper with the butt of his Havana while his wife stood by scolding him. Soon three or four fireworks would be going off at once. It was a prime example of money going up in smoke.

At twelve years old Nick Bradbury was already developing into the tiresome lout that he was destined to become. Pretty fireworks were for cissies, he jeered, bangers were the only ones worth buying. When Martin suggested that it was only cissies who asked their mates to lick their willie, Nick turned scarlet and told him – having checked there were no adults about – to fuck off. It was unfair of Martin to remind him of this – he had entered into the 'you show me yours and I'll show you mine' ritual as eagerly as Nick. It was just that Nick, who had recently discovered the joys of masturbation, had taken the opportunity to try out the oral as well as the manual approach. Both boys had equally enjoyed the experience but, at a later date, Martin had declined to repeat it.

Nick wasted no time in wreaking his revenge. He knew that Martin did not like loud bangs and so he filched a squib, tied a piece of string to it, attached the other end of the string to a clothes peg and clipped it on to the bottom of his nice blue anorak. He lit the touchpaper with a sparkler and retreated to a safe distance to watch.

When he heard the first bang Martin jumped. He swung round angrily to see who had thrown the firework behind him but – before he could say anything – the firecracker continued to explode. He screamed. The sight of him haring about the garden to the apparent accompaniment of machine-gun fire was a comical one. It was clear to everybody except Martin that he was in no real danger. By the time he had realised that the pool was empty – so there was no use plunging in – the squib was spent. He stood on the edge sobbing with relief. His mother came to comfort him while Mr Bradbury, without even bothering to ask, gave Nick a clip round the ear and sent him inside. His own father was still laughing on the way home.

✵

He twisted the plastic bag round and round until the fireworks were bunched together in the bottom. He knotted it then placed the bundle in another bag, knotted that one as well, and dropped the lot into the kitchen swing-bin. As usual it was the packaging that counted. He tapped the empty box over the sink to ensure that no grains of powder remained. He wrapped the fully-loaded gun in the tissue paper, placed it in the box and put the lid on. He picked up the parcel. It was heavier than it should be but the contents hardly shifted at all. There would be nothing odd about carrying such a box on a night like this. He retrieved another carrier bag from the cupboard under the sink.

At 7 o'clock he set out for the tube. He wore the same anonymous clothes as he had done the last time he had travelled on the Northern Line except that tonight he wore a pair of black woollen gloves over the rubber ones.

He strode up Hampstead Hill. All about him devils spurted, maroons exploded, catherine wheels spun and girandoles whirled. The smoky air resounded with squeals, screeches, shell bursts and banshee wails. Garden shrubbery was splashed with lurid light. NW3 was one colossal display of satanic *son et lumière*. No one would hear his two little bangs.

Rory and Nicola could not have lived in a better location. Their unusual house, which was half-way up the hill, could be approached by three separate entrances. Access to two of these was from Hampstead Hill Square. The first led down a dog-legged path to the front door, the second was a narrow alley that ran along the rear of the house to the back door, past the side door, through a secluded paved courtyard, up some ancient steps and out on to Hampstead Hill. It was a public right of way unknown to the public. Martin chose to enter from the third access point: ie the other end of this short cut. Unless you were looking for it, the alley was almost impossible to find. All that could be seen from Hampstead Hill was an open doorway sandwiched between a restaurant and an antiques shop. It appeared to be a dead end. Martin raised his collar and pretended to be looking in the shop window. When there were no pedestrians nearby he slipped down the side and into the darkness.

He had to wait for a moment so that his eyes could accustom themselves to the shadows. He slowly made his way down the steps and into the courtyard. His stomach rumbled. It was a shame that he would not be able to stay for dinner. Humming the moderato section of the Janacek Sinfonietta – now an almost permanent *chant intérieur* – he made for the side door. Suddenly the area was flooded in an icy glare. He froze. The carrier-bag swung against his leg. Nothing happened. Then he remembered – after their last burglary the insurance company had insisted that they have security lights fitted. He took a deep breath and rang the door bell.

TWENTY-NINE

'Hello. Come in. Punctual as ever.' Rory stepped back and held the door open. He crossed the threshold. He stood in a small, square lobby. On his right a narrow set of stairs led up to a bedroom and nowhere else. Straight ahead there was a door to a bathroom. He gave Rory a bottle of champagne and followed him through to the kitchen on the left.

'Thank you. Nicola's already opened one upstairs.'

A glutinous gumbo bubbled in a copper cauldron on the hob. The mahogany units gleamed in the light from a single, hidden, neon tube.

Rory placed the Veuve Cliquot in the refrigerator then went over to the entrance of his latest alteration. What had once been a brick wall was now an archway into a conservatory-cum-dining room. A ramshackle shed had been demolished to make way for a large glass box, the sides of which could be slid back in the summer to permit alfresco eating. Ivy-clad walls divided this part of the garden from the front so that the extension was entirely private. A new rockery filled the remaining space. Rory flicked a switch and spotlights flooded the grotto.

'All you need now is a couple of gnomes,' said Martin.

'You're only jealous,' replied Rory. He adjusted the cutlery on the table which was set for three. 'Come on, let's go and see Nicola. She's got something to tell you.'

'I can't wait.'

'What's in the bag?'

'Fireworks, of course. I thought we'd set them off before dinner.'

'OK. It's ages since I've bombed a cat. Do you want to leave them here?'

'It's all right. I'll keep them with me.'

'Suit yourself.'

They went back into the kitchen, turned a sharp left and walked through the old dining room. It was empty except for a white marble Adam fireplace and a black carpet. A black and white mandala hung on one of the white walls. In the main entrance hall they passed the triple-locked front door and another bathroom then started up a staircase that was just wide enough for one person.

The whole of the first floor was taken up by a split-level reception room which measured forty feet by thirty feet. Three square windows on one side of the room were matched by three square windows in the opposite wall. Red blinds covered them all. The lower half of the gallery was devoted to music. Free-standing speakers posed in the middle of the sprung ash floor. Ten thousand compact discs filled a specially designed alcove with stainless steel doors. In the upper half of the room Nicola lolled on a white vinyl sofa. A huge circular TV, encased in black plastic, flickered silently in a corner by the fireplace, which was flanked by a pair of Indonesian dragons.

Nicola was on the telephone. She hung up as soon as she saw them. She tried to mask her surprise by brandishing a bottle of champagne. It was less than half full.

'Hello Martin. It's lovely to see you.' When he bent down to peck her on the left cheek, the right cheek and the left cheek once again she flung her arms round his neck and pulled him on to the sofa. 'Have some fizz.'

Rory switched from Massive Attack to Portishead by ostentatiously pointing the remote that had been lying on a vast coffee table made entirely out of shattered glass. He poured some champagne into a flute for Martin.

'Aren't you going to take your jacket and gloves off?'

He had not planned to but he was enjoying himself too much

to rush things.

'Sure. I thought we were going to have the fireworks though.'

'Later, we want to ask you something first.'

'In a minute,' said Nicola. She got to her feet. 'Give me your jacket. I'll take it downstairs. I must check on the soup.'

'You better bring another bottle up as well,' called Rory as she disappeared. Martin took the firework box out of the bag. 'Tonight is going to be a celebration,' continued Rory. He was looking even more self-satisfied than usual. 'I hope you're in a party mood.' He lay back on the second sofa, running his long, brown fingers through his silky fair hair.

'You bet,' said Martin and shot him.

THIRTY

When there was still no reply the police rang the bell of the flat below. He felt the faint reverberation in his feet. Perhaps they would go away now.

His nosy neighbours opened the front door within seconds. They must have been twitching with anticipation, itching for an excuse to find out what was going on. It had been a mistake to ignore them. He could hear voices but not what the voices were saying. He stood up then sat down again. His knees were like two-way hinges. Determined not to wimp out at this stage, he crept to his own front door and opened it ever so slightly. The light was dazzling. He held his breath and listened.

'Yes, he did look rather shaken,' said she.

'We asked him if everything was all right but he didn't say a word,' said he.

'I think he'd been running,' said she. 'He must be up there because we haven't heard him go out.'

'We'd better take a look,' said the constable.

THIRTY-ONE

Rory did not die straightaway. The fifty-year-old bullet hit the twenty-eight-year old at an oblique angle, skewering into his chest and shattering the fourth and fifth left ribs. The explosion was deafening but Rory made no sound. His blood turned his white Kenzo shirt black in seconds. Rivulets ran over the white plastic couch creating a raspberry ripple effect. Martin stood up. Nicky was shouting upstairs but he was unable to hear what she said because his ears were ringing. He rounded the glass table and loomed over his school friend. He had forgotten how attractive Rory could be. His eyes gazed up at him blankly. They were bloodshot. He forced the smoking gun between Rory's expensive teeth. Saliva sizzled. He fired again.

Bits of the back of Rory's head ricocheted around the room. Martin went and stood behind the door. Nicola burst in and hiccoughed. The spray of body fluids had turned the walls into Jackson Pollock masterpieces. A miasma of singed flesh and smouldering hair floated in the air. Portishead kept wailing.

'Sorry about the mess. But then you're not bothered by stains, are you? Especially when they're on other people's carpets.' She wheeled round.

'What happened?'

'What do you think happened? I shot Rory and now I'm going to shoot you.' He pointed the gun at her. 'It's amazing what one of these things can do.' Perhaps it was the alcohol, perhaps it was shock –Nicola did not seem very scared. Martin was riled. 'Well aren't you going to scream or something? The least you could do, you stupid bitch, is beg for mercy.'

'You can't kill me. I'm pregnant. That's why we invited you here tonight. Rory wanted you to be a godfather.'

'Never mind. Just think of this as a somewhat drastic abortion. You won't get fat, you won't spend your mornings draped over the toilet bowl, you won't suffer endless sleepless nights. Now get upstairs.'

She turned and, casting one last glance at her dead lover, began to climb the steps to the second floor. Martin prodded her in the butt with the Colt. He was beginning to feel frisky. Did he have time for a quickie?

The idea was rejected before it had even fully registered. Nicola stopped by the bed. Instead of legs, four steel cables, one at each corner, suspended it from the ceiling.

'Strip,' he ordered. 'It makes quite a change having to ask.' She did as she was told. Her self-composure was remarkable. He had the daunting thought that she might actually be enjoying this, that she was under the impression that all of this was part of some elaborate hoax.

'Nicola.'

'Yes, Martin.'

'This is for real you know.'

'If you say so.' She gave a twirl.

'It's time for a Jacuzzi.'

They went through the walk-in wardrobes that formed a corridor between the bedroom and the bathroom. The ceiling was mirrored, the floor tiled in marble, the fixtures – twin basins, bath, bidet and lavatory – in the form of upturned sea-shells. Potted palms added to the tropical theme. It was a horrid, vulgar place in which to die.

When the whirlpool was frothing merrily, Nicola, without

waiting to be told, climbed in.

'Don't sit down. Stand up. I want to know who you were speaking to on the phone.'

'It's a secret. If I tell you, it will spoil the surprise.'

'I would have thought that you'd had enough surprises to last you a lifetime tonight.'

'Come on, Martin. Hurry up and join me.'

'You still don't get it, do you.' He shot her twice, once in each breast, and cursed when he missed the areolae. She collapsed. The ensuing surge of suds threatened to soak him. He sat cross-legged on the loo and watched as the remaining water turned into fizzing cherryade. A minor modern-day miracle. He looked at his watch. It was 7.45. Fifteen minutes flew past when you were having fun.

He washed his glass in the kitchen, dried it and carefully put it away. After he had cleared the table he turned off the stove but left the music and lights on. He unlocked the front door. He replaced the gun in the box and the box in the carrier bag. His hands were still tingling from firing it. He retrieved the Veuve Cliquot from the fridge. There was just one thing left to do.

He returned to the living room and, ignoring Rory's cooling corpse, picked up the telephone receiver. He pressed the button marked with his own initials: MR. Memory Recall. He listened to the series of clicks as the red Viscount redialled the last number entered on its keypad. At the other end of the line another phone began to ring. It was answered immediately.

'Hello?'

It was Alex. Martin hung up.

He closed the back door and, humming Janacek, crossed the courtyard. Whoosh! A rocket soared into the sky. He stopped and watched, enraptured. The shooting star reached its zenith and burst into a million sparks. He gulped the frosty night air. Magnesium chrysanthemums bloomed in his brain.

THIRTY-TWO

He stood by the window and swore. He had booked the cab for 7.30 but it was now 7.40 and it had still not arrived. He had called the cab company twice and been assured that his car was on its way. They were all liars and rip-off merchants. Most of the drivers were either illegal immi-grants or on income support. That was the trouble with living in N16 – it was difficult to phone for black cabs and if one did deign to come there was usually five quid on the meter before you had even set off. He stamped his foot. Was it too much to ask for people to be on time?

A Skoda slowed down in Clissold Avenue. There was no way he was going to get into that thing. He breathed a sigh of relief as it crawled past number 14. Twenty minutes later the early evening quiet was shattered by the screech of brakes and the noise of what seemed like an elephant farting. He grabbed the bottle of champagne, checked that the video and answer-phone were set, then locked his front door behind him. The bastard was only thirty minutes late.

As he closed the gate, the driver, who had his head buried in an Argos catalogue, sounded his horn again. Martin inspected the vehicle. Once upon a time, many moons ago, it had been a Datsun Cherry. In the sodium glare of the street lights it was impossible to discern what its original colour might have been. Vomit yellow was the best bet. Numerous dents and scratches suggested that his chauffeur was either an appalling motorist or indulged in stock-car racing in his spare time. At some stage someone had tried to repair the worst of the injuries but it was clear that the correct shade of paint had been unobtainable. Patches of rust, instead of being treated, had simply been sprayed with an aerosol. The bumpy surface recalled an adolescent's inexpert attempt to mask acne with make-up. The aerial had been replaced by a coat-hanger. The boot was tied shut with string. No doubt the tyres were bald as well but he could not wait any longer. He went round to the passenger side and opened the door.

'Good evening. Glad you could make it.'

A gust of hot, foul air swept over him. It had been a complete waste of time showering and putting on freshly laundered clothes – he now felt filthy. The seat was covered in an imitation sheepskin that had long since turned into a blackened mass of daglocks. As he scrabbled for the safety-belt, the driver threw the catalogue over his shoulder and said: 'Don't bother. It don't work. Where to?'

'Portman Square please.'

'That's in Kensington, innit?'

'No it is not.' Oik-speak always made Martin enunciate more precisely. 'Portman Square is behind Oxford Street, before you get to Marble Arch. Do you know where Selfridges is?'

'Course I do.' He could just see him strolling through the Food Hall.

'Well head for there then.'

It was obvious – even before they reached the end of Clissold Avenue – that he was at the mercy of a maniac. The driver was probably in his early twenties but he looked much older. Plump, unshaven, of Levantine origin, he was wearing camouflage trousers and a grubby white T-shirt, the transfers of which spelled out ONE MEAN MOTHERFUCKER. His long black curly hair had left grease marks on his shoulders. Similar hair sprouted from between the buttons of his flies. He probably considered underwear an irrelevance. Slamming an ancient Nike down on the accelerator, he steered the jalopy down the narrow corridor of parked cars with one hand and then, just as it seemed that they were going to pull straight out into Stoke

Newington Church Street, braked as hard as he could. Even though Martin had braced himself out of instinct and habit he still ended up banging his head on the fly-spotted windscreen because the seat slid forward a couple of inches.

'Sorry about that. I meant to warn you before we set off.'

'Don't worry about it. I should have expected it. Have you ever heard of the three magic letters MOT?'

'It's a pop group, innit?' Martin did not waste his breath mentioning insurance. He could feel the lump on his head swelling. It seemed to have cured his migraine.

As they waited for a gap in the traffic, the jolly Jehu lit a Marlboro with the stub of the one that had been dangling from his lower lip and sneezed, spraying his fare with ash and snot. Martin said nothing. When he tried to open the window the handle came off in his hand. He rammed it back on. Smiling slyly, the driver picked up his radio – the crackle of which had been competing with a bootleg tape of The Brotherhood Of Man – and yelled: 'zero eight, zero eight. P-O-B. P-O-B.' Never mind Passenger On Board, thought Martin. How about Piss Off Bullethead?

The car nosed its way through the back streets of Highbury like a laboratory rat in search of food in a maze. Martin sighed – since he could not get rid of the stench he might as well analyse it. The base was definitely scent of dog: old dog, moulting dog, drooling, incontinent dog. His nostrils began to prickle. That was all he needed: to arrive late among the glitterati wheezing like a redundant miner.

On top of the *parfum de pooch* there were several intriguing aromas that helped to create the toxic bouquet, most of which emanated from the animal next to him. He stank of onions. His halitosis was laced with beer. Every so often he would shift his buttocks to release a cheesy fart.

'Silent but deadly, huh?'

A tiny Christmas tree, made out of green cardboard, hung from the rearview mirror along with a pair of miniature football boots and a St Christopher medallion. It had plainly given up trying to keep the air fresh.

'Fag?'

'Excuse me?'

'D'yer wanna fag?'

'No thank you, I don't smoke.' He did not need to in this fume-filled death-mobile. Somewhat offended, Steve McQueen decided to clean out his ears with an old cotton-bud that he had found in his glove compartment. When he had collected a large enough dollop of toffee-coloured wax on each end he did not throw it out of the window as Martin expected but dropped it back into the glove compartment instead.

As the ride to hell continued he waited for the driver to go through every trick in the book. He was not disappointed. A green light meant slow down. A red light meant speed up. A single wrong turning meant a five-minute detour round a one-way system. They stopped for petrol. The horn and headlights were exploited at every opportunity. He wished he had brought the gun.

He did not relinquish his grip on the dashboard – which was plastered with stick-on inscriptions from the Koran – until the heap of Jap-crap had rattled to a stop.

'Ten pounds please.'

'You must be joking. If you're going to overcharge customers you should at least check whether they asked for a quote beforehand. I'll give you six pounds.'

When the office confirmed the fare, Zero Eight grinned and shrugged his dirty shoulders.

'You can't blame me for trying.'

He handed him a five pound note and a pound coin through the open door. 'What about a tip?'

'Fuck off.' He did not bother to close the door. A pair of plods was coming towards him on the pavement. 'I suggest you leave immediately before I lose you your licence.' He could not understand Arabic but he knew the farewell was not a fond one.

★

A butler, who came with the caterers, opened the door to David Burnstone's London apartment. Martin had been here before on a couple of occasions. Each room was designed to reflect a particular country. The dining room was supposed to be Iceland. There was nothing in the white-walled space except a glass table and a dozen chairs. They were all filled except one.

'Hello, Martin,' said the director. 'It is possible to be unfashionably late you know.'

'I'm sorry, David. The cab company let me down.'

'Don't worry about it, I'm only teasing. That's a very interesting aftershave you're wearing.' Martin was mortified: you did not get a second chance to make a first impression. 'Take a seat and I'll introduce you to my other guests. You look as if you could do with a glass of champagne.'

'I could do with several, actually.'

The other guests were a fellow director and his wife, who was at least twenty years older than her husband; a merchant banker and his Brazilian boyfriend; the designer responsible for the ice-cube in which they were eating; a journalist whom Martin vaguely knew and his fiancée who worked in advertising; Burnstone's first wife and her second husband, a lawyer; and a brace of beautiful, anorexic models who were probably only sitting on chairs because they were too large to be table ornaments. Martin was seated between them.

'Have you known David long?' he asked.

'No,' said the leggy blonde on his left.

'No,' said the leggy brunette on his right.

'We met him at a party last week,' said the blonde.

'We're going to be in his next movie,' said the brunette.

'Oh really?' said Martin. 'What as? A pair of chopsticks?'

It was always the same. He would set off brimming with optimism, convinced that he was going to make lots of connections, even find a partner, but by the time the main course – lobster on this occasion – had arrived he would have sunk into depression, defeated by the massed ranks of wealth, looks and success. His rancour made him more cynical and witty. His insecurity made him louder. He knew what was happening but could not help himself. Burnstone was delighted.

'Well you certainly sang for your supper tonight,' said the

host as he showed him out. Only the merchant banker and the models remained giggling in the sitting room.

'I felt like the monkey on top of the barrel organ,' said Martin. 'I'm sorry if I came on a bit strong.'

'Not at all, not at all. They loved you. Honestly. They've forgotten what it's like to be young and angry. Listen up, I'm going to Houston in a few days to prepare the shoot for *Kickback*. Would you like to come with me? All your expenses will be taken care of. It would make a really good piece...Have you ever been to America?'

'No, I haven't.' He looked at Burnstone. He did not seem to be winding him up. 'Thank you. I'd love to come if my editor will let me.'

As he bounced on the back seat of a black cab, homeward bound, he felt a rush of genuine excitement. He could do with time out. He had been working very hard. It would be wonderful to get away from it all. A sojourn in the land of the brave would be a useful way of putting things into perspective, of preparing for the final wipe-outs. Four down, two to go.

THIRTY-THREE

It was no good: he just could not get to sleep. He twisted and turned in his reclining seat, pulled the blue woollen blanket up to his chin and yawned. The 747 surged on through the night. Thirty-three thousand feet below him lay the Arctic Circle but all he could think of was his own bed. This was the first time that he had flown Club class. To begin with, the endless flow of champagne had been delightful but now he could feel the artificial air sucking every drop of moisture from his already dehydrated body. His head ached and his feet were swollen. His wakefulness was made all the more intolerable by the fact that all the other occupants of his compartmert were slumbering blissfully. At that moment Burnstone, who was out cold in the neighbouring seat, gave a little snore of contentment. That did it.

He tilted his seat into an upright position and summoned the stewardess. While he waited for his coffee he slid up the window-shutter and gazed out into the blackness. Sunrise over the Great Lakes would make a brilliant opening for his piece.

Although this was his maiden flight across the Atlantic he did not think that his insomnia was caused by nervous excitement. It was five days since his Gunpowder Plot and yet he had still not spoken to Alex. Every time he had called him at home the answering machine had bleeped into action. Every time he had called him at work he had been informed that Mr Fenton was out of the office, in a meeting or simply 'unavailable'. None of his messages had received a response. Was Alex deliberately avoiding him? What had Nicola said to him? Did he suspect something?

As far as he had been able to ascertain before leaving the country nothing about the double murder had been mentioned in the media. Perhaps the bodies had not yet been discovered. The notion that the Jacuzzi might still be bubbling away – and Nicola stewing in a septic cocktail of her own juices – spoiled the taste of his espresso. If Alex had gone to the police he would have received a visit from them before he left. Whatever the screaming queen did in the next few days they could not touch him until he returned to London. Perhaps this was a get-away in more than one sense.

The eastern horizon was tinged with the palest of pinks. He watched the first fingers of dawn claw their way up the sky. For a moment he forgot the non-stop drone of the jet, the merciless recycling of the dead air, the various twinges of his body and stared in wonder at the planetary pavane. It was November 11, St Martin's Day, his birthday and he was on top of the world. God's orrery spun on.

★

Houston. America's fourth city, twin town Oslo, climate the same as Calcutta's. They had arrived but his luggage had not. All that remained on the carousel was a euphonium in its black vinyl case. 'The owner is probably weeping in Heathrow at this very moment,' said Martin. He was too spaced out to maintain his anger.

'Never mind,' said Burnstone, putting an arm round his shoulders. 'We'll go shopping at Nieman Marcus. Paramount will take care of it. After all, it is your birthday.'

In the back of the yellow cab he had to clench the brown leather seat to reassure himself that he was not dreaming. He had seen so many of these vehicles in so many films that he felt as if he had osmosed through the screen, crossed over from real life to the reel world. He was in another country, they did things differently here, and so could he. It was not called the Land of Opportunity for nothing.

As the cab streaked along the twelve-lane freeway he had his first proper glimpse of the United States. Water towers like giant lollipops. Enormous one-legged billboards from where Marlboro men glowered down. And yet the view did not seem to belong to Texas. Everywhere was green. There was not a tuft of tumbleweed in sight. The freeways seemed to go on for ever and so did the construction. The ends of a new flyover soared out into mid-air and stopped – two set squares stuck in the ground. Every so often a pick-up truck, gun-rack on the back, drew alongside. A redneck would check them out before pulling away again. He found his shades and put them on.Burnstone, who was already wearing his, laughed.

'Texans don't fight, they just shoot each other.'

He would be at home in Houston then.

It all appeared simultaneously strange and familiar. The yellow school buses – life-size Tonka toys. The red and green road signs, more often than not peppered with shot. The black-and-white cop cars squatting on the verge. And suddenly there it was, downtown Houston looming out of the haze, the sun sparkling on its pillars of glass. Martin was high on adrenalin.

'Look! The Emerald City!'

'Too right,' said Burnstone. 'We're not in Kansas any more.'

Uniformed bellboys, who looked unnervingly like models from a Jeff Stryker skin-flick, hastened to fetch Burnstone's cases from the trunk. He gave three of the director's ten dollar bills to the driver and was handed a small white card in return. Two words stood out from the rest: WADY YAYA.

'What does Wady Yaya mean?'

'It's my name, sir. It's Peruvian. Call me any time you like. I give guided tours as well. I've taken lots of Australian people around.'

'Thank you,' said Martin. 'We're British.' He had crumpled up the card before he reached the check-in desk.

He could tell from the lobby alone that the Four Seasons Inn on the Park was the best hotel he had ever stayed in. The centre of the airy, marble cavern was dominated by a vast flower display. The director was glad that he seemed impressed.

'This joint spends over $15,000 a month flying blooms in from Amsterdam,' he whispered.

'How do you know that?'

'It says so in Fodors.'

It became obvious that Burnstone was a regular guest when the manager, a tall, sleek New Yorker, materialised by their side to welcome them. When he heard that Martin's luggage had gone missing he promised to have a shaving kit, plus all the usual bathroom requisites, sent up to his suite immediately.

'We have a limo service to the Galleria every thirty minutes. There are plenty of other excellent stores as well as Needless Mark-Up. Just call the hotel when you're ready to leave.' Having shaken their hands, he smiled at Martin and continued silkily, 'don't hesitate to let me know if I can be of further assistance.'

Their rooms were next door to each other. They were virtually identical, football pitches carpeted in deep blue pile. Martin wanted to get into the kingsize bed but Burnstone advised him that it was the worst thing he could do.

'You need sunshine and exercise. The sooner your body-clock can adjust itself the better. If you sleep now you won't be able to sleep tonight. Have a shower, order yourself some coffee or whatever and we'll hit the trail in half an hour. It's all right for you but I've got work to do. You can go shopping while I put in an appearance at the production office.'

Martin wandered around his suite, inspected the bathroom, felt the thickness of the fluffy, white bathrobes and flicked through the ten channels on his TV, catching as he did so a commercial for moist and scented toilet wipe. His complimentary shaving kit arrived. He showered. The force of the water took his breath away. The towelling-robe seemed even softer against his tired, tenderised flesh.

When he emerged from the bathroom two bottles of Lone Star beer were cooling in an ice-bucket on one of the occasional tables. There was a note as well.

Howdy an welcum ta Yewstun! Yew must be tuckered out after yore ramble, so jes set yorself down an rest a spell. Weer tha most friendliest critters yawl ever did see an weer jes tickled plum ta death yore here.

He opened one of the bottles and strolled over to the picture window which served as the end wall. The view from up here on the seventh floor was magnificent. Looking straight down he could see an outdoor swimming pool and an ornamental lake on which a pair of black swans glided, unperturbed by the spray from the single jet of a fountain. It was so peaceful – and yet he still felt as though he were hurtling through space.

He went over to the bed and flopped down on it. The mattress was far too soft. He propped himself up against the headboard, took another swig and watched a huge Stars and Stripes, on top of a nearby high-rise, billowing in the breeze. He had made it.

Ten minutes later the telephone rang.

'Mr Rudrum?'

'Yes.'

'I have a call for you from New York. Hold on please.'

'Hello darling. What on earth are you doing in Texas? Fancy running off without telling me. You are a naughty birthday boy.'

It was Alex.

THIRTY-FOUR

'How did you know where to reach me?'

'Araminta told me. She said that you'd been trying to contact me all week.'

He made a mental note to slice her flapping ears off with a rusty bread knife when he got back.

'I left loads of messages. Why didn't anybody tell me that you were away on business?'

'I'm not. They think I've got 'flu. I decided to have an autumn break in the Big Apple with Keith. He got me a massive discount. I've used up all my holiday allowance so it had to be done this way.'

'When did you fly out?' He held his breath.

'We caught the morning flight on the sixth. I would have called you but I knew that you were going to Rory's.'

'That's typical. I didn't go. He had to attend some sort of emergency meeting at school and I didn't fancy an evening alone with Nicola.'

'Never mind. Communications have been re-established. How was the flight?'

'Horrendous. I didn't sleep a wink and, to cap it all, my luggage decided to take a trip by itself.'

'Well just think of the insurance. What a wonderful excuse for waving your wad about. Where else would you use an Amex card if not in America? The gold's worn off mine already. I thought I might as well get Christmas done with here rather than in London. Keith can take care of the excess baggage.'

'I hope you've got me something expensive.'

'I haven't even bought your bijou birthday gift yet, choux bun.'

'Don't worry. I'm just about to take a limo to Nieman Marcus. Should I choose something on your behalf?'

'Certainly not. But you can give the chauffeur one from me if you like.'

'I don't like.'

'Suit yourself. Anyway I can't keep wittering on for ever. This is costing me a fortune. I'll call you in a couple of days. Happy birthday once again, darling. We must do something when we both get back.'

'I did have something in mind,' said Martin but Alex had already hung up.

★

The Galleria was an upmarket complex of malls on three levels. Its central tower was visible from all over the city. On the way there he asked their driver – who turned out to be one of the bellboys under a different hat – what it was.

'Dunno,' he replied, 'but it wasn't there yesterday.' Burnstone roared with laughter.

'There's nothing witty about boasting,' said Martin.

His jangled nerves were soothed by the obsequious assistants. The fact that he was British made them bow and scrape all the more. He deliberately emphasised the accent which they found so 'cute'. He bought some jeans, three pairs of Calvin Klein aviator shorts and a couple of Ralph Lauren polo shirts. A further hour of ambling through the polished arcades, muzak tinkling in his ears, and he was carrying two more carrier-bags. One contained a pair of Timberland loafers, the other a black Jaeger sweater. Burnstone had warned him that Houston was the most air-conditioned city in the world.

All three tiers of the cathedral to commerce overlooked a skating rink. He found a free table in one of the numerous cafes and treated himself to a regular Coke. Nutrasweet was useless when you needed to boost the sugar-level of the blood. Down on the ice nine-year-old Tracey Kirkland was in the middle of her routine. It went like clockwork until she collapsed during a double axel. She did not cry until she had finished and left the arena. A flyer, held in place by the napkin-dispenser, announced that local boy, dancing whizz and movie star, Patrick Swayze would be participating in the 19th Annual Arabian Azalea Classic Horse Show at the Southwestern Equestrian Center.

☆

That evening Burnstone took him to dinner in the revolving restaurant on top of the Hyatt Regency Hotel. He was more impressed by the colossal entrance hall, a towering pyramid of cantilevered balconies which meant that, no matter what floor your room was on, you could look down into the lobby to see the other guests scurrying about like ants. The obsession with height seemed strange when Texas afforded so much space. As the circular eaterie slowly turned it became clear that the Hyatt had long since been dwarfed by its neighbours who soared effortlessly past them up into the heavens. Some floors of the skyscrapers were still partially lit and others were not. The nightscape was one immense crossword. Jet-lagged and jagged on martinis, he was soon totally clueless.

It was at this stage that one of Burnstone's producers arrived with the woman from the Department of Tourism who would be acting as Martin's guide. Gloria was a buxom black. She shook his hand and bestowed upon him a killing smile. Her white teeth were dazzling, her full lips painted scarlet – a sabre slash in a charger's flank.

'You mark my words, Englishman, we're gonna have one hell of a time.'

THIRTY-FIVE

The next morning he had not even stepped out of the shower before Gloria was hammering on his door.

'Good morning, good morning. It's going to be a fine-and-dandy day. We've got so many places to visit, so many things to see and so little time in which to do it. Don't just stand there – you're dripping on the carpet. Hurry up and get dressed. Don't mind me – you ain't got nothing I ain't seen before. I used to be a care attendant.'

He was about to say that he had only managed to get to sleep at around five, that he had a suicidal hangover and that he really felt that he ought to go back to bed when there was another knock on the door.

'That'll be breakfast. I took the liberty of ordering for two. Come on, come on. Get your little butt in gear!'

★

Half an hour later, stuffed with ham, scrambled eggs, grits, Danish pastries and muffins, aswill with orange juice and coffee, Martin found himself in the passenger seat of Gloria's gold Cadillac. He lowered the window and let the cool breeze blow the crapulence away. They cruised through open park-land as natural as a golf course. Lean, tanned executives loped along the jogging-paths that followed the curve of the road. Such energy made him feel even more exhausted.

In the *Kickback* production office he was introduced to several people whose names he instantly forgot. Burnstone was already out hunting for suitable locations. Gloria gave him yet another cup of coffee and two tiny red pills. He did not know what they were – and did not care – but within five minutes they had done the trick. Suddenly he was raring to go. He was young, free and single with lots of other people's money to spend.

'OK. Let's do Houston.'

They began at the top and – having deposited their stomachs on the second – shot up to the 83rd floor of the Texas Commerce Bank. Gloria informed him that it was the tallest tower in the city and the site of Burt Lancaster's office in *Local Hero*, From the observation deck it was possible to see for 100 miles.

'It's a shame that one mile of scrub and desert looks much like another,' said Martin.

'You can quit that limey snootiness right now,' said Gloria, 'or I'll make your stay a painful one.'

He believed her. But his guide would not be the one who brought about his comeuppance.

Because Houston's economy was based on oil, the city fathers were accustomed to the rollercoaster ride of boom and bust. However, this did not prevent them searching for extra, more reliable, sources of revenue. Film was one of them. Architects had responded to the lax planning restrictions by treating the area like one big drawing board and indulging their wildest dreams. If a design did not work out they could always pull it down and start again. A second coat of paint was the hallmark of an antique. Pennzoil Place featured twin skyscrapers just twelve feet apart. 1 Shell Plaza had once been the highest tower of reinforced concrete west of the Mississippi. The fifty stories of Allied Bank Plaza were known locally as the Dunhill lighter; from the air its curves were said to resemble a fat dollar sign. On the ground the windy canyons and plateaux were graced with sculpture by artists such as Miró. The result of this exuberance and extravagance was a futuristic backdrop that appealed to film-makers. What appealed even more were the various state and municipal inducements that made filming in Houston so much cheaper than in New York or Los Angeles.

They visited the Alley Theatre, a set of concrete cubes – not unlike the Royal National Theatre in London – where part of RoboCop II was shot. They visited the Wortham Centre, a miniature – but still massive – version of Grand Central Station and home of the Houston Ballet and Opera.

'Michael Tippett's New Age received its world premiere here,' droned Gloria, who clearly preferred more exciting art-forms. 'Built entirely with private money, it symbolises the fact that, even during the oil slump of the mid-eighties, civic pride never faltered.'

'You mean that banks could foreclose but the rivalry with Dallas had to continue come-what-may,' said Martin who, as always, had done his homework.

'Dallas is a dump,' replied Gloria. 'If it hadn't been for JFK or the soap no one would have heard of it. Houston was the first word spoken on the Moon. Now be quiet – it's time for some chow.'

Instead of taking him to a swish but soulless restaurant as he had expected, Gloria drove to the Cafe Adobe, an alfresco Tex-Mex joint which also seemed to be straight out of the movies. It was the sort of place where one old buddy meets another old buddy to tell him that he has diddled his wife for the last time or the kind of venue in which the affluent tranquillity is established only to be immediately destroyed by some Uzi-toting suburban psycho. Over strawberry and peach margaritas swimming with sorbet, Gloria dropped her gung-ho routine and relaxed. It all came out – the divorce from her doctor husband, losing the battle for custody of Leroy and Patricia, leaving nursing for what she thought would be the more glamorous world of public relations but which turned out to be just one more way of shovelling shit.

'You don't look forty,' said Martin, nearly poking his eye out with a straw. He became flirtatious when he was tipsy.

'And you certainly don't look 29. If we were the same colour folks would think we were mother and son.'

'Well I feel like an old man. I can't shake off my circadian dysrhythmia'.

'Say what?'

'I've got jet-lag.'

He was not hungry but, after his third cocktail, he had no difficulty putting away an enchilada bursting with home-grown beef and a bowl of guacamole. Gloria merely nibbled some tortilla chips. When the meal was over she had a guilty cigarette while Martin, who was feeling pleasantly light-headed, watched the other diners on the patio. A fountain trickled. Big black and white birds sang a strange song. London seemed a life-time away.

'Where would you like to go this afternoon?' asked Gloria.

'I actually have some say in the matter?'

'Yup.'

'It might be easier if I say where I don't want to go. There's no way we can see everything in three days.'

'Pleasurable, no. Possible, yes.'

'Not for me. I like being in foreign countries but I don't like travelling – it just broadens the behind. The trouble with Texas is that everything is so spaced out. I'd be a hopeless American. I can't even drive.'

'You should be ashamed of yourself. No one walks anywhere in the US of A. An automobile means freedom and independence. Where would we be without my Cadillac?'

'In a cab of course.'

She snorted. 'Shysters the lot of them. I wouldn't give them the time of day. Someone around here has the right idea.'

'Meaning?'

'It don't matter. How about NASA?'

'Need Another Seven Astronauts?'

'Hush your mouth. The shuttle disaster is still a sore point down here.'

'I know plenty of Challenger jokes. Where do astronauts go for their holidays?'

'I don't know and you are not going to tell me. There are lots of museums in Houston. There's the Museum of Fine Arts, the Contemporary Arts Museum, the Menil Collection, the Rothko Chapel, the O'Kane and Blaffer Galleries, the Museum of

American Architecture and Decorative Arts, the Houston Museum of Natural Science, the Museum of Medical Science and the Burke Baker Planetarium.'

'Not my scene.'

'How about the San Jacinto Battlefield State Park?'

'Christ. If the Alamo is just a crumbling bit of wall in the middle of nowhere goodness knows what that has to offer. I've never even heard of it.'

'I can see that when the mood takes you, you can be one helluva an ornery sonofabitch.' She was getting mad. She threw a tourist map at him. 'You've got one minute to pick somewhere.'

In the end they made a deal. She would take him to Astroworld, a theme park boasting such white-knuckle rides as The Viper, Excalibur and Greased Lightning, if – first of all – he agreed to be taken round the Astrodome next-door. They hit the 610 Loop at sixty.

He was the only non-American on the tour. As they traipsed round the big daddy of domed stadia, the Hispanic guide fed them a constant stream of Fascinating Facts.

'Why should it enrich my life to know that it costs $150,000 a month to air-condition this oversized bubble?' asked Martin.

'Quiet,' said Gloria.

'If this thing is the eighth wonder of the world, the ninth must be why.'

'Be *quiet*.'

He switched his attention to the other, more willing, tourists. One family – mom, pop, daughter and son – were extraordinarily obese. Even the waistlines were bigger in Texas. They waddled about, each one munching a Hershey bar. A tall, gangly boy, bald except for a few isolated strands of hair like tadpoles – chemotherapeutic fall-out – was the only person – apart from Martin and Gloria – who was not wearing a baseball cap.

Astroworld was much more fun. Gloria basked in the sun while, time and time again, Martin was flung upside down and round about with astonishing violence. He got drenched on the

Thunder Rapids – his fury, for some reason, amusing the other, drier, punters – and got stuck on the Texas Cyclone when the brakes jammed.

'Don't worry,' said thirteen-year-old Debbie, who was strapped in beside him. She was dressed and made up like a sophomore. 'It happens all the time. By the way, there's a much bigger rollercoaster in Alabama.'

'I'll bear it in mind,' he said. 'Do you think we're going to die?' While her giggles subsided into boredom the body of Toyota salesman Roddy N MacIntosh was being discovered on the eastern perimeter of the playground, a bullet hole in his head.

Gloria dropped him back at the Inn On The Park just after 5pm. She had regained her good humour when he had expressed no desire to spend the evening stifling yawns at the Wortham Center. 'Right on! I'll give you a taste of Houston night-life. It will be an experience you'll never forget.'

She was right.

★

At 7.30, dead on time, Gloria marched into the hotel. Her fleshy legs were crammed into a pair of washed-out denims, her feet into a pair of fancy cowboy boots. Her large breasts swayed gently beneath a red plaid shirt. Martin, who was waiting for her in the lobby, was impressed.

'Hi!'

'Hello. You look stunning.'

'Why thank you. I do believe in dressing for the part. Has your luggage turned up yet.'

'Fat chance. I hope I'm not going to show you up in my Ralph Lauren.'

'Not at all. You look very debonair.'

'That was exactly what I was afraid of.'

Their first port of call was an Icehouse – so called because of the fierce air-conditioning. They drank Lone Stars and watched the wildlife. Roughnecks, rednecks and real-life wranglers played pool, groped their girls and spat on the wooden floor.

Gloria, though, seemed more interested in Martin.

'You're scared ain't you?'

'Sort of. I don't like public drinking places very much. Back home I prefer to drink champagne at my club.' She was intrigued by his refusal to be macho.

'Let's go sit at the bar.' They ordered a couple more beers. He liked the way they came with a twist of lime stuck in the neck of the bottle.

'You can tell me those gags now, if you like.' He did not really want to. Even though it was a little less noisy up here it was still difficult to make oneself heard over the moaning Country & Western.

'Have you heard of the Challenger cocktail?'

'No.'

'It's Seven Up and Teachers on the rocks.'

'What's Teachers?'

'A brand of whisky.'

'OK. I get it. Very good.' She smiled.

'Try this one.' He was beginning to lose his voice. 'Where do astronauts go for their holidays?'

'All over Florida.' The punchline was delivered by the man sitting on Gloria's left. He was short, stocky and had a kind, craggy face. He was also drunk as a skunk. Gloria almost fell off her stool laughing. Hank introduced himself.

'What y'all drinking?'

He judged it foolish to refuse. While Hank shot the breeze with Gloria he gazed around the dive, careful not to catch anybody's eye. He bought another round. It was Mickey Mouse money anyway.

Further along the bar a Viet-vet with a livid scar running diagonally across his right eye and cheek was hitting on one of the women behind the counter. Martin watched him in the mirror that faced them. He could see the GI's dog-tags dangling round his neck.

'You ate them candies I bought you?'

'Nope.'

'How come?'

'Sam, I told you. I'm dieting.' She went to the huge refrigerator and took out what was clearly an expensive box of chocolates. She opened it and started offering its contents to the other drinkers who had been following the conversation with glee.

'Yum-yum,' said one.

'Dee-lish-us,' said a second, smacking his lips.

'Well that there's one mighty fine collection of candy,' opined a third. 'Any chance of another?'

'You sure are a greedy-guts,' said the callous bargirl. 'Leave some for Sam.' The smitten soldier did not look happy.

Martin had witnessed this scene umpteen times on the screen. He knew what was coming. He was torn between sitting tight, waiting for the inevitable fight to erupt and scarpering right now under the pretext of rescuing his chaperone from danger. Fortunately the decision was made for him.

'We thought we'd move on some place else,' said Gloria. 'That OK with you?'

'Sure. You lead, I'll follow.'

The entrance to the Yucatàn was marked by a large plastic shark.

'That's just to let you know this is a place for meat-eaters,' said Hank. A dayglo pink and green stretch limo was parked outside. Inside was a vision from one of the lower circles of Dante's *Inferno*. Two thousand yuppies, smashed on tequila, stomped on tables and made out on the dance floor. It resembled the last throes of a Club 18-30 wet T-shirt competition.

'This is where they filmed *Urban Cowboy*,' yelled Gloria, arm in arm with Hank. 'Are you having a good time?' Her eyes were shining.

'Yes, thank you,' said Martin. 'I'm getting some great copy.' Ten minutes later he was back outside and ankling it down Westheimer. This was not a wise move.

From the steadily accumulating pile of promotional literature in his hotel room he had learned that Montrose was the gay area of Houston. Since the city was the largest port for foreign ships in the US he felt certain that it would cater for the needs of every sailor. He had not bought himself a birthday present because, as soon as he knew that he was going to Texas, he had promised himself a cowboy – a cowboy, moreover, who kept his boots on. And why not? No one would know.

Every so often the sidewalk and streetlights gave out, marooning him in no-man's-land. It was the midnight hour and yet there was still a prickly heat. Cicadas sawed. Cars flashed past, their occupants shouting what were presumably obscenities. This was the Stars And Bars syndrome. The vicious nightmare scenario of After Hours. He told himself to grow up. He had to get a cab. As if by magic, a yellow light came into view. Salvation! He stepped into the road and windmilled his arms. It did not stop. Nor did the next one. Nor did the one after that. He trudged on, near to tears. He shoved his hands into his pockets and found the crumpled card of Wady Yaya.

When he eventually found a pay-phone it took him a while to figure out how to use it.

'You were lucky that I was working tonight,' said Yaya. 'I usually go over to my mother's on Thursdays but she's visiting friends this week. Cabbies are very nervous at the moment. Three have been killed in the past month. That's why they won't pick up on the street. You have to call them.'

He gave him a large tip.

'I didn't have you down as the Montrose type,' he said, the cash safely stashed away. 'Still, you've come to the right place. They say that Texas only breeds two things – steers and queers.'

He liked Montrose. It was a leafy gridwork of wooden houses, many of which had been converted into shops or clubs. The dee-jay in 'Heaven' only seemed to have one record to play. Its chorus was 'the only way is up.' The atmosphere was that of a sixth form disco. There appeared to be more going on in 'JR's' next-door. There was.

The pool tables were covered with boards on which hunky go-go cowboys gyrated in nothing but pistol-packed G-strings. It was a ridiculous sight but one which made him tremble. He bought a beer and, leaning against the wall as nonchalantly as he could, let himself be mesmerised by the performances. Now he knew the meaning of culture shock.

Of course it was all about money. Observing the other punters, he discovered that you got exactly what you paid for. Five dollars allowed you to to slip the bill underneath the strap at the back of the boy's briefs. Ten got you round the front and twenty got you entry. He was on the point of making an exit, of continuing his cruise, when a pair of hands snaked round his waist. A pair of arms embraced him from behind and pulled him up against a warm, hard body. 'Guess who?' murmured a voice in his ear. Its owner gave his earlobe a friendly nibble. One of the hands dropped to Martin's groin and gripped his growing erection. 'I reckon you're pleased to meet me.'

He did know the voice but he could not recall the context in which he had heard it. An all-American voice. A little-boy-lost voice. 'I give up.' The hands held his shoulders and spun him round.

'Hello again,' said Dan Salter.

THIRTY-SIX

'What are you doing here?'
'The same as you I guess.'
'Enjoying the scenery?'
'Right.'
'Isn't it risky?'
'Not really. Fans only tend to recognise you when you're in a familiar setting. This is the last place they'd expect me to be.'
'Exactly. What about the press?'
'What about it? Unless they've got photographs of me caught in the act they can't prove a thing and, as you know, I've

a reputation for being writ-happy. Look, chill out. It's my problem not your's. Come and take a load off.'

He followed Salter to a booth at the back of the bar. The light was dimmer here but the writhing beefcake was still in view. 'So what brings you to Houston?' He flashed his famous smile.

Martin felt his heart flutter.

'David Burnstone suggested I accompany him on a recce for *Kickback*. The idea is to write a piece on how film-makers are making use of Texan locations and saving money at the same time. This is my first trip across The Pond.'

'In that case we'd better make your stay a memorable one. What are you drinking?'

He asked for a beer but Salter brought him bourbon.

'Thanks.' This was weird. *The* Dan Salter had just bought him a drink. 'I don't mean to be rude but Houston hardly seems your kind of town.'

'It isn't. We start shooting *Ice* after Christmas and, as I'd already done a couple of movies this year, I thought I deserved some R&R. When Patrick heard that I was taking time out he invited me to stay at his ranch. He and I go way back. I've been here a week and I'm just beginning to touch down. I'd forgotten what it was like to be an ordinary human being.'

'I can understand that, but you're not ordinary are you? I wouldn't have interviewed you if you were.' Shit. He should not have brought that up.

Salter grinned at his embarrassment. 'Please. Do go on.' Martin drained his glass. 'About the interview.'

'Yes?'

'I'm sorry it was so bitchy. It was nothing personal. I mean, in the piece I said I liked you. The trouble is people buy *Streetwise* for hatchet jobs. I'm probably flattering myself. Even if you did bother to read it I'm sure that what I said made no difference to you.'

'No sweat. Of course I read it. I read everything that's written about me. You're not the first to say that I can't act and I'm sure that you won't be the last. You are paid to say what you think and I'm paid to make movies that people don't have to think about. We both have jobs to do. Forget it.'

The midnight cowboys ground on through their routines. Their cache-sexes seemed on the point of bursting.

'Would you like another whisky?' said Martin.

'Sure.'

As they got drunk together and discussed the various merits and demerits of the dancers like two tipsters arguing racing form, Martin wondered why Salter was taking the trouble to talk to him. Perhaps he just wanted company. It could not be easy being a gay megastar. Even Hollywood heroes could be lonely. He had already confessed that the starlets snapped hanging on to his arm at galas and award ceremonies were to keep the studio PRs happy.

'They're beards, one and all,' said Salter.

He suddenly felt sorry for him.

'What I need now is some coke,' said Salter, running his hands through his long black hair.

'There's too much sugar in it.'

'Are you kidding me? I don't mean to drink, dummy. I mean the real real thing.'

'Have you got some?'

'No, but I know where we can get some. How much cash have you got on you?'

'I'm not sure. Two hundred and fifty dollars, maybe three hundred.'

'I've got five hundred. It should be enough. Let's split.'

The narrowed eyes of a dozen jealous queens watched him leave with Salter. He had not had so much fun in ages.

Outside, the temperature had dropped. He shivered.

'It's not far,' said Salter, slapping him on the back. 'I left the wheels a couple of blocks away. You'll understand why when you see it. Some weekends, when the ranchers come in to get laid, they drive round here in their pick-ups taking pot-shots at the homos.'

'Charming.'

'I love the way you say that. Chaaaaaaarming.' He sniggered.

Martin let out a low whistle when he saw the black Lamborghini Diabolo.

'Isn't this just a teensy-weensy bit ostentatious? Hmm?'

'It don't belong to me. Look at the license plate. He said I could use it. I didn't set out to come into this neck of the woods. I planned on taking it for a test drive, that's all.'

'DD1. I didn't know Donald Duck could drive.'

'Cute. Try again.'

'David Dimbleby.

'Who?'

'Forget it. I don't know.'

'I didn't say they were his initials. Think of flicks.'

'Dirty Dancing.'

'Bingo!'

They set off, leaving behind a set of smoking skid-marks.

'By rights you shouldn't be driving,' said Martin pompously. 'You're under the influence.'

'We'll be OK as long as we don't hit anything and I've no intention of doing that. Patrick would crucify me.'

'Does he know about you?'

'About me? About me?'

'Don't play the innocent with me, sunshine. Does he know you're gay?'

'Who said anything about being gay?' He leaned over and kissed Martin on the cheek. He blushed.

Salter turned left off Montrose and headed west along Allen Parkway. The engine purred as it ate up the asphalt. It really was a magnificent machine.

'You're back in your normal environment now. You belong behind the wheel of a car like this,' said Martin. 'Where are we going?'

'You don't want to know. Quit asking questions.'

Within minutes they were surrounded by urban dereliction. The Lamborghini rolled past low-rise, low-rent housing earmarked for demolition. A few clapped-out clapboards still stood among the graffitoed concrete blocks. It was after two in the morning and yet, here and there, huddles of two or three blacks kicked their heels on the wasteground.

'Welcome to Texas,' said Salter.

He had no time to be afraid. In the blink of an eye poverty had been superseded by plutocracy. It was as if they had driven from one Tinseltown back-lot to another.

'We are now entering Houston's own Beverly Hills,' said Salter. 'This is where you should start getting nervous.'

They slowed down to a crawl and glided past a succession of spot-lit mansions. Each one seemed to have more white pillars than the last. Acre upon acre of lawn, which were doubtless as green as the baize on a brand new pool table during the day, glowed blue in the night. There were small metal signs everywhere warning the curious that the area was protected by Pinkerton security. No living thing disturbed the silence.

'I wonder if George is at home,' said Salter.

'George who?'

'Mr Ex-President of course. He comes from hereabouts.'

He did a right then a left and swung into the drive of a plantation pavilion. Light streamed from every window. There was no sign of movement.

'Give me your cash. How much do you want to get?'

'As much as you can.' He already knew what he was going to do with the surplus.

'Wait here. Whatever happens, don't get out.'

'Can you give me some idea of what is likely to happen?'

'Nothing, all being well. Stay cool.'

He looked at his sham Gucci. It was 2.17am and yet he had never been more wide-awake. He could hear the blood rushing in his ears. Even the darkness seemed to pulsate. He waited for a figure to cross one of the uncurtained windows. No one did. What was he doing here?

Three minutes later the front door opened again and Salter emerged. He could not see anybody else.

'Success!' said Salter, turning the key in the ignition. The executive toy roared into life. They swept past the house and out of the other end of the drive. 'Where are you staying?'

'The Inn On The Park.'

'All right! Let's party!'

★

He ignored the gawping bellboys and led Salter to the elevators. He was humming 'The Only Way Is Up'.

When he returned from the bathroom he found Salter already inhaling his second monster line off a framed print that he had removed from the wall.

'Help yourself.' The screen idol handed him a rolled up dollar bill. His nostrils were rimmed with white like the salt on a couple of margaritas. 'You can keep the other packet. Think of it as a souvenir of this evening. From me to you with love. Use mine.'

As he was snorting the powder that had been prepared for him Martin noticed that the hunting scene portrayed in the picture was exactly the same as the one that hung in his grandmother's room at the nursing home.

'Wow! This is great stuff, man.' Martin could not really tell. His eyes were watering.

Salter paced around the room. When he spotted the pool – an aquamarine oblong in the black – he instantly began to strip off. Somewhere, deep in the pit of Martin's stomach, a trapdoor swung open. Salter, wearing only a pair of white Jockey shorts which contrasted sharply with his smooth, tanned skin, marched past him into the bathroom and fetched the two robes that he knew would be hanging behind the door. As usual the over-attentive maid had tied the belts in bows.

'Come on. What are you waiting for?'

'I haven't got any trunks. My luggage was lost.'

'So?'

'So I can hardly swim in these.' He pulled off his jeans aware that, compared with Salter's muscular legs, his own lily-white ones resembled the shanks of a sparrow. 'Aviators are not meant to swim.'

'It doesn't matter. Once we're in the water we'll take them off.' He watched Martin as he self-consciously finished getting undressed. He threw him a robe. 'Don't be shy.'

Down on the ground the swans were nowhere to be seen. The only sound was the plash of the fountain. Faint wisps of steam curled away from the surface of the pool. Lit from below, it looked very inviting. With a whoop Salter slid out of his robe and dived cleanly into the water. Martin lowered himself in gently. As he ducked to wet his hair he heard the unmistakable strains of Handel's Water Music.

The heart-throb began to ply up and down the pool doing a fast crawl. Martin floated on his back and watched the floodlit Stars and Stripes on the nearby high-rise rippling in the wind. The cocaine coursed through his veins. Warm water lapped at his ears. He had finally arrived. It was the moment he had been waiting for all his life.

Suddenly, hands grabbed his ankles and pulled him under. He came up gasping face to face with Salter who kissed him on the lips. They kissed again and, with their arms around each other, sank to the bottom of the pool. When Martin felt Salter fiddling with the buttons on his flies he slipped his hand down the back of his shorts and gripped his buttocks. Having released Martin's cock, Salter made for the surface, wriggling out of his underwear as he did so.

The fact that they were now both naked seemed to destroy any last restraint. They splashed around like two boyhood truants skinny-dipping in a pond. Laughing and shouting, they failed to notice that their innocent horseplay was attracting angry attention. Salter was trying to achieve the perfect back-flip and Martin was happily treading water – encouraging him and admiring the way the droplets running off his body gleamed like quicksilver – when they became aware of the manager standing stiffly on the opposite side of the pool. From this position he could only see Salter from behind but he was still clearly enjoying the view. Then Salter's backside was a miracle of genetic engineering.

The flunkey addressed himself to Martin.

'Excuse me sir. I would be grateful if you could refrain from making such a noise. I have received a number of complaints from other guests. It is after 3.30 in the morning.'

In reply Salter curled himself into a ball and plunged into the water. The resultant spray forced the hotelier to jump out of the way. Martin laughed.

'I do apologise. It really is most inconsiderate of us. I do hope we haven't caused too much inconvenience. We're frightfully sorry.'

'Hear, hear,' cried Salter. Without a trace of effort, he got out of the water. Recognition dawned. Martin thought the jumped-up janitor was going to have a heart attack. Salter pretended that he did not exist. 'Come on, Martin. It's time for bed.' Holding out his hand, he helped him out of the pool and draped a robe round his shoulders before putting on his own. They walked back towards the hotel. A dozen tousled heads disappeared behind a dozen sets of identical blue drapes.

Once they were back in Martin's room Salter prepared another four lines and, having vacuumed his own two, flung his robe to the floor and leaped into bed.

'Brrrr! I'm freezing. Desperate Dan is cold and hungry. Let's call room service.'

When he had ordered a medium steak, french fries and coffee for two Martin stood sheepishly at the end of the bed. Salter, peeping over the top of the covers, blinked at him.

'Hurry up. I'm waiting. Do the business, replace the picture on the wall and come to bed. I need warming up.' He did not need to be asked twice.

The overhead camera tracked him as he followed Salter's instructions. The man in this American hotel room taking off his robe and getting into bed with another naked man, a man whom half the world lusted after, was not Martin Rudrum. It was somebody else. Somewhere, somehow, a stupendous error had been made. Fate had fucked up. He was fulfilling a stranger's destiny. He was taking the part of a different actor. How could anybody mistake him for a sex-scene stand-in? He waited for the director to yell 'cut!', for the crew to hoot in derision. It did not happen.

His chilly white flesh pressed against warm, brown muscle. He snuggled down in Salter's arms, the smell of chlorine rising off them. They kissed. A hot, strong tongue pushed into his mouth, touched the tip of his own and tickled his gums. Salter's cock swelled against his stomach.

They ate cross-legged on the bed, their hard-ons refusing to go away. Martin was filled with a wild exhilaration. It did not matter what happened now, tonight could never be taken away from him. Life had been worth living after all. The meal over, they lay back, Martin tracing the contours of Dan's body with his fingertips. He stroked his cheek bones, licked his nipples and sucked his balls. When they eventually came – more or less at the same time – in each other's mouth Martin saw stars.

After a suitable interval he went to brush his teeth. When he returned Salter had not moved. His cock was hard.

'That was some movie premiere,' he said. 'Darling, you were wonderful.'

'Wait till you see the encore,' said Salter. When he got close enough Martin was startled to see how the colour of his eyes had deepened from blue to purple. It was an amazing special effect but one not sufficient to counteract the wave of exhaustion that was threatening to engulf him.

'Couldn't we have a nap first? It's even better when you've just woken up.'

'Yes it is, except that I'm not at all tired but I am, as you can see, horny as hell. Let's play carnival.'

'Sorry?'

'I sit on your face and you guess my weight.' Martin stopped laughing when he realised that Salter was not joking.

'Look, I'm not into that kind of thing. If you want to do it again then fine – but as far as risky business is concerned I've gone as far as I will go.'

'Excuse me! Who the fuck d'you think you're talking to? I put out for you – after all, there's hardly a shortage of people dying to give me a blow-job – and now it's time for you to put out for me. Come here you British sonofabitch.' Martin hesitated. Salter was stronger than him. Perhaps he was just winding him up to see how he would react. Perhaps it was the coke.

'OK. OK. Keep your hair on.' Salter grabbed him. When

Martin was flat on his back he knelt over him and, facing his feet, straddled his shoulders.

'Now kiss my ass.' He laughed but was immediately smothered by Salter's buttocks. A hand gripped his balls and squeezed. Hard. 'I'm waiting.' Martin obeyed, grateful that they had been swimming. The hand relaxed and began to wank him slowly. 'That's good, real good. Use your tongue, that's it. Now deeper, deeper. Yes.' The lady-killer swayed above him, crooning. Martin, as the warm satiny skin brushed his cheek bones, was appalled to find that he was actually beginning to enjoy it.

'OK. Time for a different game.' Salter stood up on the bed and looked down on him. 'Don't bother wiping your mouth, just bite the pillow. Roll over for Danny.'

'Fuck off. I don't care who you are. No one is going to stick their willie up my arse.'

'Don't you believe it. You surprise me. I thought all you English fags were cornholers. In cowboy country you have to learn to take it like a man and ride the Hershey way. Besides, think how many people would love to be butt-fucked by me.' His cock seemed to be getting bigger and bigger. Martin began to panic.

'I swear I'll kill you.'

'Quit stalling. The sooner we start, the sooner I finish. Did you really think I'd let you get away with what you said? You can't go around writing nasty things about people and expect them to take it lying down. You're the one who's going to do that. Fair's fair. You hurt me and now I'm going to hurt you.'

Martin rolled back, brought his feet up and kicked Salter in the groin. He fell off the bed clutching his balls. Martin grabbed one of the robes and ran for the door but he had scarcely managed to get the chain undone before Salter had his head in an armlock. He dragged him back to the bed and smashed a fist in his face. Purple and orange burst out of the black and, for the second time that evening, Martin saw stars.

'If you want to play rough then that's OK with me. It's up to you.' He released him from the headlock and slapped him across the left cheek and then the right cheek. Martin felt sick. This was more like it – now he knew it was him. He was not a body double. He was living his own life. There was no mistake. 'Which way is it going to be?' He lay on the messy bed and hid his face in a pillow. 'That's more like it. Just think of it as being put into turnaround.'

Salter patted his rump, parted his legs, knelt down between them and spat in the crevice. When he flinched the leading man said: 'I'm telling you now, it will be a lot easier for you if you relax.' He tried but as soon as he felt the tip of Salter's cock forcing its way in he became rigid. 'That suits me fine,' said the rapist and rammed his rod home.

The blood acted as a lubricant but it did nothing to relieve the burning agony. Martin thought that Salter would never come. As he continued to thrust, each lunge seeming to split his backside – the deeper ones prodding his stomach – Martin sobbed into the pillow, praying for the pain to stop. Salter did not say a word. Finally, with a terrible judder, he squirted his poison inside him and collapsed on top of him. Sweat cooled and trickled off them.

When his breathing had returned to normal Salter withdrew and went into the bathroom. The shower hissed into action. Martin did not stir. He could not move. His arse felt as if it had been ripped wide open. He turned his head. An ashen sky revealed that day was breaking.

Whistling 'Some Enchanted Evening', Salter dressed quickly and picked up his keys. He smacked Martin on the bottom. It was not a hard blow but it still stung.

'Tell that to your readers.'

THIRTY-SEVEN

He stared at himself in the mirror. The dark welts under his eyes could be attributed to jet-lag. He had a cut lip, and there was some slight bruising on the left side of his mouth, but otherwise there was little outward sign of his ordeal. The real damage was internal.

Before going to sleep he had asked the switchboard to hold any calls, left a message for Burnstone saying that he was ill, hung the DO NOT DISTURB sign on his door and swallowed four pink Migraleve. He woke, aching all over, at midday and immediately had to go to the lavatory. As Salter's seed sputtered out into the pan he was filled with a self-loathing even more bitter than usual. The only thing left was pain.

He bathed then dragged on some clothes. He bundled up the filthy sheets for the maid and hid the packet of coke in a boxed mug which had arrived yesterday – along with an Oilers baseball cap and a Houston Opera T-shirt – from the Tourist Centre. When he handed in his key at reception he was passed a message from Gloria asking him to call.

The limo-driver gave up trying to make conversation. He dropped him downtown. Martin tipped him and automatically murmured 'have a nice day.' For an hour or so he wandered through the network of skywalks and underground tunnels that enabled Houstonians to drive to work, eat and shop without ever setting foot outside. Air-conditioned and scrupulously clean, it was the ideal place for a zombie. He could have been anywhere on Earth. He ambled through the foyers of numerous conglomerates and browsed among the outlets of various franchises. He bought some cookies for Araminta and ate one.

The Metropolitan Rackets Club, of which he had been made a temporary member, was all but deserted. The tennis, squash and rackets courts were empty, their strip-lighting humming to itself. In the gym a lone man pedalled furiously, rapidly going nowhere. He was watching *The Bionic Woman*. At a table in the plush salad bar, which was relaxing after the lunchtime crush, he wrote his postcards. It did not matter that he was flying out that evening – they were just to prove that he had been here. His parents got one of the skyline at night; Michael and Nerissa got ones of cowboys; Alex and Keith got one of a launching rocket; and Rory and Nicola got one of the Rothko Chapel – the perfect site for a double funeral. The message was the same on all of them: 'Having a wonderful time. Glad you're not here.'

At 5pm office-workers started filing in to ogle the aerobicising secretaries. He took a cab back to the hotel but made a detour on the way. Stelzig's store contained everything a cowboy or cowgirl could possibly need from the age of three. Cattle-prods, whips and belts adorned the walls. Polished wood shone. Fans whirred overhead. In one corner a hat-press sizzled. All the assistants wore straight-leg Levis, boots and stetsons.

'Can I help you sir?' A tall, dark and acned boy smiled to reveal regulation white teeth.

'Yes. I'd like to buy a stetson.'

'Is it for yourself?'

Martin laughed. 'No. It's for a friend.'

'Do you have his size?'

'I'm afraid not. But let me put it this way, he's got a big head.'

'Bigger than yours, sir?'

'Yes.'

As he left, a woman who looked as if she had been made by the bendy-balloon man, was dithering over an ornate pair of red Tony Lama boots. The price-tag was $1,450.

They were due to drive to the airport at 8pm. Martin phoned Gloria to thank her. She was too excited to ask where he had disappeared to the night before. Hank was coming to take her out for dinner in half an hour.

'I wish you well,' said Martin and meant it.

'You too, honey. Keep in touch.'

His luggage might not have turned up but he still had plenty to carry. With straps cutting into his shoulders, a hat-box in one hand and a bag full of bumf in the other, he kicked on Burnstone's door ten minutes too soon.

'Hi. Feeling better?' He was about to say more but Martin ignored his raised eyebrows and walked straight past him.

'Much better, thanks. Sorry I'm early.' His timing was perfect. He had not finished packing. When Burnstone went into the bathroom and closed the door he was ready for him. In ten seconds he had switched the mugs. He knew that the director would have received the same merchandise as himself and had wiped his own freebie clean of prints beforehand.

Although the airline seat made his sore backside itch, it was a good night flight. After an excellent champagne dinner, Martin put out his light, put in his ear-plugs and slept all the way home. 'The good thing about flying Club is that you get off the plane much sooner,' said Burnstone.

They went through passport control and customs unhindered. As the cab rattled along the Westway Martin asked him if he particularly wanted to hold on to his souvenir mug from the Houston Post. 'Not at all. I can always collect another one when I go back next month.' He fished the box out of his overnight bag and handed it to him.

'Thank you very much,' said Martin.

London seemed squat and squalid compared with Texas but he was glad to be back. He felt safer here. The sheer weight of the capital's history slowed things down. It had been here a long time, it was un-new. The quality of life may have been lower but the quality of light was softer. After the taxi had dropped Burnstone in Mayfair it crossed Trafalgar Square. His heart swelled with foolish pride and relief. Even the *Streetwise* office seemed smaller and shabbier – perhaps that was why he felt he belonged there.

'Welcome back to civilisation,' said Araminta, giving him a hug. 'Where's my present?'

The rest of the week passed quietly. He derived inordinate pleasure from getting into his own bed each night and in catching up on his sleep. The circles round his eyes retracted to two dark smudges. The bruise by his mouth turned from purple to yellow. His cut lip healed. It did not hurt quite so much every time he had a shit. He skimmed through the copies of *The Times* that he had missed and did all the crosswords in the correct order. A delighted Michael phoned to thank him for the stetson that he had had biked round to him. It fitted. On Thursday morning he found his luggage on his desk. It had been to Russia. Nothing – not even the pair of jeans – was missing.

By Friday lunchtime he had dealt with the backlog of administration and had arranged as much of his schedule for the following week as he could. The weekend started here. Just as he was preparing to go to Marks & Spencer's Elaine came up to him. She was not smiling.

'Martin. Have you got a minute? There are a couple of policemen in my office. They'd like to talk to you.'

THIRTY-EIGHT

There were not many people in the office but those that were pretended to get on with their work while they watched him follow the editor through the maze of cubicles. What was needed here, thought Martin, was a crane shot that began as a close-up – to show his non-reaction – and then rose higher and higher as he moved further and further away from his desk. A bravura performance would not be necessary: all he had to do was to remain calm and, at the appropriate time, appear shocked.

Both the man and the woman were in plain clothes. The absence of Herbert and Monkton suggested that no connection had yet been made between Isobel's death and the shooting of Rory and Nicola.

'Martin, this is Detective Sergeant Williams and Detective Constable Galvin,' said Elaine.

'Thank you,' said Williams. He had carrot-coloured hair and a bean-pole physique: a human matchstick waiting to be struck. 'You can leave us now.' She patted Martin on the shoulder and closed the door to the conference room behind her. 'Take a seat. Cigarette?'

'No thank you. I don't smoke.'

'Very wise.' He lit one for himself and coughed. His partner, who was far too well-dressed to be chasing villains, sighed and looked out of the window. It was hardly a breathtaking view. Air-conditioning vents, satellite dishes, fire escapes and netting to keep the birds away. Sometimes a pigeon would peck its way in but be unable to get out. It would flap around until, exhausted, it would roost on a windowsill and slowly starve to death.

'Well, Mr Rudrum, this shouldn't take long. Can you tell us the last time you saw Mr Rory Patterson and Miss Nicola Armstrong?'

'Why? What's happened?'

'For the time being, if you don't mind, we'll ask the questions and you can give us the answers.'

'I can't remember. Ages ago.' Stick to the truth. He must stick to the truth as much as he could.

'Think. This is important.'

'September. They came for dinner in September.'

'And you haven't seen either of them since?'

'No I haven't. I was supposed to have dinner with them a couple of weeks ago but it was cancelled.'

'What date would this be?'

'The fifth. Bonfire Night.' The constable glanced at her sergeant but he ignored her. She picked a piece of fluff off her navy blue skirt and watched it float to the floor.

'Why was it cancelled?'

'I don't know. I remember that I was pretty annoyed because Rory left it so late to tell me.'

'How did he inform you?'

'I got a call at about four in the afternoon.'

'Where were you?'

'Here in the office.'

'Where was he?'

'At school I think. He's a total miser. Even though he's stinking rich he always uses the phone in the staff room if he can.'

'What did he say?'

'Not much. He said that he was very sorry but that something had come up and that I'd have to take a rain-check. The meal was supposed to be in return for the one I'd given them in September.'

'Nothing else?' Martin paused. He looked at the discarded polystyrene coffee cups, the overflowing ashtrays and the scraps of paper covered in doodles – the detritus of a hundred boring meetings.

'He said that he was particularly sorry because he and Nicola had something they wanted to ask me.'

'Any idea what this was likely to be?'

'I thought that they might have decided to get married and wanted me to be the best man.'

'Were they engaged?'

'I don't think so but that wouldn't have stopped them. They did as they pleased. They could afford to.'

'Mr Patterson gave no other reason why the dinner party could not go ahead? Did he sound worried or angry?'

'It wasn't going to be a dinner party. I was going to be the only guest. He sounded his usual insouciant self.'

'So what did you do on Bonfire Night?'

'Nothing. I went home. I wasn't going to start trawling around for last minute invites. I'm not that desperate. Besides, I'm not too keen on fireworks. They're dangerous.'

'Do you own a gun, Mr Rudrum?' Martin snorted.

'Oh yes. I carry a .44 Magnum around with me wherever I go and shoot people who ask stupid questions. Of course I don't own a gun. What would I want a gun for? I don't know anybody who has a gun. Look, what is this? Will you please tell me what is going on?'

'Your friends were discovered shot to death in their own home on the eighth of November. According to the pathologist's report they died late on the fifth or early on the sixth.'

Martin gasped. He had never been able to make himself go white but flushing was no problem. He looked at Williams who was blowing smoke out of his nostrils. He looked at Galvin who returned his stare. Neither of them gave a damn. He thought of Isobel. He thought of Duncan. Tears sprang to his eyes. When he was sure that they had noticed them he bowed his head and wiped them away.

'Would you like a glass of water?' This was the first time that Galvin had spoken. She sounded like a radio announcer from the fifties.

'I think I need something stronger.' Keep going. 'Are you sure it's them?'

'Both bodies have been identified. They are due to be buried on Monday.'

'Why didn't anybody tell me?'

'We did try to contact you earlier, Mr Rudrum but we were told that you were away. If we hadn't found your number in Mr Patterson's address book we wouldn't be here now.'

'Have you any idea who might have done this?'

'To be honest, no.' He dropped his fag-end into a half-empty cup of stagnant coffee. It hissed. 'Do you?'

'No. I haven't a clue.' He sniffed and ran his hand through his hair. He was gratified to note that he was trembling. 'This has been a dreadful shock. Have you no leads at all?'

'There was no evidence of a forced entry. This suggests that the murderer was known to at least one of the victims. Nobody reported hearing the sound of gunshots. The bullets used were fired from the same gun, a gun that we have no record of. The only prints that we could find matched those of the victims and the housekeeper who discovered them. It doesn't appear that Miss Armstrong was sexually assaulted although, in the circumstances, it was difficult to tell.' So she had been simmering in the hot-tub all that time.

'Well I suppose that's something to be grateful for. Did they both die instantaneously?'

'More or less. Did you know that Miss Armstrong was pregnant?'

'No I didn't. Christ. So three people have been killed.' He managed to inject a quaver into the last line.

'I realise that this must be very tough for you. There's just a couple more queries. Did either of your friends use drugs?' Martin hesitated. 'Don't worry, any information will be treated in the strictest confidence.'

It would be good to appear anxious to help. 'I guess there's no harm in telling you now. They did take cocaine occasionally and, if they went out dancing, they might take Ecstasy. But they were hardly addicts.'

'Controlled substances were found at the scene of the crime. Do you know where they might have got the stuff from?'

'No.'

'Well thank you very much for being so patient, Mr Rudrum. We're sorry to have brought you such bad news. We'll probably see you at the funeral. Mr and Mrs Armstrong are dealing with the arrangements. Oh, by the way, do you know a Mr Alex Fenton?'

'Yes I do. We were at university together.'

'Do you know where he might be? His office informed us that he was ill but, having received no response to the messages that we left on his answering machine, we called round to see him. A neighbour told us that both the men who lived at the address had gone away.'

'Well I can help you there. It's by no means as suspicious as it sounds. Alex was skiving. He and his friend are in New York. They're due back next week I think. But why do you want to speak to him? He hardly knew Rory and Nicola.'

'According to Mr Patterson's telephone bill, the final call made which lasted over three minutes before he and Miss Armstrong died was to Mr Fenton's home number. He may be in possession of vital information.'

'I see,' said Martin. 'Well you shouldn't have too long to wait now. I'm afraid I don't know where they are staying.'

They shook hands with him and left. Galvin's grip was firmer than that of Williams. After the door had closed he sat down again. He needed to think. He still did not know what Nicola had said to Alex before she had hurriedly hung up. When he had spoken to him in Houston Alex had given no indication that he disbelieved his story about Rory blowing him out. Even if Nicola had not said 'I've got to go, Martin's here' it was imperative to stop Alex speaking to the boys in blue. They were sure to ask him when he had last seen Rory and Nicola. If Alex revealed that he had also been at the dinner party in September the cops were bound to ask who the other guests were and that would be that. It was a tricky situation but not an impossible one. He had to be with Alex when he played back the messages on his machine and prevent him calling the police.

Elaine returned to the conference room to find him biting on the nail of his right thumb and staring into space. He looked haunted. 'Martin...Martin, are you OK?' He whipped round.

'Oh, it's you. I've had some terrible news. Two of my closest friends have died. Someone shot them. I can't believe it.'

She put her arms round him. 'I'm so sorry. It must be a terrible shock. Take the afternoon off. Call me if you want to. Come round this weekend if you feel up to it.'

'Thank you. You're very kind. I may take you up on that. I think I will go home.' He stood up.

'Don't worry. They'll get who did it.'

She might well be right. He had lied to the police. What he knew – and they did not – was that Alex was due back in England tonight.

THIRTY-NINE

Although Martin arrived at Heathrow with half an hour to spare, Alex's plane had already landed. A favourable wind had given the 747 godspeed. Passengers, relatives, crooks and guards milled about the concourse: iron filings drawn this way and that by a giant magnet. He elbowed his way through them and found a vantage point from which he could see the crumpled human cargo arriving without being seen. Alex had to be alone. Keith would more than likely work his way back on another flight to save money but, knowing his luck, Alex had probably picked up a woofter.

There he was. He strode out, giving no sign of having just completed an arduous journey. He looked fit, healthy and handsome. He did stand out in a crowd. Hiding behind his Persol shades, plugged into his Walkman, he moved blithely through his own private world seemingly unhampered by his Samsonite suitcase and flight bag. In his right hand he swung a gift-wrapped baseball bat.

He waited until it was clear that Alex was going to get a cab then fell in behind and goosed him. He slowly turned and peered over the top of his sunglasses.

'Martin!'

'Alex.'

'How sweet of you to meet me. Here, this is for you.' He handed him the bat. 'No prizes for guessing what it is.'

'Thank you. I've always wanted one of these. I'm sure it will come in useful.' They embraced.

'So to what do I owe the honour?' Alex leaned forward and slid the glass partition closed. 'We don't want that smelly old man listening to our sparkling conversation.'

'I wanted to warn you.'

'Oh yes?'

'Rory and Nicola are dead. Someone blew their heads off.'

'Trust it to happen when I'm not there to see it. You always said Nicky would come to a sticky end. Poor Rory. You know, I rather fancied him.'

'You were just after his money.'

'Hush your mouth.' He giggled. 'Well, I can see that you're absolutely devastated.'

'That's beside the point. The police want to talk to you.'

'Whatever for? I hardly knew them.'

'When they interviewed me they told me that the last call made on their phone which lasted over three minutes was made to your house. It was Bonfire Night.'

'You mean I was the last the person to speak to them?'

'Possibly.'

'How fabulous. I can sell my story to the papers!'

Martin sighed. 'What is your story?'

'To tell the truth a short one – but I can beef it up. You can help me – you're good at fabrication.'

'Not when it comes to dealing with nipple-heads. It will be much easier if you tell the truth, the whole truth and nothing but the truth.'

'But it's so boring.' He took his glasses off and stuffed them in his bag. They cost £200 – if the lenses got scratched he would buy a new pair. 'How funny that I should have just given you your birthday present. Nicola rang to invite me to a surprise party that they were going to inflict on you.'

So that was it. Thank God it had never taken place. He would have hated it. They were the ones that had got the surprise.

'Well someone did me a favour. Why didn't you tell me, you bastard, instead of swanning off to the States?'

'She swore me to secrecy. Anyway, you would have been out of the country as well. Can you imagine? The tarted-up guests, the food and the booze, the pile of prezzies, all for the sake of a birthday boy who would have been on the other side of the world? It would have been a classic.'

'Hmm… Why didn't you check your messages? The police rang several times. They even called round to see you.'

'That will have given the neighbours something to yack about. I deliberately left my remote interrogator at home. I was on holiday. I needed a rest. The messages would have been irrelevant to me in America. I was hardly going to drop everything and rush back for the sake of a couple of corpses. I shall listen to the glad tidings when we get home. You'll have dinner with me, won't you?'

'Of course. Thank you.'

'Good. That's settled then. Any chance of your being able to claim this on expenses?'

FORTY

The flatfoot began to stomp up the stairs. Romeo and Juliet must have made as if to follow because the WPC told them to stay where they were. He closed the door and dropped the latch. One of the first things that he had done when he had moved in was to install two bolts: one at the top of the door, one at the bottom. He had felt safer then. Now he hardly had time to slide them home before the wood shook as the panting policeman hammered on it. Martin sank to the floor with his back against it. He held his breath. The officer knocked again. The vibration passed straight through his body.

'Hello. Is there anybody in there? Hello. Can you hear me?' Silence. 'This is all I need.'

'See if there's a light under the door,' said the woman.

'OK. Turn out the landing one. It will save me kneeling down.'

'Don't be so bloody lazy.'

There was a grunt followed by the rustle of material as he stretched out on the carpet. Martin crawled into the bedroom. He stood up. Outside the evening's caterwauling had begun. The panda that he had been given on the day of his birth lay, as always, on top of the duvet in the valley between the two pillows. The black and white bear was grubby, balding and falling apart but Martin still loved it. He picked him up.

'There's no sign of life at all,' said the cop, hauling himself to his feet. 'Perhaps he has gone out.'

'Excuse me.' It was Juliet. 'I forgot to say, we have a key. You know, in case of emergencies. Here it is.'

'Now we're getting somewhere.' They thanked the ever-so-helpful member of the public and put the key in the lock.

'It won't turn. That means he must be in there.'

'Unless, of course, he's abseiled down the back.'

'Why should he? Stand back. I'm going to use a bit of persuasion.' The initial impact sent shockwaves through the whole flat. The door frame held. Martin glided into the living room. On his desk the gun gleamed in the twilight.

FORTY-ONE

There was a lot of stained glass in the house where Alex lived with Keith. The front door boasted a large multi-coloured window: it was like entering a kaleidoscope. The same abstract design – which resembled the solution to one of those games to be found in crackers when six or seven different shapes of plastic have to be made into a square – was repeated throughout the four-storey building. It was to be found in the small lights of the bay window in the drawing room, above the pair of french windows in the dining room and even in the tiny aperture that lit the downstairs lavatory. The *pièce de résistance*, however, was in the bathroom where every pane of frosted glass had been replaced with a tinted counterpart. When Martin had housesat for them it had taken him some time to get used to looking in the mirror and finding himself blue, purple and green. Although it had cost Alex a fortune Martin considered the result embarrassingly naff.

'My great-grandfather made stained glass windows.'

'Oh really?' Alex dumped his baggage in the hall and hastened to neutralise the burglar alarm. 'It's a shame he isn't still alive, he could have given me a discount.' He kicked off his Russell & Bromley tasselled loafers and marched upstairs. He began to run a bath.

'Churches were more his kind of thing.'

'Well this is a house of God. I dwell in it.' He had already stripped off and was standing naked – except for his Walkman – at the head of the stairs. Martin averted his gaze. 'Put the kettle on, darling. I'm spitting feathers. And while you're at it phone Pizza Hut. You'll find the number on the notice board in the kitchen. I'll have a *quattro formaggio* with extra mozzarella. You can have whatever you want.'

'Thank you.' He slid his hands into his pockets and drew out a new pair of rubber gloves.

He filled the autojug and plugged it in. When they had lived together as students Alex had always listened to music in the bath. It had seemed dangerous having an electric current so close to water but Alex had insisted that his superduper sports model was perfectly safe and, on one occasion, had dropped it into the bubbles to prove it. The Sony, and Alex, had played on. Obviously he had not grown out of the habit. Good. It would make it easier.

After he had ordered the fast food he returned to the hall and picked up the accumulation of mail that Alex had ignored. Most of it was junk. Among the circulars, catalogues and credit card bills there was a postcard. At first he thought it must be the one that he had sent from Houston but he was wrong. The front was a collage of American retro-chic with the message: 'Here's look-ing At You, Kid!' A man in a black and white check shirt, arms out-flung, was saying: 'What a night! I'm so hung over I can't remember a THING! Did I have a GOOD TIME!' Martin frowned at the use of a screamer in place of the question mark. A blue-eyed woman replied: 'Well, you spat on the hostess, killed their cat…And then you burned the HOUSE down!' The back was scrawled with 'Thanks for a wonderful evening. Here's to many more! Michael. xxx.' It was the kisses that did it.

Alex was pure shit. He did not give a damn about anyone or anything except for himself. He did not care about Rory or Nicola. He did not care that the police suspected him. He did not care about seducing Michael under his nose. It had to be the same Michael – he recognised his flamboyant scrawl. He took off his black training shoes, put the laces neatly inside and placed them under the kitchen table. He tiptoed down the hall and up the stairs. The bathroom door was wide open.

Alex lay back in the tub with his eyes closed. The leads from his individual ear-phones trailed over the end of the bath and down to the Walkman which was on the floor. He had opted for Radox rather than foam tonight. The still surface of the steaming green water was undisturbed except for his bobbing erection, the periscope of a toy submarine. The door was behind him but, at the very moment Martin darted into the room, the cassette ran out of tape, the machine clicked, Alex opened his eyes and glimpsed him in the foggy mirror.

'Hi. Have you come to scrub my back?' He made no attempt to hide his cock. 'Better still, you could gobble Percy.'

He put his hands on Alex's shoulders and pushed down with his whole body. A soapy tsunami immediately surged over the edge of the watery coffin and soaked the carpet. Alex opened his mouth. There were plenty of bubbles now. Martin kept pressing down. Alex's flailing arms posed no threat because he was standing behind him. Kicking feet banged painfully against the gold-plated mixer-tap. His penis swung frantically from side to side like the needle of a Geiger counter. As the drowning homosexual slid further down the out-sized bathtub, each ear-phone was pulled out of its lug-hole and floated to the top. The auto-reverse facility, unaffected by the overspill, started the twin spools turning in the opposite direction. Alex stopped struggling but he did not let go. There was going to be no reprise of the climax to *Fatal Attraction*. Mr Alex Fenton's life was going down the plug-hole.

He was brought out of his trance by the doorbell. He was drenched – he could not be seen like this. He tore off his clothes and put on Alex's bathrobe. It was by no means clean. Wallet in hand, he raced downstairs and opened the door. He tipped the crash-helmeted pizza boy but not so generously that he would be remembered.

The heat seeping through the cardboard boxes was oddly reassuring and helped to stop him shaking. The melted cheese and herbs smelled delicious. Yummy. He was starving.

FORTY-TWO

The tide had gone out when he got back. He replaced the plug and turned on the hot tap as far as it would go. While the tub was refilling he wandered next door into the box room which served as 'The Study'. Most of the space was taken up by a large double-pedestal desk. It was an expensive repro model, complete with an inlaid leather top and brass handles on the drawers. A brass lamp with a green glass shade shone down on a pristine blotter that gave the game away. No one had ever worked at this desk just as no one had ever read the leather-bound classics which lined the bookshelves. It was all a pose, a costly charade played by two good-time boys anxious to suggest that they retained some vestige of intellectual credibility.

The only other objects on the desk-top were a silver writing set and a combined telephone and answering machine. A red light was flashing. He pressed the button marked 'play'. A succession of voices enquired about Alex's health, asked him to contact the local police station and invited Keith and himself to dinner, drinks, tea and a party. Only one of them belonged to a female. Michael was not one of the callers. He set the machine to the 'At Home' mode and returned to the bathroom.

He took off the robe and tied Alex's ankles loosely together with the belt. The bath was boxed in. He stood astride it and, stooping to avoid knocking his head on the ceiling, he pulled the feet out of the tub and hooked them onto the shower-head attachment that was fixed to the wall. This left his best friend's body hanging upside down with his head, shoulders and arms under water. Rivulets streamed down the gym-enhanced musculature and off the end of the now flaccid cock. It was as if Alex were pissing into his own face. He had always enjoyed water sports. He took out his own dick and baptised the stiff.

He picked up the Kitchen Devil that he had brought from downstairs and sliced Alex's throat from ear to ear. Clouds of crimson mushroomed up, turning pinker and paler as they seeped through the water. He slashed the veins in both arms – vertically not horizontally – and watched as red snakes swam into the thickening tomato soup. It would be time for the news by now.

Although he was only wearing boxer shorts, gloves and socks – footprints could be just as revealing as fingerprints – he was not the slightest bit cold. Alex and Keith always had the central heating on too high – probably because they both liked to pad around in their natural state. He stretched out on one of the two blue sofas that were more like double-beds than couches. After the weather report he felt like snoozing but he still had work to do. There was no peace for the wicked.

The water had turned to gravy. He unhooked the feet and, holding the belt that bound them, dragged the clammy cadaver out of the vat and onto the carpet. Its tan seemed to be fading already. The cut in the neck was a deep one – the head was half hanging off. As he pulled Alex down to the kitchen it bounced bumpity-bump on the stairs, leaving behind it a trail of ooze. The floor of the hall was patterned with tiles. When it hit them the skull made a sickening crack.

He almost put his back out lifting the dead meat onto the table. He was surprised at how difficult it was to sever the head completely. The knife sawed through the sinews and gristly windpipe with ease but the top vertebrae of the spine put up more resistance. What he needed was a cleaver but this was not the home of a serious cook – only the state-of-the-art microwave oven looked as if it were regularly used.

In the end he discovered an electric carving knife. It was a little messy – bone splinters flew all over the shop – but it did the trick. Martin yowled as the head rolled off the stripped-pine and onto his bare foot. It felt as though his big toe was broken.

Cursing viciously, he grabbed the grinning mazard by the hair and placed it in the microwave. This would teach him to ask for head.

He set the timer for an hour, turned the dial to high, and switched the oven on. It whirred into action. The carousel started to rotate. The fan began to hum.

Nothing much happened for the first couple of minutes. The baking bonce slowly dried out. Alex's hair stood up, its ends glowing like a fibre optic lamp. Suddenly it burst into crackling yellow flames. The eyelids shrivelled up, creating the impression that their owner was waking. Enthralled, Martin leaned closer. It was then that the eyeballs exploded, splatting against the door. He leaped back in disgust.

Avoiding the small pools of blood that had formed on the hexagonal terracotta tiles – he would never have guessed that Alex had so much in him – he went through the utility room that led off the kitchen and into the shower room. It had seemed the height of decadence to Martin to have such an extension built when there was already a shower fitted over the bath. He let the needle-sharp jets of warm water rinse the sweat and gouts of blood away. His neck muscles felt as though they were in knots. He tried to let the tension drain away. He did not hear the telephone ringing.

After rubbing himself down he put the towel in the washing machine and turned it on. His clothes had more or less dried out on the radiators. He put them on. He returned to the kitchen and wiped the pizza cartons clean. Apart from the front door latch, they were the only objects that he had touched with his own skin. The thing in the microwave had degenerated into a blackened lump. Barbecue smells hung in the air.

He doused the hall light but left everything else on and quietly let himself out of the house. He wrapped his fist in a handkerchief, punched a hole in the stained glass window then set off down the street, swinging his birthday present as he went. As he turned the corner, chuckling at the note he had written to Keith – 'your lover's in the oven' – a Vauxhall Cavalier swept past him. It was driven by Detective Sergeant Williams.

FORTY-THREE

Thock! Michael's head flew off his shoulders like a cork out of a magnum of champagne. But it was not fizz that came bubbling out, it was claret: thick, sticky blood, spurting out of his neck. He could feel the warm, smooth wood of the baseball bat as he gripped it with glee. But – wait a minute – something was rising out of the pumping stump; something that had hair plastered to a skull; something that had a nose, mouth and eyes; bloodshot eyes that now opened to reveal an expression – half rage, half regret – exactly like Michael's; a mouth whose lips now parted to emit a banshee wail. Aieeee! Its piercing scream merged with the sound of the approaching sirens.

He flung off the duvet and let the cooling sweat stipple his skin. His internal organs felt as if they had been liquidised. When his heartbeat had slowed to a more normal rate he stretched out his right arm to check that the bat was where he had left it under the bed. It would soon be time for the home run. He rolled over onto the other side where the sheet was comfortingly dry. First, though, he would have to make a dummy one.

He was more or less certain that Williams had not seen him leaving Alex's but – even if he had been noticed – there was no way of telling if the detective had recognised him. Surely, if he had been clocked, Williams would have telephoned, called round or even arrested him by now? The fact that he had told the police he expected Alex to return tomorrow was one thing in his favour. As far as they were concerned he had no reason to lie. It was in his interest – if he were under suspicion – for Alex to be the focus of police inquiries. Secondly, as a registered key-holder to the house – in case the burglar alarm went off – why should he break into Alex's when a) it would be a noisy means of gaining access and b) it could easily set off the alarm? And, besides, an examination of the corpse would have soon ascertained that the murder weapon had not been a baseball bat.

However, there was no escaping guilt by association. Only a fool would not suspect a man who had suffered the loss of three friends in as many months. Four if he made the connection with Isobel. Five if he linked him with Trudi. He would have to do something that made it appear that he was a victim rather than a killer. He could try and turn the heat back on to Michael – the postcard that he had sent to Alex was still at the scene of the crime – but that would mean Isobel's death would be investigated again and how would he have his way with Michael if he were banged up in a police cell? No – it would be simpler and safer to keep him out of it.

He had to arrange his own attack, but how? It was a case of double jeopardy. If the assault did not go far enough it would be unconvincing. If it went too far the game would be over. For once, death was not the answer. He yawned, pulled the quilt over his endangered body and resumed the foetal position. He had no idea. He would try and sleep on it.

★

'Let me top you up, Martin,' said the company director.

'Thank you. I don't mind if you do.' He sipped the Mumm Cordon Rouge and looked out of the executive box onto the eddying tide of humanity. Arsenal were playing at home: the assembled fans formed a sea of red. Skinheads jostled flat-tops. Here and there a shell-suit flashed fluorescent green, acid yellow or electric blue. A Mexican wave rolled round the stadium. It was an undeniably stirring sight, one that made his stomach feel empty and full at the same time. He sank back into one of the leather seats. There was something decadent about wallowing in luxury while 22 men ran their rocks off on the pitch. It was like a Roman holiday at the Colosseum except that these gladiators were being paid a fortune.

From this eyrie it was hard to identify the individual footballers. His fellow spectators spent just as much time watching the racing on one of the many wall-mounted TVs. He was sure the cameraman in the bottom right-hand corner was gay. The way he zoomed in for close-ups of the players' sturdy thighs was simultaneously exciting and depressing. Adams scored. The ground erupted in a paroxysm of noise. Underneath the carpet the floor was shaking.

'Having a good time?'

'Fabulous. I realise now what I've been missing.' When he had asked the sports editor to take him to his first match he had expected to stand amid the great unwashed as a stream of beer and piss trickled over his trainers. The only way he was going to get done over here was if he chinned the oikish waiter.

'After we've won I'll take you down to meet the team.'

'Great.' It was a shame he could not tell Alex about it.

★

The call had come the morning after while he was in an editorial meeting. Williams left a number for him to ring. He did so straightaway. A working-class whine informed him that the DS was out of the office at present but would get back to him as soon as he could. Five minutes later Williams turned up in person. As he summoned obedient tears to his eyes, Martin reflected how easy acting became when you were able to practise regularly. The detective gave no hint of having seen him the night before. Martin was on the point of expressing concern that his name could be next on the hit-list when the plod suggested that he might like to apply for police protection. He pooh-poohed the idea.

'I have no enemies, Sergeant. Why should anybody wish to hurt me?' The last thing he needed was a flatfoot following him wherever he went.

★

And yet he had decided on a fracas at a soccer game precisely because of the presence of the boys in blue. They would probably have been able to prevent the deliberately antagonised yob from inflicting too much damage. Even if he had been stabbed they could have radioed for the ambulance. With hindsight he could see that the whole plan was too arbitrary, at the mercy of too many uncontrollable factors. It was unpredictability that had made him reject cottaging in the first place.

Soliciting in public lavatories made Martin want to lash out. The breaking down of the invisible barriers between waste disposal and sex incensed him. The notion that innocent heterosexual males should be ogled or interfered with when they were at their most vulnerable was appalling. He could understand the appeal of rough trade – the thrill of the risk – but he was certain that such sordid activities were largely responsible for the widespread disapproval and rejection of homosexuals. How could you blame people for thinking all gay men were perverts or paedophiles when so many of them loitered among the stinking stalls of subterranean pissoirs? It might be convenient for some but the thought of being branded a willie-waver swamped him with such terror that, ordinarily, he could not bring himself to even enter these amenities. Strangury was just one more example of him having to hold himself in.

It had seemed like a good idea at the time. Just smile at

someone who was clearly not gay and the fists would fly. It then occurred to him that there was nothing to stop his assailant kicking him to death. Worse still, they could call the police. It would probably have been a pretty policeman anyway. And what if, instead of taking offence, they smiled back? He dropped it.

★

A safe kind of danger was needed. If cottaging promised to be too private, the football match proved to be too public. As he got drunk in the bar with his colleague and observed the victors celebrating their win, thighs now flexing beneath Savile Row suits and designer jeans, single diamond ear-rings glinting, Martin knew he had to stop pussy-footing around and get himself seriously hurt. Intellectually, he knew it was the right thing to do. Physically, it contradicted his instinct for survival. But – as Michael was fond of saying now that his pumping iron documentary was in production – there was no gain without pain.

FORTY-FOUR

The twin tower-blocks, two vast and trunkless legs of stone, loomed up in the icy night and dwarfed the terraced houses that nestled at their feet. Highfield Manor was a monument to civic planning at its cheapest and cruellest. No thought had been given to context; no consideration had been devoted to scale. If the cliffs of precast concrete were supposed to create a striking contrast to the Victorian back-to-backs they failed. After just twenty-five years their clean-cut modernism looked dirty and dated. Instead of making people feel at home, the outsized dimensions of the estate served only to fill its inhabitants with a mixture of insignificance and dread. The overall effect was as though some Brobdingnagian developer, realising that the model of his special project had all gone wrong, had just thrown it to the ground. Here was brutalism with a vengeance.

The North London bomb-site had been transformed into a network of human rat-runs. Behind the pair of high-rises, the rest of the accommodation had been built on four levels that enclosed a square of dead grass. As in a ziggurat, each level was narrower than the one below it. Perhaps the architect had recently returned from a Mexican holiday. Walkways ran round the edges of each level or 'zone'. In an attempt to relieve the black-on-grey dreariness of the rain-streaked concrete, the council, in its wisdom, had decided to colour code each level. Four rows of yellow front doors were topped with four rows of blue front doors which were topped with four rows of red front doors which, in their turn, were topped with four rows of green front doors. The extra security lighting that had been installed heightened the brashness of the colours and made the rest of the place seem even duller. It was a dispiriting hole; a dizzying convergence of horizontal and vertical planes straight out of Escher. The tiny balconies which clung to the sides of all 21 floors of the skyscrapers were little more than perches for pigeons, a last-minute concession to the need for outside space, escape hatches for suicides. Surely some half-crazed denizen would ambush him here?

He started on the top level and walked all the way round. On the second circuit he slowed his pace. Strolling would be suspicious but striding out lessened his chances of being waylaid. If it appeared that he knew where he was going he might be left alone. As a white male in his twenties he belonged to the category most vulnerable to attack but, according to some criminal psychologists, you had to give out the right vibes, to exude the panicky pheromones of a victim. What was there to be scared about? He went round once again. 'Hi! I'm Martin. Mug me.' He did not meet a soul.

He descended to the blue zone. The crumbling steps were strewn with evil-smelling garbage. A discarded syringe cracked underneath his foot. The walls were sprayed with graffiti in a style familiar from a thousand New York adventure flicks. Even ghettos were now homogenised. It was darker down here. Raucous laughter echoed through the windy tunnels. Someone kicked a beer-can. Where were the desperate druggies? Where were their roller-bladed suppliers, the deals on wheels? Where was the knife-wielding psychopath when you needed one?

'Can I help you?' Martin jumped and instinctively grabbed the handrail for support. The constable smiled. 'Sorry about that. Didn't mean to frighten you.'

'Well you bloody well did. Are you supposed to sneak up on innocent people?'

'So we're innocent are we? How was I to know that you weren't up to no good?' He came closer. He was rather short for a copper. Martin got a whiff of Aramis. 'Why, I might ask myself, is a well-dressed young man like yourself lingering in this shit-pit when he could be tucked up at home in front of his 24-inch, flat-screen, remote control, colour TV with teletext and Nicam digital stereo?'

'I was not, as you put it, lingering. I'm on my way to a friend's.'

'And where might they live?'

'Right here.'

'Number?'

'Thirteen.'

'Ah, well. You're in the wrong zone. Numbers 1 to 48 are on the ground level. You want to get out of the blue and follow the yellow brick road.'

'Thank you.' The bobby nodded and went on his way. 'Isn't it dangerous to be patrolling this patch by yourself?'

'It would be if I was.' You could not expect a policemen to use the subjunctive. 'There are always three of us on duty somewhere on the estate. If things get lively backup is only half a mile away.'

'And do they?'

'Not very often. Not any more. Highfield is a shining example of how the Met can work in conjunction with the local community.'

'You mean you've shunted the pimps and the pushers on to somebody else's doorstep.'

'You could say that. Nowadays our main customers are alcohol and solvent abusers.'

'What about vandals and muggers?'

'We get the odd one or two. There are better pickings to be had in the High Street. Everyone round here is piss-poor. Removing most of the walkways has made it difficult to escape. I wouldn't be surprised if this place was flogged off to some private developer soon. The public has a short memory.' His radio squawked into life.

'Zero one six. Zero one six. Report current location over.' The PC rolled his eyes. 'Duty calls.'

He ventured into the bowels of the estate. Hell on earth. The choice of yellow for this zone was a sick joke. The sun never shone down here. He could sense the mass of stone hanging over him. Where had that pig got to?

The only creature he encountered on his first round trip was a scabby mutt – an alsatian/greyhound cross – that appeared to be happily lapping up a pool of vomit. Inside their poky apartments, the tenants slumped in front of the box, punished their eardrums with rap or engaged in short-lived slanging matches. Babies wailed, budgies chirruped. Martin was cold, bored and depressed. He could not stand this for much longer. He fell over.

He had been so intent on snooping through an uncurtained window – what was that *thing* on the mantelpiece? – that he had failed to notice the uneven flagstone which seesawed under him. He did not trip forwards: his ankle went and sent him thudding into one of the yellow front doors. His head caught the corner of the letterbox. Blood began to trickle down the side of his face. 'Shit!' He sat cursing on the damp and greasy concrete. The door opened.

'Oh my Lord. A traveller has fallen by the wayside.' A big, black momma, hands on hips, stood over him. 'Did they get your money?'

'I haven't been attacked. I just fell over.'

'You should look where you're going.' The door shut. Seconds later it opened again. He was still sitting there in a daze. She hooked an arm under his shoulder and pulled him to his feet. 'Come with me.' Kicking the door shut behind them, she led him to a white settee. The holes in its PVC had been patched with black adhesive tape. She plumped up a purple cushion and put it behind his head then waddled into the kitchen. Martin watched Trevor McDonald doling out the news. The good samaritan dressed his cut and tutted when the TCP – 'ow!' – made it sting. She put a plaster on it. 'Here, drink this.' He cupped his hands round the mug of sweet tea and let the heat seep into his numb fingers.

The couch faced an electric fire. Only one of the three bars glowed orange. The heater was set in a surround of imitation-wood. Its tiny shelves were cluttered with ceramic figurines, seaside souvenirs and horse brasses. Photographs of grinning grandchildren in gilt frames had places of honour at each end of the mantelpiece but the middle was devoted to a picture of Christ on the cross. The white plastic frame was tasteless enough but the image was covered in transparent, minutely corrugated plastic to create a 3-D effect. By shifting your point of view it was possible to make Jesus wink.

'You admiring Our Dear Lord's suffering, child? Look closely. I only do this on special occasions. She struggled to her feet and flicked a switch on the back of the icon. The Messiah's wounds glistened redly. Martin groaned.

'Do you like it? Isn't it life-like? It helps me in my prayers.' She thrust a pamphlet into his grazed hands. It was a copy of The Watchtower. Now he really did want to die.

FORTY-FIVE

He stopped outside number 66 and looked up at the majestic facade of the Belgravian terrace. Bright white stucco, glossy black front door. Business must be good. Thatcher might have gone but her legacy lived on. The privatisation of pain. He was broke but here he was, about to pay someone to break his bones. He pressed the relevant button. A buzzer sounded, a light came on and the security camera blinked into action. Thirty seconds later a voice crackled out of the intercom. 'Yes?'

'Malcolm Robinson.'

'Come in.' The door clicked open. He stepped inside.

The hall was tiled in a black and white geometrical pattern which reminded him of a Jumbo Crossword in *The Times*. A large bunch of lilies in a clear glass vase stood on a semicircular table set flush against the wall. All the mail had been taken away. There was an old-fashioned lift with a concertina-gate made out of brass but he did not need it. A door on the right, which was marked with the letter A, opened to reveal Zack, the man with whom he had an appointment.

'Hi! Come on in.'

'Thank you.'

'Can I get you a drink?'

'Yes. I think you better. Scotch please.'

'Anything with it?'

'No thanks.' He had felt in need of Dutch courage even before setting out. All that he had been able to find in the flat was a half-empty quarter-bottle of cooking brandy. He had drunk it.

Zack led the way downstairs into the gym. Apart from the rubber floor, every surface was covered with mirrors.

'Have you got the dosh?' Martin handed over ten twenty pound notes. His host counted them then folded them up and slipped them into the pocket of his army fatigues. He smiled. An olive green singlet displayed his muscular physique to menacing effect. He tightened the band that held his ponytail in place, rubbed his hands together then let his arms dangle at his sides as he shook them. The biceps wobbled. 'Now what exactly do you want?'

'The idea is to create the impression that an unknown assailant has tried to kick me to death.'

'Well in that case I better put me DMs on.' He was currently wearing turquoise espadrilles. 'I'll be back in a tick.' Martin sat down in a dentist's chair which had been screwed into the floor. It was not too late to chicken out.

As Zack returned someone walked across the ceiling.

'Who's that?'

'Don't worry. It's a friend of mine. He'll help me get you into the back of the jeep when we dump you.'

'Where will that be?'

'Near – but not too near – Charing Cross Hospital. We don't want to give the game away do we? That OK? I trust you're a member of BUPA.'

'Absolutely.'

'Good. I'll make sure you get your money's worth out of them.' Martin blenched.

'Relax, relax. I won't go too far. I'm used to this kind of thing.'

He went over to one of the mirrors which turned out to be a cupboard door and took out a set of knuckle-dusters. Before Martin could decide what the rest of the leather and chain paraphernalia might possibly be used for Zack closed the door. 'Follow me.'

'Where are we going?'

'Into the yard outside. It's no good you being duffed up if your threads remain in perfect condition. Realism must be observed.'

'Just one more thing before we go.'

'Yes?' Zack gave him a quizzical glance as if to say: 'If you think you're going to walk out of here on your own two feet you can forget it.'

'I don't want to lose any teeth.'

'Fine. Dental treatment costs the earth nowadays doesn't it? I promise you, in two months time you won't be able to tell that anything happened tonight. You never know, you might get to like it. If you do you know where to find me.' He slapped him on the back.

He had found Zack on the last page of Trudi's notebook before he had thrown it away. At the time he had had no idea why he felt it wise to note down the telephone number of a man who could provide 'bondage, torture, general rough stuff'. Then it was unlikely that he would ever need to call any of Trudi's better-known clients but that had not stopped him copying out their numbers as well. Blackmail would only have implicated him in her murder. After the previous two fiascoes he had lost patience and decided to call on the services of a professional.

It was freezing in the tiny courtyard. Although some of the apartments which overlooked it were clearly occupied, all their windows were either curtained or shuttered. He knew that any cries for help would be ignored. He began to panic. A door in the high wall at the back gave access to an adjoining mews. He ran towards it.

'Don't bother. It's locked.'

'Look. Couldn't you knock me out first?'

'It wouldn't produce the desired effect,' said Zack and punched him on the nose.

Martin saw the fist flying into his face, noticed the four white knuckles, registered the gleam of the steel in the streetlight and felt the cold metal splinter his nasal bone. Tears sprang into his eyes. Blood spurted out of his nostrils and shot down the back of his throat. His knees buckled and sent him sprawling to the ground.

Zack grabbed him by the collar and struck him in the face again and again. His bruised flesh felt hot yet numb. Before the swelling sealed his eyes completely Martin saw the stars reeling in the sky. Blow upon blow rained down on him.

'Get up, you motherfucker.' Zack sounded bored. He hauled him to his feet and rammed him up against the wall. His head bounced off the bricks. A quick one-two in his stomach doubled him up only to meet a rising knee which then homed in on his groin. He vomited, shocked at the violent way it spewed from his battered mouth. The bile and alcohol burned his split lips and the insides of his cheeks where his teeth had been mashed into them. Zack held his head tenderly while he puked then stroked the hair off his sweating forehead. 'Hang on. Not much more to go. Just the grand finale.'

He flung him on to the ground and began to methodically put the boot in. Stomach. Groin. Liver. Kidneys. Ribs. Back. Legs and shoulders. He could not speak but in his mind he was screaming for death. At last he blacked out. A warm, sweet smell seeped into the air. Zack sniffed in satisfaction but he kept on kicking.

FORTY-SIX

Martin aged ten. The school holidays. Daleside Fields. Yellow sun, blue sky, green grass. Two little boys are making dens in the hawthorn bushes on a long steep bank. Below them a stream snakes through a water-meadow sprinkled with buttercups that shimmy in the breeze. Above them Friesian cows flick flies off their black and white hides with tatty tails. As the boys play among the gnarled roots, which have been worn smooth by generations of children, they can hear the lumbering milk-machines cropping the pasture. The noise that the teeth make as they tear up the lush grass sounds exactly like 'munch, munch, munch.'

The boys are wearing shorts and striped T-shirts. Their knees and elbows are daubed with biscuit-coloured dust. It is cool beneath the bushes. Blackbirds, thrushes and sparrows hop to and fro among the branches overhead. The empty bottle which contained the dandelion and burdock that is now inside them rolls down the bank.

It bounces over rootlets and bumps until it lodges at the foot of a tree.

'We can't leave it there,' says Martin. 'Litter kills the animals.'

'I'm not going to fetch it.' Christopher burps then laughs. Martin giggles. The dead-man stays where it is. Christopher, curling up his lower lip, blows the fringe of his golden hair off his forehead. It falls back into place. He is bored. Martin is doodling with a stick in the dirt.

'Come on,' says Christopher. 'Let's go and explore the witch's cottage.' Martin does not like going right over to the other side of the fields. The roar from the traffic on the new by-pass is unpleasant. But Chris is a year older than him and has hairs where he does not. When he commands Martin obeys.

To reach the derelict house the boys have to tramp across the farmland for at least a quarter of a mile. On the way they stop by the pond where they collect frog-spawn in spring. At school a jam-jar of tadpoles is worth two merit marks. Today, though, there is little activity in the water. The boys toss pebbles into the greenish pool until a dragonfly, its diaphanous wings sparkling in the sun, scares them away with its killer sting.

The old ruin is not actually in the fields but on a plot along-side them. Although its overgrown garden backs onto the green belt, access to it is through the electricity substation next-door. The boys squeeze through the gap that has already been made in the new fence and crunch-crunch across the gravel. The circuit-boosters hum. A faint smell of creosote hangs in the air. They climb over the five-bar gate and walk on the pavement of the main road for a few yards before plunging into the under-growth that has forced its way up through the piles of broken bricks. As he does so Martin spots three bigger lads in the distance. They are swaggering along with their hands in the pockets of their long trousers. They are far away. They are on the other side of the dual carriageway. Perhaps they have not seen Chris and himself. They have.

There is not much left of the tumbledown building. Only a couple of the exterior walls are still standing. The boys clamber among the rotten floorboards, the rusting drainpipes and mildewed furniture. A cracked cup has been placed on the mantelpiece of the cast-iron fireplace. Fresh ash suggests that the grate has recently been used.

'Tramps!' whispers Christopher. He holds up an empty bottle of Bulmer's Strongbow Cider. He chucks it out of what was once a window. It smashes on a heap of bricks.

'Vandals!' shouts a strange hoarse voice. By the time Martin has turned to see who it belongs to Chris is already making his getaway. Before he can follow his example the tallest of the three youths has grabbed him by the arm. His collar-length hair is greasy. His face is dotted with yellow-headed spots. His upper lip is sprinkled with wispy black hairs.

'Lend us two bob, mate.'

'Do you mean ten pence? I haven't got any money.' The other two louts, who are standing just behind their leader, snigger. 'Don't he talk posh? Surely a rich kid like you has got lots of money. Empty your pockets.'

He does as he is told. The only thing in them is a penknife with a red handle.

'That's nice. I'll have that.'

The ugly teenager snatches the knife and examines it. He hooks a dirty thumbnail into the notch on the side of the blade and opens it out. It is not sharp but he sticks it under Martin's chin. Martin tries to step back but his tormentor simply grabs him again.

'Where d'you live?' Martin stammers out his address.

'Is it nearby?'

He is afraid that they want to take him home so that he can give them money. He does not know that bullies are cowards, that they do not want furious parents chasing after them.

'No. It's a long way away.' Why does that make the big boy smile? He has brown teeth.

The first time he is slapped across the face he is too shocked to cry. The second smack, which is harder, makes his other cheek smart. The third, which is harder still, brings tears to his eyes.

'Cry-baby!' One of the sidekicks, a fat boy who stinks of sweat, seizes a fistful of hair and drags him over to the back wall. The other, who is younger and seems nervous, follows suit. Martin falls but they do not stop. Nettles prick his bare legs. The slaps give way to punches. He is now screaming in terror. Not one of the passing drivers – who can clearly see what is happening – stops to help him. Where is Chris?

'Mummmy! Mummy! Mummy!' His jeering attackers drop him in disgust and start kicking him instead. 'Stop, stop, stop! Please stop!'

'Mr Rudrum. Martin. Can you hear me? It's all right. You're safe. You're going to be all right.' A warm, soft hand takes hold of his. He cannot open his eyes. His head hurts. The rest of his body, which seems a million miles away, is one dull ache. He is floating in space.

'Where am I?'

'You're in hospital. Charing Cross Hospital. Don't worry about anything. I'm just going to give you something to help you sleep.'

He sinks into oblivion before the hypodermic has even been withdrawn.

FORTY-SEVEN

The police came to visit.

'I did warn you,' said DS Williams. His tone suggested that it served him right. Martin remained silent. It hurt too much to talk. The detective pulled a pack of Silk Cut from one of the pockets of his shiny-elbowed jacket. He was about to light up when, seeing Martin's expression, he thought better of it and put the cigarette away.

'They certainly made a good job of it. I'm told it was touch-and-go for a couple of hours. You've had a lucky escape.'

He would have snorted if he had been able to use his nose.

Zack had taken the opportunity to display his black sense of humour by abandoning him outside an undertaker's.

'There's no doubt that you were left for dead. Did you catch sight of the attackers?'

He shook his head gingerly then raised his left arm and wiggled the forefinger. His other arm was encased in a right-angled plaster cast which was suspended in mid-air.

'There was only one of them. Are you sure?' He nodded. 'What else can you remember? Take your time.'

It was no good. He would have to speak. Williams was not going to leave without some semblance of a statement. He could always ring for the nurse if the questioning became awkward.

'I was on my way to see David Burnstone.' It sounded more like a croak than a voice. 'I was cutting through one of the streets behind Eaton Square. As I turned a corner someone punched me in the face and that was it – I didn't see another thing. I fell over and they started kicking me. After that I must have lost consciousness.' The policeman had to lean over the bed to hear him. He still had sleep in the corner of his left eye.

'Did you shout for help?'

'Yes. I think so.'

'Did anybody come?'

'I don't know.'

'What time would this be?'

'About 9.30.'

'Was there much traffic about?'

'No.'

Galvin, who until now had been working her way through all the Get Well Soon cards without smiling once, interrupted.

'Have you had the sensation that you were being followed at any time during the past week?'

'No'

'Who knew you were going to see Mr Burnstone?'

'No one, unless Burnstone told somebody.' She did not believe him.

'It does seem odd that you should be set upon miles away

from your usual haunts and that not a single witness has come forward,' said Williams. He opened his notebook. 'Severe contusions, a detached retina, three cracked ribs, a broken arm, a ruptured spleen that required an operation to remove it and internal bleeding are not injuries that one person can inflict in seconds. The bastard took his time. You were probably transported somewhere else, subjected to a further beating, then dumped where you were found off the Fulham Road. Whoever it was clearly didn't like you. God knows why they didn't check to see they'd finished the job.'

'Perhaps he wanted the victim to die slowly, to suffer some more,' offered Galvin. Williams glanced at her. She shut up.

He groaned as he tried to shift his position on the non-allergenic mattress.

'Do you think that whoever it was will try again when they find out I survived?'

'It's unlikely,' said Williams. 'We had a constable outside your door for the first 48 hours just in case but for the moment I don't see any need to continue the surveillance. Hospital security is pretty good nowadays, especially where private patients are concerned.' He looked round the room. 'I must say they don't do things by halves do they? Phone, TV, your own bathroom – it's like being in a hotel. Very comfy.'

'I'm not at all comfortable,' hissed Martin irritably. 'I ache all over. My kidneys are killing me. I'm still pissing blood and as if that weren't enough this fucking drip is making my arm very sore.' He pressed the switch that he held in his left hand. Even though he was hardly drinking anything he had to pee again. He had insisted on the catheter being taken out. This meant that every leak seared like liquid fire.

The nurse, a dazzling collage of blue and white, swept in through the swing door.

'It's time you people were on your way. Go and nick the wicked soul who did this to my favourite boy.' She gave Martin the bed-bottle then ushered the cops towards the door.

'Do you think that the person who tried to kill me is the same one who murdered Rory, Nicola and Alex?'

'Possibly. Possibly,' said Williams. 'As yet we have no evidence to link any of these incidents. The computer is not being of much assistance. We'll keep you posted.' He winked at Nurse Flynn. 'Make sure he takes it easy.'

'What else am I going to do?'

FORTY-EIGHT

Araminta came to visit. When she saw the state he was in she started to cry.

'Story of my life,' said Martin, who was feeling a bit better. 'As soon as an attractive woman claps eyes on me she bursts into tears.'

'I'm sorry. When they said you'd taken a severe beating I'd no idea it would be this ghastly.'

'It looks worse than it is. What expensive gifts have you brought me?'

She smiled and wiped her eyes. She opened the green and white Harrods carrier bag and placed a pile of cards on his bed. 'I see you got the flowers.'

'Yes, thank you. They're lovely. They don't even bother to take them out of the room at night now. I was surprised that some joker didn't send a wreath.'

'It was suggested. I knew that you'd only throw them back at me if I brought you grapes so we had a collection and brought you these.' She put two parcels on top of the cards. They were both wrapped in black tissue paper and topped in a white bow. 'Open the larger one first. If you need any help just ask.'

She spoke in vain. Even though one arm was out of commission, he had little difficulty in tearing off the gift-wrap. When he realised what it was he grinned. A small wooden crate held six miniature bottles of champagne. The other package contained a single lead crystal flute.

'Thank you.' He raised his chin and, when she leaned forward, touched her cheeks with his bruised lips. 'I'll give you a proper kiss when the laughing gear is back in working order. We don't want our body fluids mingling do we?…Now we must hide these before the Irish Terrier whisks them away.'

'Who's that?'

'My personal day-time nurse. I think she's in love with me.'

'Nonsense. How could anybody fall for you?'

She was only teasing and he knew it. Even so his eyes filled up. 'You might well ask.' He sniffed. 'Don't mind me – it's the drugs. I've become maudlin lying here. I've not been able to do anything except doze or watch TV. I do enjoy my own company – which is just as well – but nothing seems to have gone right since Isobel dumped me. It never used to concern me but now the thought of spending every night alone for the rest of my life is terrifying.'

She squeezed his hand.

'You're only feeling this way because of what's happened. It's called post-traumatic stress. Everyone gets it. When you're back on your feet it will all seem different.'

'And all this time I just thought I'd got a headache.' He winced at the effort required to shift his backside. It was numb. He sank back against the pillows.

'It's amazing what comes swimming up in your memory. After my bed-bath last night – before you ask it's still too painful to be pleasurable – I remembered having 'flu at school. The bath in the sanatorium was sunk into the floor. You had to step down into it. Sister Newton was one of the 'Cleanliness Is Next To Godliness' brigade and insisted on each boy bathing twice a day no matter how ill he might be. I hated it every time because the tub was coffin-shaped.'

He could still feel its bleached wooden rim sticking into the back of his neck. He could still smell the mixture of disinfectant and polish that lingered in the steamy air. He drifted away in his reverie. The hot water lapped about his chin. Araminta said nothing. She was still holding his hand.

'One afternoon – it must have been the last day of my sick leave – I was lying in the bath. I was bored but not so bored that I had to get out and dry myself. Sister was talking to one of the housekeepers. If things were quiet the domestic staff would drop in for a gossip. I wasn't paying much attention but when I heard my name my ears picked up. They obviously didn't know that I was still in the bathroom. "Oh that one," said Sister. "He'll never be happy." I'd totally forgotten about the incident until yesterday but, you know, I think the old cow was absolutely right.'

'What rot.' He had never seen her embarrassed before. 'How would she know? Anyway, the silly woman is probably dead and buried by now.'

'And may she roast in hell for all eternity. I'm sorry to go on like this, Minty, but I've just had my brains bashed out. Tell me who's fucking at the office. How are they managing without me?'

Fifteen minutes later his colleague left, promising to come and see him again soon. He did not believe her. He had frightened her. That was the trouble with being honest – the truth was hard to take. He had never told anyone that anecdote before and he would not do so again. Araminta had blushed because she agreed with Sister Newton.

FORTY-NINE

Burnstone came to visit. He brought a couple of books. One was David Thomson's *Suspects* which Martin had already read; the other was a proof copy of a thriller called *The Pit Of Pleasure*.

'Let me know what you think. I've bought first option.' He paced about the room then stopped by the window which looked out onto another wing of the hospital. 'God, I hate this country in winter. You probably haven't noticed but it's been raining for a week.'

'When are you going back to the states?'

'After Christmas. I'm off to Gstaad for the New Year. I'll fly on to LA from there. But enough of me. I came to see how you were getting on. I feel kind of responsible for what happened. But as I told the police, I didn't tell a soul you were coming round.'

'Don't be ridiculous. If anybody's to blame it's me.' He relished the dramatic irony. 'I should have taken the cops' advice.' The director shrugged. 'It would take ages to create a mug like yours in make-up.'

Although most of the swelling had subsided, his face resembled a road-map of Great Britain. A network of livid red lines snaked underneath his skin which was a motley mask of puce, yellow and even green.

'You should have brought a Polaroid.'

'That's not a bad idea. When do you get out of here?'

'On Saturday with a bit of luck.'

'I half expected you to be hooked up to a machine. How can you live without a spleen?'

'It's not an essential organ. Blood corpuscles are produced by other parts of the body. Apparently your bone marrow boosts production to compensate. Anyway I've always had too much spleen.' His visitor laughed tensely. What was he nervous about? He dropped into the armchair.

'I bumped into a friend of yours the other day.'

'Who?'

'Dan Salter.'

The only good thing about having a face like a rotten aubergine was that no one could tell if you were blushing. 'He's no friend of mine.'

'I use the term loosely.'

'What did he say?'

'Not much. Paladin were trying to promote their latest turkey so I went along out of loyalty. He was standing next to me at the bar. We got talking about Houston and your name came up. After all, you are a mutual acquaintance.'

'What did he say?' He looked at the dark crescents under Burnstone's eyes. They were no match for his own shiners. His Boss suit was crumpled. There were times when he could be an irritating little man. He let the repeated question hang in the air.

'He said he'd spent a very pleasant evening with you.' He hesitated. 'You never told me about it.'

'It wasn't important. It might have been pleasant for him but he turned out to be the narcissistic nerd I'd always taken him for.'

'You might have shared the coke with me though.'

He winced as the shock sent a ripple of pain through his body. 'Fuck! Don't make me do that again. There wasn't much left.'

'Ah, I see.'

'There wasn't. Why don't you believe me? What else did the great lunk say?'

'Nothing. Nothing at all.' He sighed. 'Just tell me this. You haven't been trying to sell any of the shit have you?'

'Of course not. Is that what you think all this is about? I promise you, drugs have nothing to do with this. I haven't a clue why anybody should want me dead – unless you count the myriad mediocrities whose work I've slagged off. You know me better than that. I wouldn't dare to smuggle anything like that through customs.'

'True. That's true.' He did not seem entirely convinced. He consulted the Rolex Oyster that was dripping off his wrist. 'I must be off. We'll do something before Christmas. Hurry up and get out of here. I'll be in touch. Ciao.'

Surely Salter had not regaled Burnstone with what had really happened? If he had someone was bound to spread the dirt. At least Salter would never allow it to be printed. The story was worth a fortune: HUMPED BY HUNKY HOLLYWOOD HOMO. He should write it anyway. If he died it would give his parents something to read. It would make a great epitaph.

FIFTY

Nerissa came to visit. He had only received a card from her the day before. She had found out about his 'misfortune' from a small news item in *Streetwise*. He had told Araminta that he intended to write a blow-by-blow account of the attack as soon as he was back in harness. He had paid good money for the assault. He might as well get some copy out of it as well.

It was an odd choice of card. He could not stop gazing at it. The back informed him that the untitled black and white photograph had been taken circa 1938 by one Lejaren A Hiller. It showed a fair-haired woman in a plaid dress falling through the air. Her body formed a V-shape. Her butt was her lowest point. Her high-heeled feet and outstretched right arm were her highest points. Her left arm could not be seen. Her blonde curls flew upwards; her frock billowed in the slipstream. It was a convincing picture.

At the moment the camera had clicked the femme fatale had reached a point between two floors of a white clapboard house. Above her was the open window from which she had presumably fallen. Net curtains blew in the breeze. Below her was another window which was closed. A blind prevented anyone seeing into the room. By the top left-hand corner of this window, beneath the woman, an empty pail was also falling. Was this a visual pun? Something to do with kicking the bucket? Perhaps the subject, instead of falling, had jumped. Although it was a realistic image he had no doubt that it was the result of trick photography. Perhaps the woman was in fact hanging upside down and the photograph deliberately turned on its head. No wires were visible. The shadows gave nothing away. However, it was the woman's expression that fascinated him the most. Although, at first glance, it appeared to be one of terror, closer examination suggested that it could be the beginning of a smile. Perhaps she was thinking: 'Just take the goddamn picture.' Perhaps the lensman was her lover. Whatever the truth, each time he looked at the card he simultaneously experienced a sensation of vertigo and the shock of recognition. He also was, and was not, falling.

Nerissa brought him a dozen red roses. He would have been delighted if he had not thought that she was paying off a debt. She, like him, was a sucker for symmetry. The gesture smacked of tit for tat. He was ashamed to realise how much her features had faded in his mind's eye. The mental image was nothing like the reality.

'How are you?'

'All the better for seeing you. My kidneys have settled down now. The ribs are mending. The arm itches more than it aches.

The bruising is going – that's why it's such a multi-coloured mess. My nose will never be the same again but I'll be able to say I got it boxing at school.'

'Good. I'm glad. I see you got a mention in last month's Azed competition.'

'Congratulations on your first prize.' He had not expected her to come. It was very kind of her. Perhaps she thought more of him than he knew. He had nothing to say to her though. It was too late. He wished she would go away.

'I discovered a wonderful word yesterday,' he said, trying to break the silence. 'Bumbershoot. Bumbershoot. What d'you think it means?'

'It's a facetious American term for an umbrella isn't it? It derives from umbrella and parachute. It's better than gamp but personally I've always had a soft spot for chatta. That's the Hindustani name for a brolly.'

'Well I prefer bumbershoot,' said Martin.

FIFTY-ONE

Michael came to visit.

'God you look awful.' He helped himself to a banana and sat on the bed.

'Thank you.'

'No, no. That's not the answer. You're supposed to say: you should have seen the other guy.'

'I'll save it for the next time. If there is one. I'm being released on Saturday.'

'Great. D'you want me to collect you.'

'It's OK thanks. I'll order a cab.'

'Good. I've got a date anyway.'

'At ten in the morning?'

'Preparation, my son. I've got to look my best.'

'Why? What's so special about this one? Is she anybody I know?'

'No. I've only just met her. I want to make a good impression.'

'If you'd arrived on time you would have met Nerissa.'

'Who?'

'Nerissa. The woman I met in Oxford.'

'Oh yes. I remember now. She'd be too clever for me.'

'You didn't say that when I first told you about her. Besides, I didn't think you could afford to be choosy. I'm glad to hear that you're not letting grief stand in your way.'

'Don't start.' His frown lasted for three seconds. It was as if the sun had been momentarily obscured by a cloud.

'Those apples look nice.'

'Go on then. Haven't you had any lunch? Business must be good. How's the Freaks on Four doc coming along?'

'We're going great guns. Not all body-builders are morons. Some of them have been to university. They're really quite intelligent.'

'How would you know?'

'Ha! Ha!' He got up to put the apple-core in the bin. 'Must go now the pips have gone.' He went into the bathroom and proceeded to urinate noisily. He left the door open so that his stream of wit could continue. He turned away in disgust. He would soon be seeing all that Michael had to offer.

He flushed the lavatory and, without bothering to wash his hands, returned to the bedside.

'Did you hear what I was saying?'

'Sorry?'

'Pay attention. These muscle-men sometimes need an adrenalin rush to help them lift even more weight. D'you know how they get it?'

'No. Tell me.'

'They get a friend to punch them in the face.'

He saw once more the gleaming knuckle-dusters. A wave of nausea washed over him.

'Christ. I'm sorry. I didn't think what I was saying.' He bit his bottom lip. 'Have they caught the gang who did it?'

'It wasn't a gang, Michael. This is all the work of one man. I know what you're going to say but it's difficult to defend yourself when you walk into a fist and suddenly all you can see is blood and tears.'

He said nothing. He was just a schoolboy really. Physically overgrown but mentally underdeveloped. His embarrassment was charming.

'I have to go. I'm parked on a double-yellow and the clampers always pick on cars like mine. I'll cook you dinner to celebrate your recovery. When's the cast come off?'

'Not for another month I shouldn't think.'

'I'll give you a bell before then. Bye.' He darted forward and kissed him on the cheek.

FIFTY-TWO

His parents came to visit. It was the week before Christmas. Mrs Rudrum had decided to combine some last-minute shopping with a check on her darling son's recuperation. She had wanted to come to the hospital but he had dissuaded her by playing down his injuries and only offering a vague mention of getting involved in a fight as an explanation. He did not want a distraught middle-aged woman flapping around him. The nurses were bad enough.

It was not merely a question of self-preservation, of avoiding trouble. As he and his parents got older their roles seemed to be reversing. He now felt that it was his duty to protect them. In many ways – having lived for so long safe inside the well-appointed bastion of bourgeois respectability – they were innocents abroad. As a child he had tried to tell them everything – what he did, how he felt, why he cried – but now he tried to tell them as little as possible.

'When did you get your arm back?' asked his father. He was dressed in a tweed sports jacket and fawn trousers. His mother was wearing a heather-coloured Jaeger suit with a cream blouse. He thought it was quaint the way they still dressed up to come to London. 'Yesterday.'

'How's it feel?'

'It's a bit stiff but otherwise it's fine. And it's a real luxury to be able to scratch it whenever I want. I think I'm more or less fully recovered now. I've been getting bored so I must be better.'

'I wish I could have six weeks off work.'

'Well I don't,' said his mother. 'Mrs Muckalt doesn't want you cluttering up the house all day.'

'He'd hardly be there, would you pater? He'd spend most of the time down at the golf club.'

'At the nineteenth hole I shouldn't wonder.' She smiled at her husband indulgently. It was a constant source of amazement to him how they seemed to get on with each other better and better as the years rolled past. Perhaps he had been the problem. Perhaps it was because sex no longer played a part in the marriage. At least he hoped it did not.

'Any more tea?' asked his father.

'The pot's empty,' said Martin, getting up.

'Stay where you are,' said his mother. 'I'll do the honours.' While she was in the kitchen his father handed him a cheque for £250.

'I thought you might like half your Christmas box before the 25th.'

'Thank you. I'll be able to buy you a present now. It couldn't have come at a more opportune time.' He folded the piece of paper in half and slipped it into his pocket.

'I don't know what you spend it on. You were always so careful with money when you were a kid.'

'That was before I had any idea what you could do with it.'

'Ah well, don't tell your mother. She'll only say it's tempting providence.'

As she returned with the teapot, the telephone rang. Martin leapt up to answer it.

'The tyranny of the telephone,' said his father. 'If it's important they can always ring back.'

'Hi! Did you have it off?'

'Yes, Michael, I did. I'm now fully functional.'

'Give or take the odd organ.'

'The same could be said of you.'

'Bitch. D'you fancy coming round tonight? I know it's short notice but She Who Must Be Obeyed has blown me out. One of her closest friends is having man-trouble. I was going to cook her a meal anyway.'

'OK. You're on. About eight?'

'Perfect. I'll see you then.'

'Who was that?' asked his mother. She had made no attempt to disguise her eavesdropping. Some things never changed.

'No one,' said Martin.

FIFTY-THREE

The door-frame began to splinter. Martin began to crack. He picked up the gun. The cool weight in his sweating hand was reassuring. He sat down in the centre of the black and white rug and crossed his legs. From here he had a direct view of the front door. The bolts were holding remarkably well. He had done a very good job.

The panting policeman continued to kick. When his legs got tired he started to use his shoulder as a battering-ram instead. He hoped it was hurting. The wooden frame was buckling – it would not be long now. There was no way he was going to be arrested without a fight. Pigs to the slaughter. Exhaustion and excitement warred within him. Perhaps he should save them the trouble. Why not? The thought of being confined in a tiny cell of painted bricks for 23 hours of every day with two oily, belching, farting, educationally-subnormal AIDS-infested bum-bandits for the rest of his life was insupportable. He had to make his get-away. His index finger curled round the trigger. The door flew open. He fired.

FIFTY-FOUR

In Clissold Park there stands a mountain laurel. It is not a spectacular tree – it looks like most other trees – but its bark, berries, roots and leaves contain a substance called andromedotoxin which, if taken internally, produces a devastating effect. The vegetable resin is marketed as a drug to relieve high blood pressure. It is named after Andromeda who, according to Greek myth, was rescued by Perseus from a sea-monster. The drop in blood pressure occurs because andromedotoxin acts like curare on skeletal muscle. If a large enough dose is administered the body puts itself to bed. The central nervous system eventually shuts down, the lungs breathe their last and the heart stops beating. The victim literally relaxes to death.

He only spotted the tree because a rottweiler was cocking its leg against it. On his visit to the local library it had taken him three times as long to find out what the plant looked like in the gardening section than it had to discover a suitable poison in the health section. Michael was the last on the list. It was important that his murder be the best of the six.

The laurel stood in a sheltered position among a clump of trees. Numerous kissy-kissy adolescents had carved their names in its trunk. Some of the couples had encased themselves in misshapen hearts. How apt: the tree was a heart-stopper. He scrutinised the branches. Although it was December they were covered in leaves. The book had been correct – it was an evergreen. There were even some purplish-black berries but he ignored these and, having glanced over his shoulder to check that no one was watching him, started to pluck the elliptical leaves. It was not easy with one hand. Their dark-green sheen was clouded by an accumulation of dust. If you ate these you were more likely to die of lead–poisoning than anything else. When he had collected enough to fill the pocket of his leather jacket he resumed his daily constitutional. His heart pummelled his mending ribs and he felt uncomfortably hot. He had been out of hospital for a fortnight now but it did not take much to bring back the shakes.

★

His parents left at 4pm in a bid to beat the rush-hour.

'It seems to start earlier and earlier,' said his mother, pecking him on the cheek. 'Take care, dear, we'll see you next week.'

As usual, in spite of swearing in January that he would never spend another Christmas with the assembled Rudrum clan, he had caved in to his mother's low-key but persistent pressure. It was a time of good will, not free will. Besides, who else would he spend it with?

As soon as he had waved them off he scurried to the airing-cupboard and removed the baking-tray of laurel leaves. After harvesting them he had washed them and left them to dry out on the rack above the hot-water cistern. The heat had turned them into greyish curlicues. They looked harmless enough – the ash of indoor fireworks. Thirty minutes of feverish chopping reduced them to a fine off-white powder.

The cocaine from Houston was hidden in the terracotta jar marked FLOUR. He put half of it straight into an envelope which he marked with a tick. Then, making sure that he did not inhale any of the two drugs, he spliced most of the poison with the remaining coke and carefully tipped the mixture into another envelope which he marked with a cross. In a dim light a drunk would not notice the difference. He placed the rest of the toxin in a third envelope but saved just a little to determine whether it would dissolve in water. It did. Great. The final solution.

FIFTY-FIVE

It was a bitterly cold night. Highbury Fields was shrouded in freezing fog. The invisible lamp-posts suspended fuzzy balls of soft white light in the air. He did not meet a soul.

He had decided to wear exactly the same outfit that he had assumed to kill Trudi – ie a pair of white cotton boxer shorts from Marks & Spencer, black Levis 501s, a white T-shirt, a navy blue woollen sweater, black trainers and a black leather jacket. It added to the sense of occasion, to the sense of an ending. The only light remaining was six down. It began with M. M for Martin, Michael and Murder.

This time round he carried a plastic shopping bag. It contained a magnum and a Colt. Every so often the gun clinked against the bottle. The right-hand pocket of his jacket held the three packets of drugs; the left-hand one the rubber gear – the last pair of surgical gloves and a packet of condoms.

At the top of the hill he could hear water trickling into the cistern of the tiny gents. The cottage doorway was blocked by a gate of iron bars. A single yellow bulb glowed above the entrance to Christ Church but he strode on past the clock tower – which had stopped at one minute to eleven – and tramped up the gravel drive and round to the door marked 1A. He took the Colt out of the bag and, lifting up his jacket and jumper, stuffed it down the back of his jeans. The icy barrel sent a shudder up his spine as it nosed between his buttocks. He must remember to hide it before he sat down. He rang the bell. No one answered. Butterflies began to flutter in his empty stomach. He rang again.

After a minute he could hear someone charging downstairs. 'Sorry. I was in the shower. Come in. Is that for me?'

He handed Michael the champagne. The drops of water on the end of his black curls glistened. He resisted the urge to tousle them.

Michael shut the door and led the way back upstairs. The thick hairs plastered to his wet legs resembled ogamic runes. What did they say? It was hard to keep his back ramrod stiff as he climbed. The steel pressed into his flesh.

His host went into the kitchen and put the Bollinger in the freezer.

'I'll just go and get dressed. Make yourself at home.'

He retracted the gun with relief and placed it on the parquet flooring beneath the sofa. He took the envelope containing the pure poison out of his jacket and slipped it into the pocket of his Levis. He hung his jacket in the hall closet. As he stepped back onto the spiral staircase he could hear Michael humming in his bedroom.

When he reappeared the white towelling robe had been replaced by faded denims and a white T-shirt. His hair was slicked straight back. Nothing could have been simpler; nothing could have been more seductive. Martin not only envied the effect but also the short amount of time it had taken to create. It always took him ages to dress for dinner. Sex appeal, savoir faire, *je ne sais quoi* or oomph – whatever it was called Michael had it and he did not. All his life – but without much success – he had tried to make the best of what he had got. What were you supposed to do if your best were not good enough?

Michael opened the champagne then slid a compilation of Bach concerti into the CD player. Small talk. After a couple of glasses he padded barefoot into the kitchen. He pottered about chatting as he did so. Martin lolled on the sofa watching him. The red and gold baubles on the large artificial Christmas tree twinkled in the firelight. This was how it was supposed to be. This was what it was all about. Domestic bliss. Affluent affection. Two people – one clever, the other beautiful – sharing their lives. He and Michael should have been lovers. If they had known each other before Michael had met Isobel he could have derived some consolation from the possibility that Michael may have been fucking him through Isobel. Surrogate sodomy. He knew that Michael went chutney-ferreting with females. Isobel had told him. As it was, all that could be said with any certainty was that Michael, in spite of everything, liked Martin and that Martin, in spite of himself, liked Michael. And when did liking translate into loving?

'Martin. Are you asleep?'

'What? No. Sorry. I was fantasising.'

'Oh yes? What about? I hope it was about me.'

'God you're arrogant. I may have been thinking about you. Then again I might have been thinking about someone else. If you're a good boy I'll consider telling you the truth after dinner.'

'Please sir. Please sir I'll be a very good boy. Please sir may I have some more?'

'Of course. Coming right up.' He sprinkled some of the poison into Michael's glass and poured in the fizz. It did not dissolve straightaway. He stirred it with his finger. The master chef would be too concerned with his pheasant in crème de menthe to do more than swig it. He took it over to him. 'Here you are.'

He was afraid that the doctored coke would not be toxic enough to cause death within two hours. Consequently, whenever Michael left the table, he added a little pure poison to his champagne, Australian Chardonnay, mineral water and even his home-made raspberry ice-cream. And, by restricting his own alcohol intake, he ensured that his unwitting host drank twice as much.

'Christ I feel odd,' said Michael. He tried to stand up. 'I hope that salmon mousse was OK. I only bought it yesterday.'

'And I thought you said that the whole meal had been cooked by your own fair hands. You cheated.'

'Only with the first course. You don't really mind do you?' He was breathing heavily now. Two wet stains fanned out from beneath his armpits. 'I think I'd better lie down.'

'Good idea. Leave this lot to me. I'll clear away and put the coffee on. Then I've got a surprise for you.'

This was not a vain attempt to sustain the illusion of domestic harmony but an essential ploy to remove his fingerprints from every object that he had touched. He could hardly have worn gloves at the table. Once the dishwasher was sloshing away he switched on the coffee machine then retrieved the two packets of cocaine from his jacket in the hall downstairs. When he returned Michael was sitting up with his eyes closed.

'Here we are.' He did not reply. Martin tipped out the adulterated cocaine in front of him on the glass-topped coffee table and, having sat down, emptied his own envelope out in front of himself.

'You can open your eyes now.'

'Crikey! This must have cost you a fortune.' His brown face was ashen. 'Where did you get it?'

'An American source. Think you can manage it?'

'You bet. I'll feel great after this magic powder. Just you wait and see.'

'I intend to.'

Michael tottered over to the stainless steel bookcase and picked up the coke-kit that Isobel had given him.

'I must be getting 'flu or something. I ache all over.' Martin raised his eyebrows. 'Not there, silly. Everywhere else though.' He knelt down with difficulty and chopped up four lines. Using the chrome toot-tube he hoovered a double dose up each nostril and immediately proceeded to divide up the rest.

'Slow down. What's the hurry? Don't snort it all at once. I'm not going to let you have any of mine. Let the stuff do its stuff.'

He proffered Martin the tube but he already had a twenty pound note furled in his hand. Should he have a couple of lines? Why not? It might be useful. He lay back in the armchair. God it was good. As the brass band marched through his veins he saw Michael take his last toot. He could not get back on the sofa. Exultation bubbled up in his belly. Two more would not do any harm.

★

He lay on his front. His eyes and mouth were open. Martin thought he was dead. He put on the gloves and stuffed the wrapping into his pocket. Grabbing hold of his ankles, he pulled Michael out from between the table and the sofa and across the slippery wooden floor. He rolled him on to the rug and placed a hand on his heart. It was still beating, albeit in an erratic fashion. His breathing was so shallow that his chest hardly moved.

'Still with us, Michael? Good. I wouldn't have you miss this for the world. Hang on. I won't be a minute.'

He wiped the table clean then flushed the J-cloth and the remaining drugs down the lavatory. He had not budged an inch. Martin licked his lips. 'Right. All we need now is Mr Janacek.'

FIFTY-SIX

He turned up the volume until it would go no higher. The mournful horns blasted out. He stripped slowly, folding each item of clothing until he had formed a neat pile on the sofa. What better music to sin to than a sinfonietta?

Michael's sloe-black eyes were wide open. Martin, aware that he could not blink, gazed into them. His blank expression disappointed him: the least he could have done was to try and look as though he were surprised or terrified. He got hold of the bottom of his T-shirt and pulled it over his head. It was not difficult – the arms flopped upwards as if he were helping him. His torso had a gorgeous tan. It was exactly the same shade of brown as the smooth variety of Sun-Pat peanut butter. A faint line of black hairs travelled down the centre of his washboard stomach and disappeared into his jeans. Martin undid the top silver stud of the flies. His own prick started to stiffen.

Michael was not wearing any underwear. Martin grabbed the bottom of both legs and tugged the 501s off the dying man. He was circumcised. The exposed head made the shaft look thicker. He flung the trousers aside and knelt down by his friend. He traced the outline of the expensive musculature with his fingertips. All those hours spent toiling in the gym had come to this. Still, he appreciated it – except for the uncontrollable sweating. He crumpled up Michael's T-shirt and wiped down the imminent corpse. Then, having instinctively and furtively glanced round to ensure that he was alone, he lowered his head and took him in his mouth. It was a pity that an erection was out of the question. The jaw action and the sudden tang of salt brought Duncan into his mind. He spat on the floor in self-disgust. It was time to stop messing about.

He turned him over and shivered at the sight of his buttocks. He knew it was ridiculous, he knew it was demeaning, but he thought that this arse was one of the most beautiful things he had ever seen. The intensity of their perfection was enough to make one believe in God. He stroked their silken curves and spread his palms over their bulging muscle. It was the arrogant way they just surged up out of nowhere. He kissed the dimples of Venus – tiny hollows on either side of the base of the back. V. Be my Valentine. Vengeance is mine; I will repay saith the Lord. Vanity, vanity, all is vanity. How could two wads of flesh exert such power over him? He pounded them with his fists. The bastard had fucked up his life and now he was going to fuck him.

The third, moderato, section began. Martin put on a condom. He opened Michael's legs and knelt inside them. He parted his cheeks. The anus looked like the knot in a pink balloon. Holding his aching cock, he positioned its tip and, with a vicious thrust of his hips, plunged straight in. He gasped at the heat. It was like poking a fire. There was not much grip though: either Michael was a closet bum-boy or the drug had penetrated every part of his body. Was it his imagination or did Michael just let out a sigh?

The tempo of the music increased. He started to pump away. God, if he had known it felt as good as this he would have been doing it all his life. Salter had a lot to thank him for. The brass neared its climactic crescendo. He could not hold back. It was too late. He came as the metallic cascade crashed in his ears, filling the penthouse with furious sound. YES… YES… YES… The exultant grunting gave way to sobbing.

It was over. He collapsed on top of him, the slight convex of his belly matching the shallow concave of the small of Michael's back. He closed his eyes and did not see the single tear roll down his victim's cheek. Bliss. The acrostic was complete.

The fifth and final section began. He did not hear the front door close. He did not hear the footfalls on the stairs.

FIFTY-SEVEN

'**M**ichael? MICHAEL? I'm home.'

He leapt to his feet. His knees were trembling. He had withdrawn so fast that the condom had come off. It trailed out of Michael's backside, an aberrant umbilical cord. A woman's hand appeared on the rail of the spiral staircase. He went for the gun.

When she saw Martin standing naked over an equally naked Michael, Nerissa's first impulse was to laugh.

'What's going on here?'

'I might ask you the same question.'

When she saw the revolver in his gloved right hand, when she saw that her new lover was not moving, her next impulse was to run. He fired at her. He missed the bitch. A pane of golden glass shattered, allowing the freezing night to gush in. He fired again. This time he hit her but not before she had pressed the panic button on the keypad at the top of the stairs. A piercing wail shrieked out. It made the Janacek seem off-key.

He ran across to her. The bullet had entered her chest through the left breast. The next smashed her right temple. He returned to Michael and shoved the smoking shooter up his arse and fired. The corpse jolted off the floor. Now he really did have shit for brains.

He got dressed. He was shaking so much that he fumbled with every button. As if to assist his getaway the music sped up as it reached the allegretto coda. He made himself knot his laces twice. Then, grabbing the gun, he rushed downstairs to flush the spunk-filled condom down the toilet and collect his jacket from the closet in the hall. The front door slammed shut. The laser cut out. The compact disc stopped spinning. The 23 minutes and 34 seconds were over. The tocsin kept on screaming.

He did not check to see if there was a reception committee. He could hear at least two police cars approaching from opposite directions. Their sirens were out of sync but the fog muffled the cacophony. He burst out of the drive. If there were any bystanders they were taking no chances. The best escape route would be one that vehicles could not follow: Highbury Fields. He tore down the path by the side of the church. The deserted soccer pitches were still floodlit. The ice forced him to slow down. It was no good breaking a leg. The frozen puddles cracked underneath his feet. The cops were getting closer. He reached the grass. As the rigid blades sank under his weight it felt as though he were walking on carpet.

When the ground began to dip he stopped. That meant he must be on the crest of the hill, near the centre of the largest field. The fog swirled about him. He could make out the dim white lights that followed the road around the edge of the vast open space. The police did not know who they were looking for. They did not know exactly where he was. All he had to do was stay put and wait. The cold snatched at the back of his throat as he panted, the clouds of breath mixing with the smog. His whole body ached. He had been stamped on all over again.

It was eerie standing alone in the middle of nowhere. If asked, he could say that he had lost his dog. The more mundane the excuse, the more likely it was to be accepted. The sirens trailed off. He was on the point of moving when he saw red and blue flashing lights on his right. They were joined by more on his left. The patrol cars began to circle. He flung himself to the ground, wincing as his ribs hit the rock-hard earth. He rolled over and stared up at where the sky ought to have been. He gripped a tuft of grass in each fist. The frost melted in them. If he was blind then so were his pursuers.

The earth began to shake.

FIFTY-EIGHT

'Nearly there,' said Mr Rudrum as they cruised along the M6. 'If it hadn't been for this damn fog we'd have been home by now.'

Mrs Rudrum did not answer. She had given up begging her husband to slow down. He would insist that 70 mph was the minimum speed for the outside lane – if you did not want someone to run into the back of you. The amber flashing fog lights recommended a limit of 50 mph. It was motorway madness. What was the hurry? What did they have to get back for? A lasagne from Marks & Spencer and the TV news. She did not know that they would be on it.

In an attempt to mollify his wife Mr Rudrum fed a James Last cassette into the tape-deck. The saccharine sound of swooning strings reverberated in stereo round the snug passenger compartment, the bass merging with the hum of the engine. The dashboard lights glowed in the dark. She tipped back the reclining seat and closed her eyes. She was too anxious to sleep. It was silly – she had nothing to worry about. These Volvos were the safest cars on the road. She peeked at the digital clock. Ten more minutes and they would be leaving the motorway.

It was not to be. As Mr Rudrum adjusted the volume of the muzak a black Porsche cut in front of an articulated lorry that was in the middle lane. The driver of the sports car – who had been tailgating the Audi ahead to no effect – had decided to overtake the slowcoach from the left instead of the right. In his frustration he had under-estimated the speed of the juggernaut. As he saw it loom up in his rearview mirror he automatically tried to accelerate out of trouble but he was trapped. The Audi sped on in safety. The Porsche rammed the transit van in front. The lorry driver instinctively slammed on his brakes and jack-knifed, slewing across all three lanes of the carriageway. Petrol from the ruptured tanks of the Porsche and van trickled on to the Tarmac.

When he saw what had happened Mr Rudrum tried to brake but it was too late. The bonnet of the Volvo shot under the main body of the eighteen-wheeler and was slammed in further by the company car behind. All across the northbound M6, rubber was burning, bumper was bending bumper, heads were bouncing off windscreens and blood was spraying plastic fascias and acrylic seating.

The Volvo's crumple zones worked like a dream and absorbed impact upon impact. The safety-belts held the Rudrums in their seats. The headrests had prevented whiplash. The steering-wheel had telescoped and the airbag in its centre had inflated to protect Mr Rudrum's chest. James Last smooched on but the smoke made them choke. People were screaming. Men and women were screaming again and again.

The steel cage that had stopped the roof being sliced off became a tomb. The fact that the doors do not jam is irrelevant when you are surrounded by a mass of twisted, jagged metal. The fog glowed orange. The thick black plumes of smoke vanished in a blast of blinding white-hot light as the fireball exploded and the air was filled with the sickening smell of frying flesh.

Martin did not like barbecues. They were naff. But this human one had served him up around £400,000.

FIFTY-NINE

The air began to vibrate. His bones began to judder. His ears were filled with an alternate whooshing and roaring. Twigs, dead leaves and litter whirled up about him. It was a helicopter.

He got to his feet and tugged the Colt out of his inside pocket. The patrol cars continued to cruise round the perimeter. The wash from the chopper sent the smog eddying around him, a host of ghostly dervishes. The cops were trying to blow his smokescreen away.

At first the whirly-bird flew this way and that – they clearly did not know where he was – but then it elected to hover. A powerful pencil-beam of light probed the murk. It formed a white disc on the black earth. It reminded him of the laser-targets on high-tech rifles. Either way, if the dot touched you the game was up.

After a tense five minutes of hide-and-seek he became impatient. It must be costing a fortune to devote all this manpower and equipment to the hunt for a single criminal. When would they call it a night? The ground crews had halted. The lights on the top of their cars were still flashing. Suddenly the roar increased. A giant vacuum cleaner tried to suck the hair from his scalp. It was time to leg it.

Thermal imaging had pinpointed the suspect and shown the police exactly where to land. He careered down the hill towards what he hoped was the swimming pool. Dogs began to bark. Sirens resumed their whooping. A black figure came out of nowhere and tried to cut across his path. He fired a shot into the air. The man dropped to the ground. Now only one bullet remained in the chamber.

The black square was not the pool but the public conveniences nearly opposite Barclays Bank. He had expected to meet the Firearms Squad not a lonely cottager. Shoving the gun into his jacket, he ran out into the street and sprinted round the corner. Although the red man was standing guard at the pelican crossing Martin ignored him and, to a cat's chorus of honking horns, weaved through the traffic on Holloway Road and entered Highbury station.

He had planned to catch the tube to Kings Cross and then get a cab home but when he heard a train on the North London Link clanking to a halt he changed his mind. It was even going east! Someone, somewhere, must be on his side.

As soon as he sat down – gasping, sweating, trembling, aching – he realised that he was going to throw up. The journey to Canonbury took less than a minute. He made it on to the platform and vomited the whole lot up: coffee, ice-cream, pheasant, smoked salmon, champagne. A meal in visceral rewind. A gaggle of teenage girls giggled. He could shoot one of them. He wiped his mouth on his sleeve and set off on the short walk home.

His legs felt like lead but the nearer he got to safety the faster he went. The shooter swaying against his breast was awkward and heavy. He resisted the temptation to dump it. He peeled off the rubber gloves and dropped them in a litter-bin. He had got away with murder once again. Did he feel satisfied or triumphant? No. Success had merely left him with a sour taste in the mouth.

By the time he turned into Clissold Avenue he was running. He opened the gate. Romeo and Juliet were on the doorstep.

'We've been to the Barbican,' said Romeo.

'Splendid,' said Martin. 'Goodnight.' His neighbours lingered in the hall.

'Are you all right?' said Juliet.

'Never been better,' said Martin. He was already halfway up the stairs.

SIXTY

He should not have done it.

The police were not there to arrest him. They had come to break the tragic good news that his parents were dead. They were fearful that he had already found out, that he was on the point of doing something stupid. He was.

Convinced that he had failed once again, that white was black, Martin blasted the top of his head off as the officer crossed the threshold. At the last moment he realised that he had forgotten to reload the gun. He could not kill all of them but the single bullet would do for him.

Juliet screamed. Romeo gawped. The constable sighed – he had seen it all before.

'Was it something I said?'

The digital clock on the video recorder blinked: 10.59 became 11.00.

Also available from The Do-Not Press

Ray Lowry: INK
1 899344 21 7 – Metric demy-quarto paperback original, £9
A unique collection of strips, single frame cartoons and word-play from well-known rock 'n' roll cartoonist Lowry, drawn from a career spanning 30 years of contributions to periodicals as diverse as Oz, The Observer, Punch, The Guardian, The Big Issue, The Times, The Face and NME. Each section is introduced by the author, recognised as one of Britain's most original, trenchant and uncompromising satirists, and many contributions are original and unpublished.

Paul Charles: FOUNTAIN OF SORROW Bloodlines
1 899344 38 1– demy 8vo casebound, £15.00
1 899344 39 X – B-format paperback original, £6.50
Third in the increasingly popular Detective Inspector Christy Kennedy mystery series, set in the fashionable Camden Town and Primrose Hill area of north London. Two men are killed in bizarre circumstances; is there a connection between their deaths and if so, what is it? It's up to DI Kennedy and his team to discover the truth and stop to a dangerous killer. The suspects are many and varied: a traditional jobbing criminal, a successful rock group manager, and the mysterious Miss Black Lipstick, to name but three. As BBC Radio's Talking Music programme avowed: "If you enjoy Morse, you'll enjoy Kennedy."

Jenny Fabian: A CHEMICAL ROMANCE
1 899344 42 X – B-format paperback original, £6.50
Jenny Fabian's first book, Groupie first appeared in 1969 and was republished last year to international acclaim ("Truly great late-20th century art. Buy it." –NME; "A brilliant period document" –Sunday Times). A roman à clef from 1971, A Chemical Romance concerns itself with the infamous celebrity status Groupie bestowed on Fabian. Expected to maintain the sex and drugs lifestyle she had proclaimed 'cool', she flits from bed to mattress to bed, travelling from London to Munich, New York, LA and finally to the hippy enclave of Ibiza, in an attempt to find some kind of meaning to her life. As Time Out said at the time: "Fabian's portraits are lightning silhouettes cut by a master with a very sharp pair of scissors." This is the novel of an exciting and currently much in-vogue era.

Miles Gibson: KINGDOM SWANN
1 899344 34 9 – B-format paperback, £6.50
Kingdom Swann, Victorian master of the epic nude painting turns to photography and finds himself recording the erotic fantasies of a generation through the eye of the camera. A disgraceful tale of murky morals and unbridled matrons in a world of Suffragettes, flying machines and the shadow of war.
"Gibson writes with a nervous versatility that is often very funny and never lacks a life of its own, speaking the language of our times as convincingly as aerosol graffiti" –The Guardian

Miles Gibson: VINEGAR SOUP
1 899344 33 0 – B-format paperback, £6.50

Gilbert Firestone, fat and fifty, works in the kitchen of the Hercules Café and dreams of travel and adventure. When his wife drowns in a pan of soup he abandons the kitchen and takes his family to start a new life in a jungle hotel in Africa. But rain, pygmies and crazy chickens start to turn his dreams into nightmares. And then the enormous Charlotte arrives with her brothel on wheels. An epic romance of true love, travel and food…

"I was tremendously cheered to find a book as original and refreshing as this one. Required reading…" –The Literary Review

Ken Bruen: A WHITE ARREST Bloodlines
1 899344 41 1 – B-format paperback original, £6.50

Galway-born Ken Bruen's most accomplished and darkest crime noir novel to date is a police-procedural, but this is no well-ordered 57th Precinct romp. Centred around the corrupt and seedy worlds of Detective Sergeant Brandt and Chief Inspector Roberts, A White Arrest concerns itself with the search for The Umpire, a cricket-obsessed serial killer that is wiping out the England team. And to add insult to injury a group of vigilantes appear to to doing the police's job for them by stringing up drug-dealers… and the police like it even less than the victims. This first novel in an original and thought provoking new series from the author of whom Books in Ireland said: "If Martin Amis was writing crime novels, this is what he would hope to write."

Maxim Jakubowski: THE STATE OF MONTANA
1 899344 43 8 half-C-format paperback original £5

Despite the title, as the novels opening line proclaims: 'Montana had never been to Montana". An unusual and erotic portrait of a woman from the "King of the erotic thriller" (Crime Time magazine).

Jerry Sykes (ed): MEAN TIME Bloodlines
1 899344 40 3 – B-format paperback original, £6.50

Sixteen original and thought-provoking stories for the Millennium from some of the finest crime writers from USA and Britain, including **Ian Rankin** (current holder of the Crime Writers' Association Gold Dagger for Best Novel) **Ed Gorman, John Harvey, Lauren Henderson, Colin Bateman, Nicholas Blincoe, Paul Charles, Dennis Lehane, Maxim Jakubowski** and **John Foster**.

Geno Washington: THE BLOOD BROTHERS
ISBN 1 899344 44 6 – B-format paperback original, £6.50

Set in the recent past, this début adventure novel from celebrated '60s-soul superstar Geno Washington launches a Vietnam Vet into a series of dangerous dering-dos, that propel him from the jungles of South East Asia to the deserts of Mauritania. Told in fast-paced Afro-American LA street style, The Blood Brothers is a swaggering non-stop wham-bam of blood, guts, lust, love, lost friendships and betrayals.

The Do-Not Press
Fiercely Independent Publishing

Keep in touch with what's happening at the cutting edge of independent British publishing.

Join The Do-Not Press Information Service and receive advance information of all our new titles, as well as news of events and launches in your area, and the occasional free gift and special offer.

Simply send your name and address to:
The Do-Not Press (Dept. AP)
PO Box 4215
London
SE23 2QD
or email us: thedonotpress@zoo.co.uk

There is no obligation to purchase and
no salesman will call.

Visit our regularly-updated web site:
http://www.thedonotpress.co.uk

Mail Order

All our titles are available from good bookshops, or (in case of difficulty) direct from The Do-Not Press at the address above. There is no charge for post and packing.

(NB: A postman may call.)